EDWARD MARSTON was born and brought up in South Wales.
A full-time writer for over forty years, he has worked in
radio, film, television and theatre and is a former chairman
of the Crime Writers' Association. Prolific and highly
successful, he is equally at home writing children's books
or literary criticism, plays or biographies.

edwardmarston.com

By Edward Marston

THE BRACEWELL MYSTERIES

The Queen's Head • The Merry Devils • The Trip to Jerusalem
The Nine Giants • The Mad Courtesan • The Silent Woman
The Roaring Boy • The Laughing Hangman • The Fair Maid of Bohemia
The Wanton Angel • The Devil's Apprentice • The Bawdy Basket
The Vagabond Clown • The Counterfeit Crank •
The Malevolent Comedy • The Princess of Denmark

THE RAILWAY DETECTIVE SERIES

The Railway Detective • The Excursion Train
The Railway Viaduct • The Iron Horse
Murder on the Brighton Express • The Silver Locomotive Mystery
Railway to the Grave • Blood on the Line • The Stationmaster's Farewell
Peril on the Royal Train • A Ticket to Oblivion • Timetable of Death

Inspector Colbeck's Casebook:
Thirteen Tales from the Railway Detective

The Railway Detective Omnibus:
The Railway Detective, The Excursion Train, The Railway Viaduct

THE CAPTAIN RAWSON SERIES

Soldier of Fortune • Drums of War • Fire and Sword
Under Siege • A Very Murdering Battle

THE RESTORATION SERIES

The King's Evil • The Amorous Nightingale • The Repentant Rake
The Frost Fair • The Parliament House • The Painted Lady

THE HOME FRONT DETECTIVE SERIES

A Bespoke Murder • Instrument of Slaughter
Five Dead Canaries • Deeds of Darkness • Dance of Death

THE BOW STREET RIVALS SERIES
Shadow of the Hangman

The Malevolent Comedy

An Elizabethan Mystery

EDWARD MARSTON

Allison & Busby Limited
12 Fitzroy Mews
London W1T 6DW
allisonandbusby.com

First published in 2005.
This paperback edition published by Allison & Busby in 2015.

A CIP catalogue record for this book is available from
the British Library.

10 9 8 7 6 5 4 3 2 1

ISBN 978-0-7490-1819-1

Typeset in 10.5/16 pt Sabon by
Allison & Busby Ltd.

The paper used for this Allison & Busby publication
has been produced from trees that have been legally sourced
from well-managed and credibly certified forests.

Printed and bound by
CPI Group (UK) Ltd, Croydon, CR0 4YY

The Malevolent Comedy

Chapter One

Nicholas Bracewell had worked in the theatre for many years but he had never known a silence so complete and reverential. The hush that fell on the audience that Sunday afternoon was extraordinary. Those standing in the pit stopped munching their apples or shuffling their feet, spectators in the galleries ceased fidgeting, and pickpockets who operated in every part of the playhouse abandoned their craft momentarily lest the noise of a purse being lifted should cause a disturbance. Some people did not even dare to breathe.

A searing tragedy had reached its climax with the death of its eponymous hero, Lamberto, an Italian potentate. The silence that followed seemed to reach out beyond the walls of the theatre to embrace the whole of Shoreditch. For a full minute, the world itself stood still. Then the final speech took *Lamberto* to its poignant conclusion.

Our ruler brought great joy unto the state,
A single fault, enough to seal his fate.
His tragedy so stark, unkind and grim,
To love his people more than they loved him.

Before the rhyming couplets ended the play and released the audience from the unbearable tension of the closing scene, tears were flowing freely on all sides. A profoundly moving drama had touched the hearts of all who watched it. Having devoted himself to the care of his subjects, Lamberto, a benevolent monarch, betrayed by some of the very people he had served so well, sacrificed his life for his country. His nobility had been an example to all. To the sound of solemn music, he was borne away by his stricken subjects.

After such a stirring performance, it was almost sacrilegious to break the mood by resorting to something as banal as clapping and there was a collective reluctance to do so. When the first pair of hands did eventually meet in gratitude, however, others soon followed then the torrent burst forth. Everyone in the galleries rose to acclaim a triumph and Nicholas Bracewell was among them. Nobody clapped harder or with more enthusiasm. He had seen a fine play, cleverly staged and beautifully acted. Book holder for Westfield's Men, one of London's leading theatre companies, Nicholas was a keen judge of drama and he acknowledged without hesitation that *Lamberto* was unquestionably the best thing he had seen on a stage all season. It had one glaring defect.

It did not belong to Westfield's Men, but to their deadly rivals.

'You went to see Banbury's Men?' said Lawrence Firethorn with disgust. 'How *could* you, Nick? Nothing on God's earth would make me sit through a performance by that crew of mountebanks.'

'London takes a very different view of their work. What I saw this afternoon was the ninth successive staging of *Lamberto*. Like today, the other performances filled the Curtain till it was fit to burst.'

'I care not if it was the hundredth time the piece was aired. I'd sooner be stretched on the rack, and have my eyes pecked out by ravens, than watch Giles Randolph strut upon the boards. He and his company are pigmies beside Westfield's Men.'

'They were more than a match for us today.'

Firethorn's anger flared. 'What!' he exclaimed with a voice like a wounded buffalo. 'You dare to compare those ranting buffoons with us? You have the gall to mention the name of that vile toad, Randolph, alongside my own? Shame on you, Nick!'

'I speak as I find,' said Nicholas, firmly. 'It's folly to be blinded by naked prejudice. Giles Randolph will never eclipse you as an actor but Banbury's Men have nevertheless put us in the shade this past week. While our audiences have dwindled, they have unleashed this new tragedy on the capital and won golden opinions from everyone.'

'Including you, it seems.'

'I went merely to see if reports of its excellence were true.'

'Have you no better way of spending the Sabbath?'

'Yes,' retorted Nicholas, 'the best way of all is to be on our stage at the Queen's Head, competing with our rivals. That's where I'd love to spend my Sunday afternoons. But we're kept idle by edicts that prevent us playing on the Lord's Day because we are within the city limits.'

'A rank injustice,' agreed Firethorn. 'While we sit on our hands, Giles Randolph and his miserable actors can ply their trade out here in Shoreditch, free from city restraints. Both playhouses – the Curtain and the Theatre – flourish at our expense. It's monstrous, Nick, all the more so for me, living cheek by jowl with our rivals. There's no more devilish sound for an actor's ears than that of thunderous applause for others.'

They were in the parlour of Firethorn's house in Old Street, only minutes away from the theatre where *Lamberto* had been performed. It was impossible for the actor not to hear the lengthy ovation that it had earned. Each second had been a separate dagger through his heart. He sat down heavily in a chair and turned a melancholy eye on his visitor.

'Did the play really deserve its plaudits?' he asked.

'Every one of them,' replied Nicholas, honestly.

'What of Randolph?'

'Inspired. The best I've seen from him.'

'That's not saying much,' growled Firethorn, stung by the praise of the one actor in London who could threaten his primacy. 'The fellow is a raw beginner, still green and untried. It were an achievement for him simply to stand upright and remember his lines.'

Nicholas Bracewell showed his usual tact. His friend had suffered enough. It would be cruel to point out that Giles Randolph had given a towering performance in a remarkable new play. And the actor-manager of Westfield's Men needed no reminding that his company had hit a difficult patch. Takings were down, audiences cool, morale among the actors low. Unable to offer a new play for several weeks, the troupe had fallen back on its stock of old dramas, many of which now looked tired and stale. Westfield's Men were no longer leading the way in the theatre. Their supremacy was fading and Firethorn knew it only too well. His head sank to his chest.

'Who wrote this tragedy of theirs?' he muttered.

'John Vavasor and Cyrus Hame.'

'Why did they not bring it to us first?'

'Because of the way you dealt with Master Vavasor,' explained Nicholas. 'When he offered you his *History of Edmund Ironside*, you told him your children had written better things on their slates.'

'And so they had!'

'That was untrue and ungenerous. The play had faults, and many of them, but there was great promise locked away inside it. Had you seen fit to encourage that promise, instead of condemning it outright, Master Vavasor's loyalty would have been bought. Instead,' said Nicholas, pointedly, 'he found a co-author in Master Hame, who has lifted his art to new heights. On his own, John Vavasor was lacking

11

but, with Cyrus Hame beside him, he's transformed.'

Firethorn was dismissive. 'This success of theirs is like a beam of sunlight,' he said with contempt. 'It dazzles for a while then vanishes forever behind the clouds. We'll not hear of Vavasor and Hame again.'

'Assuredly, we will.'

'Why so, Nick?'

'The rumour is that they have already finished a second play,' said Nicholas, trying to break the news gently, 'and it goes into rehearsal soon. It's a tragedy about Pompey the Great.'

'Never!' howled Firethorn, leaping to his feet. '*I* am Pompey the Great. It is one of my finest achievements. I'll not let that vulture, Giles Randolph, pick the bones of my role. I am a greater Pompey the Great than he could ever be. Send for my lawyers, Nick. This must be stopped.'

'There's no law to stop an author writing about Ancient Rome,' said Nicholas, reasonably. 'The play in which you shone was masterly, I grant you, but there have been others on the same subject. Master Vavasor and Master Hame clearly believe they can conjure a new shape out of this old material.'

'Theft! Plagiarism! Iniquity!'

Firethorn stormed around the room as if he were Pompey the Great on receipt of bad news about a battle. He roared, cursed and made violent gestures. Pompey was one of his favourite roles. Too possessive to let anyone else take it on, he was appalled by the notion that Randolph would usurp him. It was insupportable. Stopping beside the wooden table, he thumped it so hard with a fist that the manuscript lying on it was tossed inches in the air. The sight of the fluttering pages took all the rage out of him. It was replaced by cold despair.

'A pox on it!' he cried, picking up the manuscript. 'They have this wondrous *Lamberto* with a new-minted tragedy to follow it and what can we set against them?' He flung the sheaf of papers down. 'This dull and feeble comedy about a lovesick milkmaid. Pah!'

'*How to Choose a Good Wife* has its merits,' said Nicholas, defensively.

'Enough to put before a paying audience?'

'Edmund has written better plays, it's true.'

'Answer my question, Nick.'

'Barnaby liked it.'

'Barnaby Gill likes any play that allows him to pull faces at the audience and dance those tedious jigs of his. And what does *he* know about choosing a good wife?' he added, raising a meaningful eyebrow. 'Unless the wife in question is a pretty boy with sweet lips and a compliant body. Don't fob me off with Barnaby's opinion,' he warned. 'Give me your own. Is this play fit for performance?'

Nicholas took a deep breath. 'No,' he admitted. 'Not yet, anyway.'

'Not ever. It's the worst thing that Edmund has ever penned.'

'It needs a little work, that's all.'

'What it needs is another plot, another set of characters and another title. Most of all, Nick,' he insisted, 'it needs what every comedy needs and that is comic substance.

There's not a decent laugh in it from start to finish. Worse still – there's not an *indecent* laugh.'

'That's too harsh an opinion.'

'It's the one that Edmund will hear when he arrives, and he's due here any moment. I'm in no mood to spare his feelings. He's contracted to supply us with plays of quality – not with this base, brown paper stuff.' He gave a snort. 'Edmund Hoode may know how to choose a wife but he's forgotten how to write a comedy. I'll tell him so to his face.'

Right on cue, there was a knock at the front door and they heard Firethorn's wife, Margery, going to answer it. Nicholas glanced down at the fateful manuscript. Edmund Hoode was a close friend of his and he wanted to protect him from the actor-manager's scorn. A man who had provided so many good plays for the company over the years deserved due consideration. Nicholas stepped forward.

'Let *me* speak to him,' he volunteered.

'I commissioned the play,' said Firethorn. 'I'll hurl it back at him.'

'That's what you did to Master Vavasor.'

Sobered by the reminder, the actor retreated into a sullen silence. When his wife conducted Edmund Hoode into the room, Firethorn spared him no more than a curt nod. Nicholas, by contrast, gave him a warm greeting. Margery looked on with a hospitable smile. She was a handsome woman in her thirties, still vivacious and blossoming in male company. The tall, pale, moon-faced, ever-anxious Hoode always aroused her maternal instincts. She touched his arm.

'Can I get you anything, Edmund?' she enquired.

'You can get us all something strong to drink,' said Firethorn. 'I have a feeling that we'll need it.'

'Yes, Lawrence.'

'Open that bottle of Canary wine.'

'I will.'

Margery lifted the hem of her dress and tripped out of the room. Hoode's eye went straight to the play that lay on the table. Before Firethorn could speak, Nicholas interrupted him.

'Why don't we all sit down?' he suggested, lowering himself into a chair. The others sat opposite him. 'How are you, Edmund?'

'Keen to hear your opinion of the play,' replied Hoode. 'I know that you went to the Curtain today. How did *Lamberto* fare?'

'Very well indeed.'

'Enough of this turgid tragedy!' protested Firethorn. 'I'll not have Banbury's Men praised under my roof. The only play that concerns me is the one that lies on that table.'

'That's what I came to discuss,' said Hoode. 'I worked long and hard on *How to Choose a Good Wife*. When will it go into rehearsal?'

'Never!'

'What Lawrence means,' said Nicholas, trying to soften the blow, 'is that the play is not yet entirely ready to be put before an audience. It lacks your usual deft touch, Edmund.'

'It lacks anything that might commend it,' announced Firethorn.

15

Hoode was distressed. 'You thought it that poor?'

'Poverty itself.'

'But not without its finer points,' said Nicholas, keen to offer his friend some solace. 'Barnaby was delighted with his role and I believe the scene at the fair was a small masterpiece. Taken as a whole, however, the piece does not hang together.'

'Then it is *rejected*?' said Hoode, shaken to the core.

'For the time being, perhaps.'

'That's all eternity in my book,' declared Firethorn. 'I'd not dare to feed an audience on such a half-baked matter as that. It would stick in their throats.' Margery came into the room with a tray. 'This is the way to choose a good wife,' he went on, cheerfully. 'Follow my example. Pick a comely creature who knows when and how to satisfy your appetites.' He patted Margery on the rump. 'Thank you, my love.'

'We've company,' she scolded, gently. 'Behave yourself, Lawrence.'

'Why? Nick and Edmund know how much I adore you.'

'Tell me about your adoration at a more seemly time.'

After handing each man a cup of wine, she went back to the kitchen. Firethorn took a long sip of his drink while Nicholas set his cup down on the table. Hoode stared bleakly into his own wine as if seeing the dregs of his career as a playwright. A pessimist at the best of times, he now sank into complete despondency. Seeing his gloom, Firethorn repented of his bluntness and felt sorry for him. Nicholas, for once, was unable to find words of comfort for his friend. It was Hoode who finally broke the awkward silence.

'You are both right,' he conceded, sadly. 'You tell me nothing that I didn't know myself when I laboured on it. *How to Choose a Good Wife* is a case of *How to Write a Bad Play*. Barnaby was pleased with his role because I gave the Clown several scenes and let him dance in each one. All that he bothered to look at were the parts in which he appeared. You, on the other hand, read the whole play and saw how shapeless it was.'

'That can be remedied,' said Nicholas.

'Not by me, Nick.'

'You have a gift for construction.'

'Then it's left me,' said Hoode. 'I'm not the man I was. My wit no longer sparks, my pen no longer flows. The well of creation has dried up.'

'How oft have we heard you say that?'

'This time, I mean it.'

'You meant it when you spoke the very same words about your last play,' Nicholas reminded him, 'and with some justice. When you were writing *A Way to Content All Women*, you were struck down with such a pernicious disease that you never thought to recover. Yet, when you did, you finished the play within a week and it turned out to be the sprightliest comedy of the season. Your well has not gone dry, Edmund. You simply have to lower the bucket a little further in it.'

'Yes,' said Firethorn, showing some sympathy at last. 'We love you and respect your work, Edmund. It would be cruel to offer this new play under your name and undo all your credit. Nick speaks true.' He inflated his chest. 'A Way to Content All Women was a triumph for me – and a sparkling comedy to boot. That was the *real* Edmund Hoode at work.'

'I am merely his ghost,' said the playwright with a sigh.

'We put too much upon you,' argued Nicholas. 'You are not only obliged to provide us with a steady flow of new plays, but to keep old ones in repair, and to lend your guidance to novice authors. And if that were not enough, you also hold your own as an actor.'

'My duties wore me down. I am posthumous.'

'Drink up, man,' said Firethorn. 'Enough of this nonsense about the death of your art. All you need is a good rest. If your pen has molted, give it time to grow its feathers again.'

'That's sound advice,' said Nicholas, sampling his wine.

'Watch and pray.'

'But what do we do meanwhile?' asked Hoode, taking a welcome sip of his own drink. 'Novelty is ever the life-blood of theatre. While our rivals can assuage the demand for new plays, our offerings are bent with age and covered with dust.'

'I may have the answer to that,' said Firethorn, reflectively.

'Oh?' Nicholas was very surprised. 'It's the first I've heard of it. Are you talking about a new play?'

'A new playwright. Since we were in such straits, I took it upon myself to commission a comedy from him. Yes, yes,' he went on, quickly, before Hoode could interrupt, 'I know that I exceeded my powers. Before a new play is accepted, it must be read by you and Barnaby as well.'

'And by Nick,' said Hoode. 'He may not be a sharer but there's no shrewder judge of a play in the whole company. Why did you not at least take him into your confidence?'

Nicholas was disconcerted. 'I could ask the same thing,' he said. 'You made no mention of this new playwright before Edmund arrived.'

'I wanted you both to hear the news together,' claimed Firethorn. 'And I look to one of you to pass it on to Barnaby because I know he'll have a tantrum when he realises that he was kept in the dark.'

'Like the rest of us.'

'Do not censure me, Nick. Nobody is better placed than you to know what a parlous state our finances are in. To reduce our commitments, we had to part with three hired men last week and manage without them. Desperate situations call for desperate measures.'

'So what have you done?' asked Hoode with unaccustomed sarcasm. 'Written a play yourself?'

'No,' returned Firethorn, 'I relied on my instinct. I met a fellow, lately come to London with an ambition to be a dramatist. Most who entertain that dream will never have it fulfilled but Hibbert is different.'

'Hibbert?'

'That's his name, Edmund. Mark it well. Saul Hibbert.'

'I've never heard of him,' said Nicholas.

'You soon will,' prophesied Firethorn, 'and so will all of London. He has a rare talent and we must harness it. All that he was able to show me were three acts of his comedy but they were enough to make me offer him a contract. Saul Hibbert is our man.'

'How did you meet him?'

'He wrote to me and asked if we would consider his work.'

'And we would have done so,' said Hoode, peevishly, 'had you had the grace to ask us. This is most irregular, Lawrence. We've always discussed new work before and not proceeded with a commission until all three of us – Nick, too, of course – were thoroughly satisfied.'

'I think I can guarantee satisfaction in this case.'

'Yet you only saw three acts of the play?' said Nicholas, worried.

'One was enough to tell me that he is a true dramatist.'

'And when will his comedy be finished?'

'By the end of next week,' said Firethorn. 'Why these long faces?' he went on as the others exchanged an apprehensive glance. 'You should be rejoicing with me. I've found a second Edmund Hoode.'

'The first one has not departed yet!' yelled Hoode, indignantly.

'A moment ago, you were talking from the grave.'

'I've climbed out again.'

'Be still, Edmund,' said Nicholas with a calming gesture. 'These tidings may yet lead to our salvation. If this fellow can furnish us with a new play, we should bid him welcome to the company. He's no threat to *your* position,' he emphasised. 'There's only one Edmund Hoode.'

'Lawrence would do well to remember that.'

'It's graven on my heart,' said Firethorn, a hand on his chest. 'I've a play or two left in me yet.'

'A dozen, at least,' said Nicholas, delighted to hear the pride in Hoode's voice. 'Rest awhile and the words will come teeming out of you. In the meantime,' he added, turning to Firethorn, 'it seems that we have to take Saul Hibbert on trust. What is his comedy called?'

Firethorn opened his mouth to reply but, before he could speak, there was a pounding on the front door that made all three of them look in the direction of it. The knocking continued until Margery opened the door. After a brief conversation, she ushered the visitor into the parlour.

'This is Master Hibbert,' she said, clearly impressed by the newcomer. 'He claims that he has urgent business with you, Lawrence.'

Firethorn was on his feet. 'Why, so he has!' he confirmed. 'Come in, Saul. Come in, come in.'

Though he gave a smile of thanks, Saul Hibbert preferred to stay framed in the doorway where he had struck a pose. Tall, slim and flamboyantly attired, he had a natural elegance that would make him stand out in a crowd. He also had an actor's assurance and charm. Seeing that Margery wished to leave, he stood back and gave her an elaborate bow. With a little giggle, she went past him. Hibbert came into the room to be introduced to the others.

Hoode was slightly unnerved to see that the man who had been compared to him was ten years younger and twenty times more good-looking. Nicholas's first impression was that Hibbert was too fond of outward show but he reserved his judgement on his character. Beaming at Firethorn, the newcomer thrust a sheaf of papers into his hand.

'Finished at last!' he boasted.

'But your play was not due for another week,' said Firethorn.

'I was enjoying the act of creation so much that I could not break off. I've worked night and day to complete it.'

'That's heartening news!'

'It is, indeed,' said Nicholas. 'Tell me, Master Hibbert, is this the first play you have written?'

'No, Nick,' replied the other, familiarly, 'it's the third. One was performed at Norwich and the second at Oxford.'

Hoode was suspicious. 'Oxford. You're a University man, then?'

'I am, Edmund. I started my learning in the gutter and took my degree in the university of life. Oxford?' he said with a sneer. 'Why waste time in a cap and gown that could be better spent elsewhere?'

'Quite so,' said Firethorn, starting to read the first page.

'I have enough Latin to get by and enough Greek to show that I have a gift for languages. On my travels, I've also picked up a tidy amount of German, French and Italian. The necessities of courtship, you might say.' Firethorn let out a guffaw. 'Ah, you're reading the scene in the apothecary's shop?'

'Reading it and loving it,' said Firethorn, turning to a new page.

'Welcome to the company, Master Hibbert,' said Nicholas.

'We're delighted to have you,' added Hoode, guardedly.

'You certainly need me,' said Hibbert, tossing back his long, wavy black hair. 'When I saw you perform last week, I could not believe how much Westfield's Men had declined since my last visit to London. The play was billed as a comedy but it did not raise a smile from me. Whoever thought that such a tame piece could be offered as entertainment?'

'Which play did you see?'

'*A Way to Content All Women.*'

Hoode gurgled as he realised that his own work was being vilified. His discomfort was intensified by another burst of laughter from Firethorn. While Hoode was being ridiculed, Hibbert was being lauded. Nicholas came to his friend's defence.

'You may not have smiled, Master Hibbert,' he said, 'but the rest of the audience was shaking with mirth for the whole two hours.'

'It shows how easily pleased the fools were.'

'Include me in their folly. I admire the play immensely.'

'Thank you, Nick,' said Hoode.

Firethorn waved the manuscript. 'Wait until you read this,' he said, grinning broadly. 'It's the very essence of wit.'

'I'll leave you to relish it,' decided Hibbert, putting his hat on at a rakish angle. 'When you have read it through, I'll hold you to your contract. Send my fee to the Queen's Head. I lodge there at the moment.' He gave another bow. 'Gentlemen, it was a pleasure to meet you. Together, I am sure, we can lift Westfield's Men above the mundane.'

He swept from the room and let himself out of the house.

'Above the mundane!' echoed Hoode, puce with anger. 'Did you hear what he said about *A Way to Content All Women*? It was insulting.'

'He's entitled to his opinion,' said Firethorn, tolerantly.

'But not to express it so rudely before the author,' said Nicholas.

'Saul meant no harm.'

'It was felt, nevertheless,' said Hoode.

'Read his play and you'll forgive him everything.'

'I doubt that, Lawrence. I found him boorish and arrogant.'

'He has the confidence of his genius, that's all.'

'And what has that genius actually produced?' asked Hoode, waspishly. 'Does this hilarious new play of his have a name?'

'Of course. It's called *The Malevolent Comedy*.'

'An apt title for such an author,' observed Nicholas, drily.

Chapter Two

Opinion about the company's new playwright was sharply divided. When the actors adjourned to the taproom of the Queen's Head after the first rehearsal of Saul Hibbert's comedy, they had all reached a very firm conclusion about the author and his work. The taproom was filled with noise and tobacco smoke as Barnaby Gill joined Owen Elias and Francis Quilter at their table. Gill was a walking paradox, a morose, brooding, self-centred man offstage, he turned into a comic delight in front of an audience, genial, outgoing and full of energy. Some of that energy had been put to good use during the rehearsal.

'It's a fine play,' he said, reaching for his Canary wine, 'and it enables me to be at my finest. I'm grateful to Master Hibbert for that.'

'He'll not get my gratitude,' warned Quilter. 'I think that Saul Hibbert is an arrant popinjay and that his comedy, like him, is neat and trimly dressed without any real essence. A hollow piece of work.'

'I fill the void with my dances.'

'They are mere distractions, Barnaby. Every time our author runs short of ideas, he brings the Clown on to perform a jig. You are simply there to conceal the fact that the play lacks substance.'

'I disagree, Frank,' said Elias, keen to take part in the argument. '*The Malevolent Comedy* is the best new offering we've had for months. Where I do side with you, however, is in the matter of Saul Hibbert's character. I found the fellow haughty and irritating.'

'I like him,' said Gill.

'I hate the jackanapes,' asserted Quilter.

'Saul has a sharp eye for talent.'

'You only say that because he applauded you today.'

'And you only decry him because he said your performance was too shallow and weak-willed. And I'm bound to confess,' added Gill, waspishly, 'that I felt the very same. You struggled badly, Frank.'

Quilter was hurt. 'No, I did not!'

'We were all floundering at a first rehearsal,' said Elias, quaffing his ale. 'I know that I was. Even Lawrence lost his footing in the role a few times. You were better than most, Frank.'

'I was as good as the play allowed me to be, Owen.'

Quilter was a tall, lean, sharp-featured young man of considerable talent. Proud of belonging to Westfield's Men, he was dedicated to the troupe. He was also fond of reaping the benefits of appearing in major roles with such an important company, and was never short of female admirers. Elias realised that Quilter's dislike of Saul Hibbert was partly based on jealousy. No sooner had the handsome playwright moved into the Queen's Head than he began to capture the attention that formerly went to actors like Francis Quilter. Elias did not feel the threat in quite the same way. A stocky Welshman with a natural ebullience, he was inclined to take people on trust. Hibbert was an exception to the rule. From the moment that they met, Elias knew that he could never befriend the conceited newcomer.

'He showed no respect for Edmund,' he complained.

Gill was sour. 'Edmund does not deserve any at the moment.'

'That's a terrible thing to say!'

'Truth is often painful.'

'So is a punch on the nose,' said Elias, roused by the insult to his friend, 'and that is what you'll get if you disparage Edmund Hoode. Have you so soon forgot all the wondrous plays that he has given us over the years? More than any of us, you have cause to get down on your knees to thank him. His comedies *made* you.'

'I'll bear witness to that,' said Quilter. 'Without Edmund, there would never have been a Barnaby Gill.'

'Calumny!' howled Gill.

'Truth is often painful,' goaded Elias.

'My art is unique and irreplaceable, a jewel that would shine in any setting. I bow to no playwright. It is I who make *their* reputations by enhancing their work with my very presence.'

'No wonder you like Saul Hibbert,' said Quilter. 'The two of you are blood-brothers to Narcissus. Each of you has fallen in love with his own image. You spend so much time courting a looking glass that you can no longer see anyone but yourselves.'

'I recognise bad acting when I see it,' replied Gill, loftily, 'and that is what you inflicted on us today, Frank. Learn from my example. Study your part with more diligence and play it with more spirit.'

'If the role were in any way worthy of me, I'd do so.'

'Follow in my stead and rise above your role.'

'You malign Frank unfairly,' said Elias with truculence, 'and you were equally unkind about Edmund. Who else will feel the lash of that wicked tongue of yours?' He bunched a fist. 'Take care, Barnaby. I'll not suffer any of your reproaches. Carp and cavil at me and I'll make that ugly face of yours even uglier.'

Gill was unruffled. 'Why are the Welsh always so needlessly bellicose?' he asked with a sigh.

'Pour scorn on my nation and you'll answer for it!'

'Leave off, Owen,' advised Quilter. 'Unless he is boasting about himself, Barnaby is ever full of slights and slurs. The wonder is that he has such words of praise for Saul Hibbert.'

'He has written an excellent play,' said Gill.

'Yet when you first caught wind of *The Malevolent Comedy*, you shrieked like a turkey with a butcher's hand around its neck.'

'With good cause. Lawrence chose the play entirely

on his own, in direct violation of our policy. Neither Edmund nor I was asked for an opinion.'

'Nor was Nick Bracewell.'

'An even more serious omission,' Elias put in.

'Nick is only a hired man with the company,' said Gill, petulantly, 'and not a sharer like us. His approval does not count.'

'It does with me.'

'The point is that Lawrence – not for the first time – exceeded his authority. He went over our heads and I rightly chastised him for doing so, especially as there was another instance of his tyrannical behaviour. He rejected Edmund's new comedy without even raising the possibility with me. The one person in whom he did confide on that occasion,' he went on, bitterly, 'was our book holder.'

'I have no quibble with that,' affirmed Elias.

'Nor me,' said Quilter. 'Nick Bracewell can see the defects in a play more acutely than any of us.'

'You value his judgement, then?' asked Gill.

'Above that of anyone else in the company.'

'Then you've surely betrayed him. Where you censure *The Malevolent Comedy*, Nicholas commends it highly. So do I, won over by its biting wit and merriment. Everyone admires it save Frank Quilter.'

'I told you, Barnaby. I find the play empty.'

'Not as empty as Edmund's *How to Choose a Good Wife*. That was so full of cavities that we were in danger of falling through them.'

'Yet you liked it at first,' challenged Elias. 'I remember

you telling us so. You said that it gave you the chance to dominate the stage.'

'*Every* play does that,' said Gill, grandly. 'Were I to take on the humblest role in any drama, I would still steal all the glory. And, yes, I did smile upon Edmund's new comedy but only out of friendship. In all honesty, it really is a barren construction. Place it beside *The Malevolent Comedy* and it pales into invisibility.'

'Edmund Hoode is still the better playwright,' said Elias, loyally.

'And a truly loveable man,' said Quilter.

'You talk of the past but I look only to the future. Edmund was supreme at one time, I grant you,' conceded Gill, 'but that time is gone. His star is in decline. We have been carrying him this last year.'

'That's unjust,' protested Elias.

'Mark my words, Owen. The days when Edmund Hoode wore the laurel wreath are behind us. Westfield's Men need a sparkling new talent. I believe that we have it in Saul Hibbert.'

'God forbid!' cried Quilter.

'He's a proven master of comedy.'

'But that's not what we crave, Barnaby. Comedy will cheer the ignorant in the pit, and spread some cheap laughter among the gallants, but it will not stir their souls. Only tragedy can do that yet we have abjured it and are set to dwindle into mere comedians. Look to the Curtain,' urged Quilter. 'See what great success Banbury's Men have had with *Lamberto*. Nick Bracewell says that it outweighed anything that we have presented this year. Tragedy is in demand and we should strive to provide it.'

'Not when we have something as priceless as *The Malevolent Comedy*. It will be the envy of our rivals. Saul Hibbert is not just a playwright of rare promise,' insisted Gill, wagging a finger, 'he is a saviour in our hour of need.' The others exchanged a sceptical glance. 'Laudable as his achievements have been, talk no more of Edmund Hoode. He will soon fade into oblivion. The man we should toast,' he said, raising his cup of wine, 'is our redeemer – Saul Hibbert.'

Saul Hibbert stood in the middle of the empty inn yard and gazed at the makeshift stage that was being dismantled. What he saw in his mind's eye were actors, strutting to and fro in his play, provoking laughter at every turn and winning spontaneous applause. After the modest success of his plays in Norwich and in Oxford, he was ready to test his mettle in the more demanding arena of the capital. Hibbert had no fear of failure. Convinced of his prodigious abilities, he felt that it was only a matter of time before he conquered London audiences. When he closed his eyes, he could hear an ovation filling the dusty inn yard where Westfield's Men performed. Saul Hibbert's name was on everyone's lips.

'Master Hibbert! Master Hibbert!'

It was also on the thin, down-turned, ulcerous lips of Alexander Marwood, the landlord of the Queen's Head, a gaunt, wasted man of middle years with sparse hair and a nervous twitch that animated his face. The twitch was currently located at the tip of his nose.

'Master Hibbert – a word with you, sir!'

Hibbert came out of his reverie to find that he was looking at the unsightly visage of the landlord, nose twitching violently as if not quite sure in which direction to settle. Alexander Marwood loathed actors, detested plays and despised those who wrote them. Though he regarded Westfield's Men as a form of pestilence, he relied on the income that they brought in. As a consequence, he felt as if he were being crushed between the millstones of revulsion and need. In his codex, theatre was an abomination. Saul Hibbert was as disreputable and unwelcome as the rest of the company. Marwood was characteristically blunt.

'You are slippery, sir,' he said with open resentment. 'Every time I try to speak with you, you wriggle out of my grasp like a fish.'

Hibbert was dismissive. 'We have nothing to say to each other,' he replied, flicking a wrist. 'I am a guest here. You are at my beck and call.'

'Guests are expected to pay for their rooms.'

'Did I not give you money on account?'

'Ten days ago. More rent is now due.'

'In time, in time.'

'Now,' said Marwood, firmly. 'If you want the best room that the Queen's Head can offer, you must render up fair payment.'

'Best room!' echoed Hibbert with disgust. 'If that is the finest you have, I would hate to see the others. My chamber is too small, too dirty and too poorly furnished. The linen is soiled and the place stinks almost as much as its disagreeable landlord.'

'I'll not hear any complaint against my inn.'

'Then put your fingers in those hairy ears of yours or I'll give you a whole catalogue of complaints. The room is unfit for human habitation.'

'That should not trouble a rutting animal like you.'

Hibbert rounded on him. 'Do you dare to abuse me?'

'I state the facts,' said Marwood, taking a precautionary step backwards. 'If the room is dirty, then you have brought in the filth, for it is cleaned from top to bottom every day. As for the linen being soiled,' he added, knowingly, 'you and your visitors are responsible for that.'

'Away with you!'

'Not until I get my money.'

'You'll feel the point of my sword up your scrawny arse.'

'Then I'll send for officers to arrest you.'

'I dignify the Queen's Head by staying here.'

'You've done nothing but drag it down to your own base level.'

'I'll not haggle with a mere underling like you,' said Hibbert as he saw Nicholas Bracewell approaching them. 'Talk to this fellow instead. He'll vouch for me.' He raised his voice. 'Is that not so, Nick?'

'What say you?' asked Nicholas.

'This cringing knave has the effrontery to demand money from me. Tell him that my credit is good. Rescue me from this hideous face of his.'

'The landlord is entitled to be paid,' said Nicholas, reasonably.

'There!' shouted Marwood. 'There's one honest man among you.'

'Then you can discuss the matter honestly with him,' decided Hibbert with a supercilious smile. 'I'll not speak another word to you. Nick,' he said with a lordly gesture, 'see to this rogue, will you?'

'What am I supposed to do?'

'Get the whoreson dog off my back.'

'This sounds like a matter between you and the landlord.'

'Resolve it, man. That's what you're here for, is it not?'

'No,' said Nicholas, stoutly.

'You're a book holder, paid to fetch and carry for the rest of us. So let's have no more hesitation. Do as I tell you or there'll be trouble.'

'I take no orders from you, Master Hibbert.'

'Neither do I,' said Marwood, emboldened by the presence of Nicholas. 'Settle your bill or I must ask you to quit your room.'

'I'd have more comfort in a pig sty,' returned Hibbert with a sneer. 'Now keep out of my way, you apparition, or you'll live to regret it.' He pointed to Nicholas. 'Badger this fellow in my stead. He'll tell you who and what I am. Nick will solve this petty business in a trice.'

'Why should I do that?' asked Nicholas.

'Because I *tell* you.'

Saul Hibbert turned on his heel and strode off towards the door to the taproom. Nicholas contained his anger. Upset by the playwright's cavalier attitude towards him, he resolved to take it up with Hibbert at a latter date. Meanwhile, he had to placate Alexander Marwood, a task he had been forced to undertake many times on behalf of the company.

'Master Hibbert treats me like a cur,' wailed the landlord.

'His manner is indeed unfortunate.'

'He has brought nothing but trouble since he has been here. If I am not showing a tailor up to his room, I am telling a succession of women – I dare not call them ladies – where they might find him. It's more than a decent Christian like me can stand.'

'If he has rented a room, he can surely entertain friends there.'

'That depends on how he entertains them,' said Marwood, darkly. 'When she happened to be passing his chamber last night, my wife heard sounds that brought a blush to her cheek.'

Nicholas doubted very much if Sybil Marwood had passed the room by accident. Knowing the landlady of old, he suspected that she had an ear glued to Saul Hibbert's door every time he had female company. Marwood's wife was a flinty harridan, a formidable creature of blood and stone, who had never blushed in her life. Politeness, however, required Nicholas to show a degree of sympathy for her.

'I'm sorry that your wife has suffered embarrassment,' he said.

'She was too ashamed to give me the full details.'

'I'm surprised that either of you is shocked, however. This is an inn, after all, not a church. You must surely be accustomed to the sound of your guests taking their pleasures in private.'

Marwood gave a visible shudder and the twitch

abandoned his nose to move to his right eyebrow, making it flutter wildly like a moth caught in a cobweb. The landlord had not enjoyed any pleasure with his wife since the night their only child had been conceived, a fact that accounted for his deep melancholy. Deprived of any fleshly enjoyment himself, he begrudged it to others. Those with obvious sexual charm, like Saul Hibbert, earned his particular rancour.

'The man should be gelded,' he argued.

'From what you tell me,' said Nicholas, 'that would cause upset to number of ladies, and would, in any case, be too harsh a penalty for someone who has not paid his bill. How much does he owe?'

'Five shillings.'

'A paltry amount to Master Hibbert.'

'Then why does he not hand it over?'

'He will,' promised Nicholas, 'when I speak to him. He can well afford it. Master Hibbert was paid handsomely for his new play.'

'That is another thing. I do not like the title.'

'Why? What is wrong with *The Malevolent Comedy*?'

'It unsettles me.'

'It may come to reassure you.'

'In what way?'

'Audiences have been thin of late,' said Nicholas, sadly, 'because we've been guilty of putting on meagre fare. Our gatherers took less money at performances while you sold far less beer and food.'

'It was a matter I meant to take up with you, Master Bracewell.'

'Our new play may put everything right.'

'I am more worried about the new playwright.'

'Give him time to settle in. He is still something of a novice and needs to learn his place. I'll endeavour to instruct him.'

'Make him treat me with respect,' said Marwood. 'When he talks to my wife, he is all smiles and flattery. I get nought but insults and threats from him. And ask him to change the title of his play.'

'It is too late to do that. Playbills have already been printed.'

'Then I fear for the safety of my inn.'

'You need have no qualms,' Nicholas told him. 'You have my word that this is one of the most cunning and spirited comedies we have ever staged here. It will fill the yard time and again.'

'You said that about *The Misfortunes of Marriage*.'

'Another work that was touched with genius.'

'And what happened to its author, Master Applegarth?' asked the landlord, ruefully. 'He was murdered at the Queen's Head under our very noses. Think of the trouble that caused me.'

'We all suffered together.'

'It drove me to despair, Master Bracewell.'

'Jonas Applegarth did not get himself hanged in order to torment *you*,' said Nicholas, sharply. 'It was a most cruel way to die and we should mourn him accordingly.'

'I mourn the damage that it did to the reputation of my inn.'

'The Queen's Head survived.'

'But for how long?' demanded Marwood, anxiously. 'Master Applegarth was a load of mischief from the start and this prancing peacock, Saul Hibbert, is cut from the same cloth. He is dangerous. I feel it in my water. Your clever playwright is a harbinger of disaster.'

'I'll take pains to ensure that he's not hanged on your property,' said Nicholas with light sarcasm.

'Do not jest about it, Master Bracewell. If he continues to put on airs and graces at the Queen's Head, your Master Hibbert may well finish up at the end of a rope,' said the landlord, 'and I'll be the hangman!'

George Dart had always been the lowliest member of the company in every sense, a diminutive figure, toiling manfully in the background as an assistant stagekeeper, while those with more talent, more presence and more confidence received all the plaudits. Dart accepted his role as the whipping boy for Westfield's Men with resignation, never expecting to shed it. The arrival of Hal Bridger, however, transformed his existence. Dart was no longer the most junior person in the troupe. Tall, gangly and hopelessly innocent, Bridger was a fair-haired youth whose passion for the theatre was not matched by a shred of histrionic skill. Unable to tread the boards with any style himself, he wanted nothing more than to serve those who could, worshipping actors such as Lawrence Firethorn and Barnaby Gill as if they were minor gods.

George Dart finally had someone beneath him, a gullible

lad who deflected the mockery away from its usual target. It was Hal Bridger who was now teased, shouted at, sent hither and thither, scorned, ridiculed and given all the most menial jobs. Dart was his friend and advisor. When he saw Thomas Skillen, the irascible old stagekeeper, box the newcomer's ears, he took his young friend aside.

'Remember to duck, Hal.'

'Duck?'

'Whenever he tries to hit you,' explained Dart. 'Thomas's back is so stiff that he cannot bend. Duck under his hand and he'll not be able to touch you. Life will be much less painful that way.'

'Thank you, George.'

'I should be thanking you. Since you joined the company, Thomas no longer turns his fury on me. It's aimed at you now.'

'Only because I deserve it.'

Hal Bridger gave a toothy grin. To be part of such an illustrious theatrical enterprise, he was very willing to endure daily beatings and constant verbal abuse. To be yelled at by Lawrence Firethorn was, to him, a signal honour. At the same time, he did not wish to jeopardise his position by failing in his duties. Guided by Nicholas Bracewell, and helped by Dart, he had become an efficient servant to the company. Bridger had been rewarded with what he saw as the ultimate accolade.

'I never thought I'd ever be given a role to play,' he said.

'You are onstage for less than a minute,' Dart noted.

'It will seem like an hour to me, George. I'll bask in its

glow. And I'll share my precious moment of fame with no less an actor than Master Firethorn. I'll be in heaven.'

'It was more like hell to me.'

An unwilling actor at the best of times, Dart had a fatal habit of forgetting his lines, dropping anything that he was carrying and bumping into scenery. Even though confined to tiny roles, he could be a menace. The part assigned to him in *The Malevolent Comedy* had filled him with his customary apprehension, until Nicholas Bracewell took pity on him and suggested that Hal Bridger might take his place. One man's intense relief was another's joy. Day after day, Bridger had rehearsed his single line with alacrity.

'I will take anything from your fair hand,' he declared.

'What?'

'That's what I say to Mistress Malevole when I take the potion from her. I know that she is only Dick Honeydew in a wig and skirts, but she is the most convincing lady I ever saw.'

'Dick is the best of our apprentices,' said Dart, proudly. 'He can play queens or country maids with equal skill. Wait until you see him as the Countess of Milan in one of our tragedies.'

Bridger was eager. 'Will there be a part for me in that?'

'Several. I played four the last time we performed it.'

'I'll *buy* one of them off you, George.'

'You can have all four *gratis*.'

'Thank you,' said Bridger, striking a pose. 'I will take anything from your fair hand.'

'It will be a clout if Thomas catches you dawdling here,'

warned Nicholas Bracewell, coming up to them with an affectionate smile. 'The spectators will begin to dribble in soon and the first scene is not set. About it straight.'

The pair of them gabbled their apologies and ran off. They had been talking in the tiring-house, the room at the rear of the stage that was used by the actors during a performance and filled with their costumes. Nicholas checked that all the hand properties were set out in the correct sequence on the table, and was pleased to see that Dart and Bridger had done that job well. He went through the curtain and onto the stage, making sure that they put the settle, chairs and small table in the right positions for the opening of the play. Hal Bridger broke off to stare up in wonder at the galleries.

'Our patron will be up there this afternoon,' said Nicholas.

Bridger was overawed. 'Lord Westfield himself?'

'He's coming expressly to hear you, Hal,' joked Dart.

'But I only utter a single line.'

'Make sure that it is loud and clear,' said Nicholas. 'That is all we require of you. Except that you do not knock anything over when you fall to the floor.'

'As I'd be certain to do,' admitted Dart.

'Ah, yes,' Nicholas went on, struck by an afterthought, 'there is perhaps one thing more, Hal.'

'What's that?'

'*Enjoy* yourself.'

'I will, I promise you!'

'It's more than I ever managed to do,' confided Dart.

But his remark was drowned out by Hal Bridger's happy laughter. The assistant stagekeeper was on the brink of one of the most thrilling experiences of his life and Nicholas was pleased for him. Like everyone else in the company, Hal Bridger could not wait to perform an exciting new play before its first audience. Heaven was at last at hand.

Spectators flocked to the Queen's Head in droves, spurred on by the promise of novelty and by rumours that they would be present at a remarkable event. The galleries were soon crammed to capacity, the pit a seething mass of citizenry. Food and beer were served in large quantities, putting the watching public in the ideal frame of mind. Saul Hibbert wore a new suit of blue velvet for the occasion, looking more ostentatious than ever as he settled onto his cushion in the upper gallery. While the author of *The Malevolent Comedy* oozed a conviction that bordered on complacency, the cast was troubled by the doubts and fears that always afflicted them on such occasions.

Veteran actors knew the horrors that could attend first outings of a play. If the work did not find favour, they would be booed, jeered and even be hit by ripe fruit, hurled at them by disappointed spectators. More than one of the new plays they had performed in the past had sunk without trace beneath the wrath of their audience. In two cases, the actors had not even been allowed to finish the play, hounded from the stage by riotous behaviour. While they all had faith in the excellence of *The Malevolent Comedy*, their confidence was not unmixed with dread.

It was a situation in which Lawrence Firethorn came to the fore. If he had the slightest tremor, it did not show in his face or bearing. As he gathered his company around him in the tiring-house, he was the epitome of poise and assurance. Resplendent in his costume as Lord Loveless, he addressed his actors.

'Friends,' he said, solemnly, 'we have been given an opportunity today that we must seize with both hands. Westfield's Men have lost something of their lustre and we must repair that loss. Our rivals boast that they are now supreme but we have a new play that can restore all our fortunes. It was Edmund's joyous comedies that helped to forge our reputation,' he continued, indicating Hoode, who looked like more like a disconsolate sheep than the proud steward he was supposed to be playing, 'and we must follow in the tradition that he set for us. I believe that, in Saul Hibbert, we have another Edmund Hoode. Let us show our new author how much we appreciate his work by playing it to the hilt.' He drew an imaginary sword and thrust it into the air. 'Onward, lads!' he exhorted. 'Onwards to certain victory!'

Buoyed up by their leader's encouragement, the actors were keen to begin, looking in the mirror for the last time and making final adjustments to their costumes. Edmund Hoode remained forlorn. Wanting the play to succeed, he believed that it would mark the end of his own career as playwright. Nicholas Bracewell went across to slip a consoling arm around his shoulders.

'There is only one Edmund Hoode,' he told him.

'Thank you, Nick.'

'And we will soon be staging his next matchless comedy.'

'In truth,' said Hoode with a wan smile, 'I'm in no mood to provide humour. My muse has deserted me. She is gone forever.'

Nicholas had no time to reassure his friend. With the play due to start, a signal had to be given to the musicians in the gallery above the stage. A flag was hoisted, a fanfare blared and Owen Elias stepped out in a black cloak to deliver the Prologue. Within a matter of seconds, he got the first titter from the audience. Firethorn glanced over his shoulder at the other actors and beamed regally.

'Let's make them laugh until their sides are fit to burst,' he said.

The Malevolent Comedy secured a firm and immediate hold over the spectators. From a simple plot, Saul Hibbert had built up a complex series of comic effects. Lord Loveless, a wealthy nobleman, was looking for a wife who would marry him for love and not for his money. To that end, he enlisted the aid of Mistress Malevole, a white witch whose potions could achieve magical results. Loveless required her to make three separate women – unattainable beauties until now – swallow a potion that would make them fall instantly in love with him. By courting all three, Lord Loveless could decide which he would take as a wife.

What he did not know was that Mistress Malevole had a malevolent streak that made her give the three women the wrong potion. Secretly in love with Lord Loveless herself, she was not prepared to yield him up to another. One of her rivals was turned into a cat, another believed she was an owl and the third capered around the stage like a monkey. Barnaby Gill complicated matters even more with his clowning, stealing some of his mistress's other potions to slip into the wine cups of the men.

Edmund Hoode, a stately steward, conceived a passion for his master that led to all kinds of comic friction. Francis Quilter, in the guise of the ancient Martin Oldman, regressed into childhood and became a gibbering infant. Sir Bernard Graball, the rapacious knight played by Owen Elias, took a sip of his wine and became so afraid of women that the very sight of them threw him into a panic. Antidotes that were administered to counter the effects of the potions only made things worse. At one point, everyone in the play thought that they were in love with the Clown. Ironically, the person who most wanted affection was denied it and Lawrence Firethorn revelled in his misery with hilarious consequences. Reviewing the possibilities, he turned on the grinning Mistress Malevole.

'Am I to marry a cat and spend nine lives, chasing mice and fornicating with black fur? Is that what you offer me? Or would you rather have me wed an owl and pass my nights upon a cold bough, letting my manhood wilt untouched beneath my feathers? My other choice is this moonstruck monkey. How can I mate with such a creature when I cannot even catch her? And what sort of progeny would I father on these zanies? Cats, owls and monkeys! Two of each, bearing my loveless name, going forth into the world to multiply like so many dumb animals, issuing from Noah's ark. A pox on these freaks of nature! Give me a woman I can love as a woman, and be loved in return by her. Is that too much to ask?'

Mistress Malevole assured him that she would answer his plea, only to create further confusion with another round of potions. In the leading female role, Richard Honeydew, the youngest of the apprentices, showed a delight in merry mischief that earned Mistress Malevole the complete sympathy of the audience. They rejoiced in the endless potions and the multiple changes of character. It was only in the last act that Loveless himself was prevailed upon to drink one of the concoctions himself. Seeing the havoc they had wreaked on others, he insisted that his servant tasted it first and he beckoned Hal Bridger forward.

His moment had arrived. Trembling nervously and with a throat that had suddenly turned into a parched desert, Bridger summoned up all his strength to say the one line that he had been given. He watched Mistress Malevole mix the potion then pour it into a cup. When it was offered to him, he forced a smile.

'I will take anything from your fair hand,' he said, bravely.

Accepting the cup, he drank deeply. Bridger was supposed to sway for a few moments before falling gently to the floor. Instead, he let out a cry of agony, flung away the cup and grasped at his stomach with both hands. When he keeled over, he went into a violent paroxysm, arching and kicking with such uncontrollable force that he knocked over the table, spilling its contents across the stage. The audience roared with mirth, thinking it was part of the play that had been carefully rehearsed.

Nicholas Bracewell was not fooled. Watching with dismay from behind the scenes, he knew that Hal Bridger was in real pain. No compassion was shown by the throng. The greater his convulsions, the more the spectators laughed. When he kicked over a chair and sent it cart-wheeling from the stage, there was a round of applause for him. But the hapless servant was no longer acting a part.

He was, literally, dying before their eyes.

Chapter Three

Bemused by the frantic display in front of them, the actors were quite uncertain what to do. They stood in a circle around Hal Bridger and watched him writhe dramatically on the boards to the misplaced amusement of the roaring onlookers. Lord Loveless's servant then twisted upward in torment one more time before lapsing into immobility. It was Nicholas Bracewell who reacted first. Realising that the play could founder if it lost its impetus, he set his prompt copy aside and stepped onstage, nodding deferentially to Lord Loveless as if he were another of his retinue. With great gentleness, he scooped up the body and carried it quickly into the tiring-house. Lawrence Firethorn showed his presence of mind by turning the incident into a jest.

'Is *that* what your potion does, Mistress Malevole?' he asked. 'I'll have none of it or there's not a piece of furniture in my house will be safe from my flailing limbs?'

The rest of the cast followed where he led, using all their skills to disguise the fact that they had been deeply disturbed by what had just happened. With a combination of witty dialogue, vivid gestures and the comic business carefully devised in rehearsal, they took the play at breakneck speed into its closing scenes. No more magic potions were needed. Restored to normality, the three beautiful women sought the same rich husband, but each was rejected in turn by Lord Loveless because they were only interested in his wealth. It was the scheming Mistress Malevole – renouncing her malevolence – who emerged as his true love and he disclosed his own secret passion for her. The happy couple were promptly married by a priest, and Barnaby Gill, as the effervescent Clown, brought festivities to a close with an hilarious jig. Cheers, whistles and loud applause reverberated around the inn yard.

Westfield's Men had a resounding success on their hands.

Nicholas Bracewell took no pleasure from the ovation. All that concerned him was the fate of the youth who lay on the table in the tiring-house. Though he tried to revive Hal Bridger, he knew that his efforts were in vain. What the audience had found so diverting were, in fact, the death throes of a young and innocuous assistant stagekeeper, making his very first – and last – appearance before the public. Nicholas was shocked and saddened. He used a cloak to cover Bridger's face and hide it from the actors who were staring with ghoulish fascination at the contorted features. George Dart was appalled.

'Hal is *dead*?' he gasped.

'I fear so,' said Nicholas. 'The poor lad was poisoned.'

'Poisoned?'

'I could smell it on his lips.'

'God forgive me!' exclaimed Dart. 'I prepared that potion.'

'You were not to blame, George.'

'And I let Hal drink it in my place. *I* should have played that servant.' He began to quake. 'In giving the part to Hal, I killed him!'

Dart was inconsolable. Weeping copiously, he retired to a corner of the room with his head in his hands. At that moment, Firethorn led the company offstage. Actors who had acknowledged the applause with broad smiles now gathered around the corpse with a mixture of sorrow and bewilderment. Lord Loveless gazed down at the body.

'What on earth happened, Nick?' he demanded.

'Hal's drink was poisoned.'

'Send for a doctor at once.'

'He's beyond the reach of medicine,' said Nicholas.

There was a collective sigh of despair. Rising above it was a piercing cry of horror from Richard Honeydew, who pushed forward to stand beside the table and pulled back the cloak from Bridger's face. The apprentice was no longer the guileful Mistress Malevole but a frightened boy with blood on his hands.

'This is my doing!' he said, aghast.

'No,' said Nicholas.

'But I gave him that drink.'

'You were not to know that it was poisoned, Dick.'

'I murdered Hal Bridger.'

The acclaim in the yard reached a new pitch of hysteria and Firethorn responded at once, calling his actors to order so that he could take them back onstage to harvest the applause. Fixed smiles returned to their faces but grief burnt away inside them. Stunned by the gruesome death of the servant, Mistress Malevole had difficulty in standing and Lord Loveless had to wrap an arm around her shoulder to prevent her from tumbling over. Spectators clapped and shouted until their palms were sore and their throats hoarse.

Nicholas Bracewell, meanwhile, remained in the tiring-house. His only companions were the distraught George Dart and the body of Hal Bridger. Closing his eyes, he sent up a silent prayer for the soul of the deceased. When he lifted his lids again, he saw the head of Alexander Marwood peering around the door at the corpse on the table. There was a note of grim satisfaction in the landlord's voice.

'I told you that this play would bring trouble,' he said, baring his blackened teeth. 'You should have changed the title.'

There was so much for the book holder to do that the next half an hour passed in a blur. Nicholas had to send for constables, report the murder and set an official investigation in motion. He also had to calm George Dart, reassure the tearful Richard Honeydew, keep the irate Lawrence Firethorn at bay and supervise the storing of costumes and properties. The first thing that he did was to slip onstage to retrieve the poisoned cup that had been tossed aside by Hal Bridger, sniffing it as he did so and noting the pungent odour. The potions that were given throughout the play were contained in a series of phials, filled with nothing more harmful than red wine, heavily diluted with water. Nicholas took charge of them all so that he could examine each one at leisure. As soon as the audience began to disperse, he was able to order the dismantling of the scenery and the stage.

After such an exultant performance, the tiring-house was usually a Bedlam of revelry and congratulation. There was no hint of celebration this time. Hushed by the death of Hal Bridger, the actors moved around in bruised silence, all too aware of the fact that the poison might have been given to one of them instead. In meeting his grisly end, the youth had saved someone else from the identical fate. It was only when the body was removed that most of the company felt able to talk. They drifted away to the taproom in a sombre mood.

Lawrence Firethorn stayed behind to consult his book holder.

'How could this happen, Nick?' he wondered.

'Someone put poison into one of the phials.'

'Then why was nobody struck down during this morning's rehearsal? We drank the same liquid then as this afternoon.'

'No,' said Nicholas, thinking it through. 'After the rehearsal, I told George Dart to refill the phials and watched him as he did so. They were set out on the table so that Mistress Malevole could use them during the performance.

Before that happened,' he concluded, 'one of the potions was poisoned. Some knave must have sneaked in here.'

'Why? Did he have reason to hate Hal Bridger?'

'He had no idea that he would be the victim because he could not possibly know which of the potions Hal would drink. It could just as easily have been Owen, Frank or Edmund who took the fatal dose.'

'Or even me!' said Firethorn in alarm.

'The obvious intent was to commit a murder that would interrupt the play and bring it to an untimely end.'

'Villainy!'

'We were fortunate,' Nicholas pointed out. 'That particular potion was not used until late in the play, and our actors were sufficiently alert to cope with the situation. Thanks to your example, the play was saved.'

'At what great cost, though! I'd rather lose a dozen plays than sacrifice the life of one member of my company. *The Malevolent Comedy* has been fringed with tragedy. It makes me sick to my stomach, Nick.'

'I'll find the man behind all this,' vowed the other.

'At least, you'll know where to start looking.'

'Will I?'

'Of course,' said Firethorn with growing fury. 'Go to the Curtain. I'll wager all I own that it was Giles Randolph who hired this killer.'

'I doubt that,' said Nicholas.

'Naked envy is at work here. He heard about our new play.'

'That would not make him stoop to murder. The best

weapon that Banbury's Men have is their own success. That hurts us most.'

'I still believe that Randolph is behind all this somehow.'

'And I'm just as certain that neither he nor his company is involved in any way. If they wanted to inflict real harm on Westfield's Men,' Nicholas pointed out, 'they would strike directly at you and bring us to our knees. Why use a poison that might only lead to the death – as it did, in this case – of a mere hired man? I mean no disrespect to Hal,' he added, quietly. 'A willing lad and a pleasure to work beside. I'll miss him sorely. But we'd all miss Lawrence Firethorn much more.'

Firethorn pondered. 'Perhaps my wager was a little hasty,' he said.

'You stand to lose everything you have.'

'Margery would skin me alive if that happened. Let me retract at once. But, if it was not one of Giles Randolph's minions,' he went on, scratching his beard, 'then who, in God's name, was it?'

'Who and why?' said Nicholas. 'I think that motive is important here. The person we want most probably has a grudge against the company, against Master Hibbert or against the Queen's Head itself.'

'If we talk of grudges against the Queen's Head, then add me to the list of suspects. I have a thousand grudges against that miserable reptile of a landlord. Come, Nick,' urged Firethorn, 'I saw you put those phials aside. Give me the one that contained the poison and I'll push it down Marwood's throat until he chokes on it.'

'What purpose would that serve?'

'My satisfaction.'

'We search for a more dangerous enemy than our landlord,' said Nicholas, briskly. 'I'll take the phial, and the cup into which the liquid was poured, to Doctor Mordrake. One sniff of either will tell him what poison was used. That must be our starting point.'

'What of Hal Bridger?'

'When the body is examined, they'll reach the same conclusion.'

'Then why not apply to the coroner?'

'Because he will only decide the cause of death,' said Nicholas. 'Doctor Mordrake does business with every apothecary in the city. He'll know where that poison can be readily bought. I'll try to trace its origin. Before that, alas,' he went on, shaking his head, 'there's a prior duty that calls.'

'A prior duty?'

'Hal's family must be informed of his death.'

'I'll send them a letter,' suggested Firethorn, anxious to evade the responsibility of delivering the bad tidings in person. 'Fetch me pen and paper. I'll write it now.'

'They deserve better than a few choice words scribbled down,' said Nicholas with reproach. 'I'll take on the office. His parents will want a full account of what happened.'

'Thank you, Nick. You knew the lad better than me.' He nodded in the direction of the taproom. 'Will you take a cup of wine before you go?'

'No, I'll clear up here then slip quietly away.'

'So be it.' Firethorn stepped forward to embrace him warmly. 'We are indebted to you once again, dear heart. Had you not made that entrance and carried the body away, we would all have faltered. You came to our rescue.'

'Too late for Hal Bridger, alas.'

Firethorn nodded then left the tiring-house. Nicholas put all the phials on the table and sniffed each one until he found the offending bottle. It went into the pocket where he had concealed the cup from which the potion had been drunk. He was still tidying things away when Saul Hibbert came swaggering into the room.

'What?' he asked. 'Are my actors all fled?'

'You'll find them in the taproom,' replied Nicholas.

'Then I'll buy them their beer. They brought my play to life this afternoon and made me famous. A hundred people must have fought to shake my hand. I have only now been able to shake off my admirers.'

'The congratulations were deserved, Master Hibbert.'

'I'll share the kind words with Lawrence and the others. Most of them, anyway,' he said, curling a lip, 'for there's one idiot who'll get no praise from me. That wretched servant to Lord Loveless did his best to ruin my work by pretending to have the falling sickness. I'll make him fall in earnest when I catch up with him. What was the fool *doing*?'

'Dying from poison.'

'What?'

'Hal Bridger was not acting out there,' said Nicholas. 'What you saw was a foul murder. The poison that he

56

drank killed him within a matter of minutes. Officers took details of the crime and the body has been now removed. You'll not be laying a finger on the lad.'

'Can this be so?' said Hibbert in amazement. 'You believe that there was deliberate murder?'

'We kept the truth of it from the audience.'

'Thank heaven that you did, or my play would have been ruined!'

'Can you not spare a sigh of regret for the victim?'

'I am the real victim here,' said Hibbert, angrily. 'Someone set out to halt my work when it was at the very zenith of its power. I would've have been robbed of my triumph.'

'Hal Bridger was robbed of his life,' Nicholas reminded him.

'I care nothing for that. How can you compare the death of a stripling to the violation of my art? You heard that acclaim out there. *The Malevolent Comedy* has made me the talk of London.'

'Is that all that matters to you?'

'Of course.'

'Then it's high time you learnt to feel some compassion,' said Nicholas, squaring up to him. 'Because of your play, a blameless lad lost his life in front of a baying audience. He stepped onto that stage to serve you and your ambition. You might at least show thanks.'

'I need no lessons in behaviour from you,' snarled Hibbert.

'It seems that you do.'

'Step aside, man.'

'No,' said Nicholas, standing his ground. 'I want an apology first.'

'Apology? For what?'

'Putting yourself before Hal Bridger.'

Hibbert was contemptuous. 'He means nothing to me.'

'Well, he does to us,' said Nicholas, vehemently. 'When he joined Westfield's Men, he became part of a family and we cherish each member of it dearly. Spurn him at your peril, Master Hibbert.'

'Who are you to give orders to me? Be off with you!'

He reached out both hands to push Nicholas aside but he soon regretted doing so. His wrists were grabbed and he was swung so hard against the wall of the tiring-house that it knocked the breath from him. Putting a hand around his throat, Nicholas forced his head back.

'You may be the talk of London,' he said, 'but it's clearly not because of your manners. You're a disgrace to the name of gentleman, Master Hibbert. You'll start treating the members of this company – from the highest to the lowest – with the respect that's due to them, or you'll answer to me. And the same goes for the landlord. Talk to him civilly and pay your bills on time.' He banged the playwright's head against the wall. 'Do you understand?'

'I'll kill you for this,' yelled Hibbert, struggling in vain to escape.

Nicholas tightened his grip. 'Do you understand?'

'No,' croaked the other, defiantly. Nicholas applied

more pressure until Hibbert's eyes began to bulge. The playwright was eventually forced to capitulate. 'Yes,' he gurgled. 'I understand.'

'Good,' said Nicholas, releasing him with a cold smile. 'And if you should still wish to kill me, Master Hibbert, I'll be happy to indulge you at any time. You can have choice of weapons.'

'Oh, I will!' warned Hibbert, rubbing his throat. 'Nobody treats me like that – least of all an upstart book holder. I'll be back, I promise you. I'll be back to get my revenge.'

Cursing under his breath, he reeled out of the tiring-house.

The atmosphere in the taproom was strangely subdued. Though the actors were entitled to celebrate, they did so in muted fashion, all too conscious of the fact that one of their number had been poisoned in the course of the play. Guilty feelings had been stirred by Hal Bridger's death. Those who had mocked him and exploited his good nature now felt pangs of remorse. They wished that they had been kinder to him when he was alive, and more tolerant of his shortcomings. Lawrence Firethorn shared the general contrition, aware that he, too, had been unduly harsh to the assistant stagekeeper at times. Seated at a table in the corner, the actor-manager reflected on the situation with Barnaby Gill and Edmund Hoode.

'This changes everything,' he said, gloomily.

'I do not think so,' countered Gill. 'We must make the most of our success and play *The Malevolent Comedy* again tomorrow. When word of it spreads, we'll be able to run for a week or more.'

'And must we poison someone in each performance?' asked Hoode, sardonically. 'For that is what they saw and loved onstage this afternoon. Whose turn will be next? Yours, Barnaby?'

'Cease this jesting.'

'I speak in all seriousness.'

'And so do I,' said Firethorn. 'Edmund is right. We owe it to Hal Bridger to let a decent interval pass before we tackle the play again. We'll stage *Black Antonio* tomorrow, as planned.'

'That's madness!' chided Gill. 'You throw away our advantage.'

'*The Malevolent Comedy* will keep for a few days.'

'I never thought to hear such stupidity coming from the mouth of a blacksmith's son. Strike while the iron is hot, Lawrence. Is that not the first thing you learnt at your father's anvil?'

'No,' replied Firethorn, nostalgically. 'The first thing I learnt was not to put my hand on the anvil because it was usually still hot from the horseshoe that had just been hammered into shape upon it.'

'I do not think we should play at all tomorrow,' opined Hoode.

'Then you must have taken leave of your remaining senses,' said Gill, pouting with outrage. 'Leave our stage empty? Our rivals would love that, I am sure. Why not simply surrender our occupations altogether?'

'I have already done that, Barnaby.'

'And not before time, I may say.'

'No more of this nonsense!' ordered Firethorn, putting down his empty wine cup with a bang. 'It's folly to say that we'll deny our audience tomorrow and double folly to say that Edmund is a spent force as a playwright.'

'He admitted it himself,' noted Gill.

'Willingly,' said Hoode. 'I yield the palm to Master Hibbert.'

'Westfield's Men need more than one playwright to keep up a steady flow of new work,' said Firethorn, 'and I look to the time when we have you back at your incomparable best.'

'Earlier today, you talked only of a second Edmund Hoode.'

'Give me a third, a fourth or even a fifth Edmund Hoode and none of them would hold a candle to you.'

'Saul Hibbert does,' said Gill, flatly. 'He holds a dozen candles in both hands to light up the stage with his brilliance.'

'I see none of that fabled brilliance now,' observed Firethorn, as the playwright strode across the taproom towards them. 'Master Hibbert looks as if he has sat upon those twenty-four candles of yours before he had the sense to snuff out their flames.'

Still enraged by his confrontation in the tiring-house, Saul Hibbert was puce and beetle-browed. He ignored the congratulations that were called out to him and charged over to Firethorn.

'I crave a word in private, Lawrence,' he said.

'There's privacy enough at this table,' explained Firethorn. 'I have no secrets from Barnaby and Edmund. We form the triumvirate that runs the company. If you wish to discuss business, pray do so in front of my honoured fellows here.'

'We were less than honoured when you commissioned Saul's play,' recalled Gill, spikily. 'You did not mention it to either of us.'

'Do you disapprove of my choice?'

'No, Lawrence. *The Malevolent Comedy* is unsurpassed.'

'I rest my case.'

'Then let me put mine,' said Hibbert, sitting on the empty stool at the table. 'I want some recompense for providing you with the outstanding play of your season.'

'You've had your fee in full.'

'I need more than that, Lawrence, and I feel that I'm in a position to demand it. I talk not of money – that's irrelevant here. I ask only this of you.' He took a deep breath. 'Dismiss your book holder.'

The others were so astounded that they could say nothing for a full minute. It was only when Hibbert repeated his demand that Firethorn found his voice. He burst out laughing.

'Get rid of Nicholas Bracewell?' he exclaimed. 'That's like saying that we should disband the whole company. Nick is its heart.'

'Yet he's only a hired man,' argued Hibbert.

'And blest are we that were lucky enough to hire him.'

'I take issue with that,' said Gill, contentiously.

'Do not listen to Barnaby,' said Hoode. 'He has never appreciated Nick's value. Nor do you, Master Hibbert. Did you not see what occurred today? But for Nick Bracewell's speed in removing a corpse from the stage, your play might have twitched to death like poor Hal Bridger. You owe our book holder some gratitude.'

'All that I owe him is enmity,' said Hibbert. 'He insulted me.'

'That does not sound like him. Was there any provocation?'

'None whatsoever.'

'Then why did he speak roughly to you?'

'He did more than speak,' complained Hibbert. 'He threw me against a wall and held me by the throat.'

'I beg leave to question that,' said Firethorn. 'Nick is the gentlest of men. He'd not hurt a fly. And you tell me that he attacked you?'

'Attacked, insulted and abused me. Dismiss him at once.'

'I'd like to hear his side of the story first.'

Hibbert was incensed. 'You'd take *his* word against mine?'

'Every time,' said Hoode. 'And even if he did lay hands upon you, I'm sure that he had a sound reason to do so. Dispense with our book holder? I'd sooner part with Barnaby.'

'I resent that!' shouted Gill.

'We'll keep both you and Nick,' said Firethorn, with an appeasing pat on his shoulder. 'Rest easy on that score, Barnaby.'

'Do you deny my request, then?' asked Hibbert.

'A moment ago, it was a demand.'

'You'll not get rid of your book holder?'

'No,' said Firethorn. 'He holds this company together.'

'You had better search for someone else to serve in that capacity,' warned Hibbert. 'If you will not throw him out, then I will do so myself with the blade of my sword. He more or less challenged me to a duel.' Firethorn put back his head and laughed. 'What is so comical now?'

'The thought that you could kill Nick in a duel,' said Hoode with a chuckle. 'Make your will before you lift your weapon because your heirs will be sure to inherit. Am I right, Lawrence?'

'Yes,' agreed Firethorn. 'It's Nick who instructs us in swordplay on the stage. He has no equal with a rapier. Do not offer him any other weapon either, Saul, for he is a master with every one of them. Nick Bracewell sailed around the world with Drake in younger days. He was trained to fight with sword, dagger and musket. And there's no better man to have beside you in a brawl. Fight a duel with him and you commit certain suicide. I think you'd best mend this quarrel with Nick.'

'Never!' said Hibbert.

'He's the most reasonable man alive.'

'What he did to me was unforgivable.'

'Yet not without cause, I suspect,' said Hoode.

'Nicholas does get above himself at times,' remarked Gill.

Firethorn grinned. 'Would *you* cross swords with him, Barnaby?'

'Not for a king's ransom!'

'There's your answer, Saul. Make your peace with him.'

Hibbert was fuming. On a day when his play had bewitched a full audience, when it had introduced a striking new talent to the capital, when he expected to be feted by everyone he met, he had instead been thoroughly humiliated. Someone was going to pay for it. Rising abruptly from his seat, he stalked out in a temper.

'He's too rash to be the second Edmund Hoode,' said Hoode with a contented smile. 'I'd not dare to challenge Nick to a duel even if his sword were made out of paper. Saul Hibbert may be a clever playwright but he's no judge of a fighting man. One of us needs to speak to Nick about this.'

'Well, it won't be me,' said Gill.

'I'll gladly take on the role of peacemaker here.'

'You may have to wait a while, Edmund,' said Firethorn. 'Nick has other business in hand. He's gone to speak to Hal Bridger's family.'

Nicholas Bracewell did not have far to walk. The Queen's Head was situated in Gracechurch Street, only a hundred yards or so from the house near Bishopsgate, where Hal Bridger had been born and brought up. The boy's father was a leather-seller and the family lived over the shop that he had kept for some thirty years. As he entered the premises, Nicholas inhaled the distinctive smell of tanned leather. Like his son, Terence Bridger was tall and slim but there was a hardness in his face that he had not passed on to his only child. Nicholas was surprised to see how old the man was – close to sixty, if not beyond it.

'Can I help you, sir?' asked Bridger, gruffly.

'My name is Nicholas Bracewell,' replied Nicholas, 'and I belong to Westfield's Men. I need to speak to you about your son.'

'I have no son.'

'Are you not Hal Bridger's father?'

'Not any more.'

'But he always speak of you with such respect.'

'Then it's a pity he did not show more of it when he was here.'

'Your son *loved* you.'

'Love is not love if it turns its back on obedience.'

Nicholas could see that his task was going to be even more difficult than anticipated. Terence Bridger's stern tone and unforgiving manner marked him out as an enemy of the theatre. Nicholas sensed that the leather-seller had distinct leanings towards Puritanism.

'He made his choice and must live by it,' said Bridger.

'I can see that he joined us without your permission.'

'He defied both me and his employer. I had him apprenticed to a saddler in Cheapside. It was an honest trade, a chance to work with leather that I supplied. But Hal betrayed his calling. Instead of learning his craft, he was forever sneaking off to watch a play at the Queen's Head, the Curtain or at that other devilish place in Bankside.'

'The Rose?'

'Theatre corrupted him. It turned a God-fearing young boy into a shameless heathen that I refuse to acknowledge as my own.'

'Hal was no heathen,' said Nicholas, firmly. 'He attended church every Sunday, as do most members of the company.'

'His church was *there*,' snapped Bridger, pointing towards the Queen's Head. 'He worshipped in that foul pit of iniquity, where painted women consort with evil men to watch disgusting antics upon the stage.'

'I can see that you've never actually attended a performance.'

'Nothing would make me do so, sir!'

'Then you condemn out of sheer ignorance.'

'I do so out of Christian conviction,' said Bridger, thrusting out his chin. 'If you are party to the profanity that goes upon a stage, you are not welcome in my shop. Good day to you!'

'I've not delivered my message about your son yet.'

'He no longer exists. I tell you this, Master Bracewell,' said the other, eyes glinting, 'that I'd sooner wish a son of mine in his grave than fall into the clutches of a theatre company.'

'Then your wish has been granted,' said Nicholas, softly. 'That's what I came to tell you – Hal, I fear, is dead.'

Terence Bridger's face was impassive. His voice was icily cold.

'He died the moment that he walked out of here,' he said.

Owen Elias laughed until the tears trickled down his rubicund cheeks.

'He intended to fight Nick Bracewell in a *duel*?' he asked.

'Yes,' said Firethorn, 'until we warned him against such lunacy.'

'Saul Hibbert would not last a minute. I'm no mean swordsman but I wouldn't chance my arm against Nick. He moves like lightning. Did you tell that to the reckless author?'

'Saul is too choleric to listen to sound advice.'

'Speak to him when he's cooled down, Lawrence, or we'll be bidding an early farewell to him at his funeral.'

They were still in the taproom at the Queen's Head, where strong drink had now lifted the prevailing sadness a little. Seeing that Gill and Hoode had left the table, Elias had moved across to join Firethorn for a private talk. The Welshman sipped his ale ruminatively.

'We've not had good fortune with new playwrights, have we?'

'No, Owen. I thought we'd found a gem in Michael Grammaticus, but he turned out to be passing off his friend's plays as his own. And since that friend was no longer alive, we could hope for nothing more from his cunning brain. Nor from dear Jonas Applegarth,' said Firethorn with deep regret. 'The poor fellow was hanged by the neck in this very building – though how they found a rope strong enough to bear his weight, I'll never know.'

'Then there was Lucius Kindell, full of promise, seduced away from us by Havelock's Men. And was there not one Ralph Willoughby, before my time with the company?'

'Burnt alive during the performance of *The Merry Devils*.'

'Do all our dramatists have a death wish?'

'One of them does, Owen,' said Firethorn, seriously, 'and he's the man we must discuss. Forget the new and cleave to the old. I'll do my utmost to keep Saul Hibbert alive to write more plays for us, but my chief concern is for Edmund. He has abdicated his position.'

'Tie him back on his throne and force a pen into his hand.'

'It's not as easy as that. Edmund has lost all appetite.'

'He's a creature of moods, Lawrence, as you well know. When his juices flow,' said Elias, 'he'll write all day and night without a break. There's not a playwright in London who has produced so much work of such high quality.'

'You'd not say that if you read *How to Choose a Good Wife*.'

'I did read it – the first act, anyway. I lacked the courage to go any further. It made my toes curl with embarrassment.'

'I could not believe Edmund had put his name to it.'

'Nor me,' said Elias, pursing his lips. 'It was not a new work at all but a collection of everything cut out of his earlier plays, strung untidily together like washing on a line.'

'It contained a frightening message for me, Owen.'

'Yes. Edmund is unwell.'

'Worse – he's fallen out of love with the theatre.'

'You've hit the mark there. Except that it is not only the theatre that has made him jaded. Edmund is out of love. It's as simple as that. Only when he's pining for a pretty maid can he write from the heart. We've seen it before, Lawrence.'

'Too many times.'

'Edmund is happy in his work when he's unhappy in love.'

'Then there's our solution,' announced Firethorn, snapping his fingers. 'We must find him a good woman.'

'A bad one would have more chance of exciting his interest,' said Elias with a grin. 'She must have enough respectability to lure him and a touch of wickedness to close the trap.'

'Let's draw a portrait of her in our minds.'

'She must be tall and slim.'

'But not too tall,' said Firethorn, warming to the task, 'for she must appeal to Edmund's protective instinct. And not too slim, either. He likes the bold curve of a breast as much as any of us.'

'And a pair of shapely hips.'

'What of her hair?'

'Raven-black with eyebrows to match.'

'He's always had a weakness for fair-haired ladies before.'

'Then we must wean him off it with a darker siren. Black hair, white cheeks, red lips and a pair of eyes to tempt a saint.'

'I want her for myself!' cried Firethorn, rubbing his hands gleefully together. 'By all, this is wonderful! I see the lovely lady, forming before my eyes as we speak, Owen. We are co-authors, bringing her to life as readily as Edmund creates a beauty on the page.'

'Is she rich or poor?'

'Neither. We'll have no wealthy widows or menial

servants. Our lady must be young, of middling sort and independent.'

'Yet not too forward. She must be schooled in that.'

'How much shall we need to pay her?

'Not a penny, Lawrence. This is no work for a hired enchantress.'

'Then how do we find her?'

'London is full of such comely creatures.'

'And just as full of rampant satyrs to chase them.'

'She is here somewhere,' said Elias, thoughtfully, 'and I believe I know the very woman. Yes, *she* would be ideal for Edmund Hoode. Pert, fetching and full of accomplishments.'

'Not one of your discarded mistresses, I hope.'

'No, no, this lady is not for me. She's too refined and intelligent. I like redder meat in my bed. Edmund has subtler tastes. He'll adore her.'

'Who is this paragon?'

'Buy me some more ale,' said Elias, 'and I'll tell you her name. Just wait, Lawrence. Our worries will soon be over. One glance at her and Edmund will start writing as if his life depended on it.'

Chapter Four

Nicholas Bracewell had been to the house in Knightrider Street many times. It was a rambling edifice, whose half-timbered frontage bulged sharply outwards as if trying to break free of its foundations. Sagging heavily to the right as well, it was supported by the adjacent building, like a hopeless drunk being helped home by a considerate friend. With all its structural faults, it was an amiable place and Nicholas always enjoyed his visits there. He was not shown much amity on arrival. Had he not glanced upward in time, he would have been drenched by the pot of urine that was emptied through an open window into the street. As it was, he jumped nimbly out of the way of the downpour.

At least, he knew that Doctor John Mordrake was at home.

'Come in, come in, Nicholas.'

'I hope that I'm not disturbing you.'

'Oh, no. Now that I've emptied my bladder, I'm at your service.'

'Thank you, Doctor Mordrake.'

Nicholas was pleased to see him again. Mordrake was a big man whose contours had been cruelly reshaped by age so that he was bent almost double. Skeletal hands poked out from the sleeves of his shabby black gown. Out of the mass of wrinkles that was his face, two eyes shone with astonishing clarity, separated by an aquiline nose. Silver-grey hair fell to his shoulders and merged with his long, straggly beard. Around his neck, as usual, he wore a chain fit for a Lord Mayor of London, though no holder of that august office could ever equal his extraordinary range of achievements.

Detractors accused him of sorcery, but Doctor John Mordrake was a philosopher, mathematician, alchemist and astrologer of note and, on occasion, physician to Her Majesty, Queen Elizabeth. He shuffled across to a chair and lifted a dead squirrel from it so that his guest could sit down. Filled with a compound of rich odours, the room was his laboratory and the huge, dust-covered, leather-bound tomes that lined the walls spoke of a lifetime's study. Jars of herbs stood everywhere and on one table, in a series of large bottles, a number of small animals had been preserved in green liquid. In the fireplace, something was being heated in a small cauldron and giving off an acrid blue steam.

'How can I help you, Nicholas?' he asked.

'I want a poison identified.'

'That's easily done.'

'I'll pay you for your time,' said Nicholas.

Mordrake flapped a hand. 'Keep your money in your purse, dear fellow. I would never charge a friend like you. My services are expensive to others but free to Nicholas Bracewell. I've not forgotten the favour you once did me when Westfield's Men travelled to Bohemia to play before a Holy Roman Emperor.'

Nicholas remembered the visit to Prague only too well but had so many misgivings about the venture that he did not wish to revive any memories of it. Instead, he launched into a concise and lucid account of the tragic death of Hal Bridger. Listening intently throughout, Mordrake took especial interest in the symptoms displayed by the victim. He then asked to see the vessels that had contained the poison. Nicholas handed over the cup and phial, hoping that they retained at least some of the smell of the poison. Mordrake put both to his nose in turn. With so many competing aromas in the room, Nicholas feared that the old man would be unable to detect anything at all but he had reckoned without the sensitivity of the beak-like nose. It inhaled deeply through both nostrils.

'Well?' asked Nicholas.

'It's a fiendish compound.'

'What can you detect?'

'Monkshood, belladonna, henbane, even a hint of foxglove. And something more besides that I cannot quite name. A lethal dose for any man, however strong his constitution.'

'Hal was young and delicate.'

'Then the poison worked more swiftly on him.'

'Could anyone mix the compound?'

'No, Nicholas,' said Mordrake, taking a last sniff of the phial. 'This is the work of some corrupt apothecary, paid to dishonour his calling. You must check the phials more carefully if you stage the play again.'

'We'll not use any liquid at all next time,' resolved Nicholas. 'If the phial is held right inside the cup, nobody in the audience will be any the wiser. It was the author who insisted that the potion should be seen.'

The old man raised a shaggy eyebrow in surprise. 'Since when has Lawrence Firethorn taken much note of authors?'

'A good question, Doctor Mordrake.'

'He has a reputation of being a law unto himself.'

'A well-earned reputation,' said Nicholas, fondly, 'but he paid the playwright more attention in this case and abided by his every request. What the audience saw is what Saul Hibbert asked for and received.'

'So *he* is indirectly responsible for the murder.'

'Nobody would ever be able to convince him of that.'

'Have I been of any use?' asked Mordrake, handing the cup and phial back to him. 'I like to feel that I've earned the exorbitant fee I might have asked from you.'

'The names of renegade apothecaries would not come amiss.'

'There are not many. Most are proud to uphold their standards.'

'What of those who do not? There are villains in every profession.'

'One moment, my friend.'

Mordrake sat on a stool at one of the tables and reached for a piece of parchment that was already half-covered with abstruse drawings. After chewing meditatively on the end of his quill, he dipped it into the inkwell and wrote down some names. Without bothering to dry the ink, he handed the list to Nicholas.

'The first man has a shop in Trigg Alley,' he said. 'Find him and you'll find the others, for he'll direct you to them. They are all of them men who have sadly fallen from grace in their time.'

'I can't thank you enough,' said Nicholas, studying the list.

'Preparing a fatal poison does not make a man a killer. Bear that in mind. If it did, I'd have been hanged long ago, for I've made up some venomous concoctions to rid a house of vermin. At least,' he went on, 'that was what I was told when it was purchased from me. How would I know if the potion was instead used to remove a shrewish wife or send a troublesome husband to his Maker?'

'I'm only after the person who *bought* the poison.'

'Take great care. He's an evil man.'

'He must be called to account,' said Nicholas, gravely. 'I'll track him down somehow. I owe it to Hal Bridger to do that.'

Sobbing quietly, George Dart and Richard Honeydew sat side by side on the bottom step of a staircase at the Queen's Head and hugged each other for comfort. They looked so small and insignificant that most of those who went in and out of the taproom did not even notice them. Edmund Hoode saw them at once as he was leaving. Taking pity on them he sat between the pair and enfolded them gently in his arms.

'What's this, what's this?' he said, softly. 'Crying will not bring Hal Bridger back to us. You must bear his loss with courage.'

'But we *killed* him,' whined Dart.

'Away with that silly thought!'

'We did,' said Honeydew. 'George made up that potion and I handed it to Hal in the cup. We are accomplices in a murder.'

'You are nothing of the kind,' said Hoode, 'and, were he here now, Hal would be the first to tell you that. George did not put the poison in the phial any more than you, Dick, knowingly poured it into the cup. You loved Hal and would not harm him for the world.'

'That's true,' said Dart, offering evidence in his defence. 'I was his friend. I taught him how to duck under Thomas's blows and keep out of Master Firethorn's way when his temper was up. I tried to save Hal from any pain and not inflict it.'

'You'd never hurt anyone, George,' soothed Honeydew. 'The same is true of you, Dick.'

'You're the kindest two lads in the company,' said Hoode, giving them an encouraging squeeze. 'George is a martyr to endure all the teasing that he gets, and Dick is the one apprentice who never stoops to silly mischief. I'd trust my life with either of you.'

'That's what Hal thought,' said Dart, tears forming again.

Honeydew sniffled. 'And he paid dearly for his mistake.'

'We'll never be able to forgive ourselves.'

'Hal Bridger will haunt me in my dreams.'

'And so will I, if we have any more of this,' said Hoode, adopting a sterner tone. 'Neither of you bears any blame. You might just as well blame Saul Hibbert for writing the play, or Lawrence for deciding to commission it, or the landlord for allowing it to be staged here. If you want to find a culprit, there's a great long line of them to choose from and it includes me.'

'*You?*' they said in unison.

'Yes. *The Malevolent Comedy* was only bought because I was unable to supply a new play myself. Had my rustic tale been deemed worthy enough, then *that* would have been staged here today, and Hal would still be alive. No, lads,' Hoode continued. 'There's only one true culprit and we must all help to find him.'

'How can we do that?' asked Dart.

'By keeping your eyes and ears open. If he's struck once, he may do so again. We must be on our guard.' The others began to shiver. 'The search for the villain has already begun. I've just spoken with Nick Bracewell, who managed to get the poison identified. We know exactly what killed Hal now. Tomorrow, Nick will try to find the apothecary who mixed the lethal potion.'

Honeydew was frightened. 'And you think the killer is still here?'

'It's a possibility that we must consider.'

'Then none of us is safe!'

'We are, if we stay together, Dick – and take care what we drink.'

'I'll be afraid to touch a drop of anything.'

'So will I,' said Dart, querulously.

Hoode smiled. 'You'll drink when you get thirsty enough,' he said. 'The main thing is that you absolve yourselves of any blame. Nobody is pointing the finger at you. We understand your fears and want to help you overcome them. The worst is over, lads. Bear up.'

'But the worst is *not* over yet,' said Honeydew.

'What do you mean?'

'Hal has a family and they will want to know how he died. They are bound to come looking for George and me. *You* may say that we were not at fault,' he went on, biting his lip, 'but his parents may think that we are the murderers. I'm terrified to face them, Edmund.'

'We both are,' said Dart.

'Then let me put your minds at rest,' said Hoode, discreetly. 'Nick spoke to Hal's father and told him of the tragedy. For personal reasons, the parents will not come anywhere near the Queen's Head. Shed that anxiety as well, lads. You are safe.'

'Disowned his own son?' asked Anne in a tone of disbelief. 'Surely not.'

'It is sad but true.'

'Sad and reprehensible, I'd say. What sort of father turns his back on a boy who has been murdered? It's bad enough if a child dies by natural means, but a calamity when he's poisoned to death. Do the parents have no hearts?'

'I only spoke with the father,' said Nicholas, 'and his heart was made of stone, hewn, I suspect, from some Puritan quarry. Theatre is anathema to him. Left to himself, he'd tear down every playhouse in London. Hal was very brave to defy such a man, braver still to join Westfield's Men.'

'Why?'

'He left a secure trade as a saddler to trust his luck with the most precarious profession in the city. His bravery verges on heroism, Anne. And it cost him his young life.'

After the rigors of the day, Nicholas was glad to get back to the haven of his lodging in Bankside, and to relax in its welcoming parlour. Anne Hendrik, the English widow of a Dutch hatmaker, was a handsome woman in her thirties with skills she did not even know that she possessed until she was forced to run her late husband's business in the adjoining premises. During the early months of struggle and financial restraint, she took in a lodger to defray expenses and found, in Nicholas Bracewell, a man who became her friend, confidante and, in time, her lover. Married in all but name, they shared a closeness that was a source of continual solace during times of strife. Nicholas could always rely on her support and sympathy.

'Why did *you* have to take on this duty?' she said, touching his arm. 'It should have fallen to Lawrence, as manager of the company. This is so typical of him, Nick. He always shuffles off his own responsibilities onto you.'

'I was happy to accept in this case,' explained Nicholas. 'I liked Hal and worked more closely with him than anyone. The lad did all that we asked of him, willingly and without complaint. In view of what happened,' he added with a wry smile, 'it's perhaps just as well that Lawrence did not bear the bad news to the father.'

'Why not?'

'Puritanism brings out the worst in him. He'd have started an argument with Hal's father and that would have been very unseemly in the circumstances. The boy deserves to be mourned, not haggled over. If Lawrence had gone to the leather-seller's shop,' he said, 'he would have been seen as the Prince of Darkness.'

'Would he and the father have come to blows?'

'Most likely.'

'I'm sure that you behaved more peaceably.'

'I was far from peaceable this afternoon, Anne,' he admitted. 'As a result, I may have to fight a duel.'

'A *duel*?' she repeated, eyes widening in distress.

'Unless the matter can be settled amicably.'

'And can it?'

'We shall see.'

Nicholas told her about his altercation with Saul Hibbert, conceding that he had been unduly robust with the man yet showing no regret. He felt that he was repaying him for the disdainful conduct they had all endured for weeks. Having already heard some bad reports about the playwright, Anne was not surprised that he had behaved so selfishly, but she was dismayed to learn that he had dismissed the murder of Hal Bridger with such scorn.

'Did he show no sign of sorrow at all?' she asked.

'Only at the way that Hal's death interrupted his play.'

'Master Hibbert is a monster.'

'You might change your mind if you met him, Anne.'

'Why?'

'He's a man of great charm when he chooses to be,' said Nicholas, 'and the ladies flock to him. Saul Hibbert is careful to flatter Lawrence as well, so that he can secure a more permanent place with the company. When it comes to the rest of us, however,' he continued with a frown, 'he has nothing but disregard. He treats hired men as if we were a lower order of creation, and he's even shown contempt towards Edmund.'

'That's unpardonable. Edmund would not strike back.'

'I did so on his behalf, Anne, and on behalf of all the others whom our arrogant author has seen fit to bully and criticise.'

'Someone had to stand up to him,' said Anne, admiringly.

'That's what I felt.'

'But I'm worried that it might lead to a duel.'

'Lawrence wants me to apologise to Master Hibbert.'

'For what? It's *he* who should apologise to you.'

'He's already done so,' said Nicholas with a half-smile, 'though I had to squeeze it out of him. That's the reason he wants me dismissed.'

'He has no right to do that, Nick.'

'Lawrence made that clear.'

'Yet he still takes Master Hibbert's side?'

'No, Anne. He simply wants the two of us quickly reconciled. Saul Hibbert may be a tiresome man but *The Malevolent Comedy* carried all before it. We need such an author to compete with our rivals,' he said, 'and Lawrence knows that full well. He urges me to woo Master Hibbert.'

'You can hardly do that with a sword in your hand.'

'I'll not shirk a duel, if one comes along.'

'Duelling is against the law.'

'It makes no difference, Anne. What he did this afternoon

was against the more sacred laws of humanity. An innocent life is snuffed out in the course of his play and all that he can do is to protest about it. Truly,' he went on, gritting his teeth, 'I don't know which of them I despise the more. A father who pretends that his son does not exist, or a playwright who treats the lad like a piece of dirt to be kicked aside.'

'Both are equally hateful,' said Anne without equivocation.

'The problem is that I have to go on working with Saul Hibbert, for we'll stage his play again and again. We are yoke-fellows.'

'What will happen next?'

Nicholas gave a shrug. 'That depends on him.'

Lawrence Firethorn gave him plenty of time to calm down but, after a few hours, Saul Hibbert was still simmering with rage. They met in the author's room at the Queen's Head and shared a bottle of sack. A haunting aroma of perfume hung in the air but it was clear to Firethorn that even time spent in the arms of a woman had failed to dispel the playwright's sense of grievance. He continued to brood.

'I'll not let this pass, Lawrence,' he warned.

'Be ruled by me. Try to forget the whole incident.'

'Why should I do that?'

'Because that's what Nick Bracewell is prepared to do.'

'The devil take him!'

'Be reasonable, Saul.'

'Was that ruffian book holder of yours reasonable when he took be by the throat? No!' he exclaimed. 'Do not waste your time by appealing to my reason, Lawrence. I'm beyond that.'

'All may seem different in the morning.'

'Not to me.'

Hibbert seemed more indignant than ever and more vengeful. Two cups of sack did nothing to still his anger. Over a third, Firethorn tried once again to placate him.

'Circumstance was against you both,' he said. 'After your play was such a triumph, you were rightly on fire with joy. By the same token, Nick Bracewell – after the death of Hal Bridger – was also profoundly stirred. Blood was up when the two of you met.'

'Mine still is.'

'Nick is mildness itself now. He accepts that he acted on impulse.'

'I knew that you'd take his side.'

'That's not what I'm doing.'

'It's the thing that annoys me most,' said Hibbert, tossing back his long, wavy hair. 'You listen to a hired man before an author. You prise a lackey above someone who's just delivered you the best success you've enjoyed all season.'

'Nick is no lackey,' rejoined Firethorn, hotly.

'What else is the fellow? He's a servant, a slave, a hireling, a nothing man, a minion, a menial, a faceless creature, who holds a book at a performance. Ha!' he snorted with distaste. 'Cancel his contract and you could replace him in five minutes.'

'Five years would not be enough to replace Nick Bracewell.'

'And how many years would it take to find another Saul Hibbert?'

He almost spat the challenge at Firethorn and the actor had to bite back his initial reply. Having come to pacify the man, he did not wish to alienate him further by having an argument with him. In two bare hours that afternoon, Hibbert had proved his worth. His was a talent that had to be kept, nurtured, developed, refined and, at all costs, put beyond the reach of rivals such as Banbury's Men. In *The Malevolent Comedy*, as in no other new play, Firethorn had something able to hold its own against *Lamberto*, the pride of the Curtain. However contentious he was, however intemperate his language, Hibbert had to be wooed.

'And I've another complaint,' said the playwright, returning to the fray. 'I'm told that you play some mouldy old tragedy tomorrow.'

'*Black Antonio* is popular with our audiences.'

'But staged so often as to be threadbare.'

'It was always our intent to offer it again tomorrow.'

'But only if my play disappointed. Instead of which, it dazzled like the sun and left an audience begging to feel its warmth again. Why fall back on *Black Antonio* when you have a wonderful new play to offer?'

'It was not felt proper, Saul.'

'By whom? Barnaby felt it proper. He told me so. He believes that *The Malevolent Comedy* could occupy the stage for a fortnight.'

'And maybe it will,' said Firethorn, exasperated by the mention of Barnaby Gill, 'but the final decision about tomorrow lies with me, and, in deference to the company's feelings, we'll rest your play awhile.'

'The company's feelings? What on earth are they, Lawrence?'

'I can see you are not well-versed in the ways of the theatre. Actors are ever at the mercy of superstition. If something goes awry during a performance, it plants a fear in their mind. And there cannot be a more worrying mishap onstage than the death of a member of the cast.'

'Do you mean that the actors *refuse* to play it again?'

'No,' said Firethorn, choosing his words carefully, 'they will do as they are told, but they'd prefer to leave your comedy aside tomorrow. They are not in a mood to do it justice and believe, in any case, that we should rest your play as a mark of respect to Hal Bridger.'

'An assistant stagekeeper?' scoffed Hibbert.

'Nick Bracewell agreed.'

'Who manages Westfield's Men – you or him?'

'I do,' said Firethorn, straightening his shoulders.

'Then why bother with the riffraff of the company, for that is all they are. Assistant stagekeepers and book holders!' He gave a derisive laugh. 'Any fool could do such an office. It's work for trash, for rabble, for scum, for the sweepings of the streets.'

'It's work that has to be done well,' said Firethorn with passion, 'or playwrights like you and actors like me are made to look ridiculous. Never condemn those behind the scenes, Saul. Our success rests on them as much as on our own abilities.'

'I dispute that.'

'Then we must agree to differ.' Firethorn rose from his chair. 'I'll bid you good night and hope that wiser counsels prevail on the morrow, and that you come to see Nick Bracewell in a fairer light.' Hibbert stifled a retort. 'It's another reason why *Black Antonio* holds the stage in your place, Saul. It will keep you and Nick apart.'

'We'll meet again ere long, I assure you.'

'Then do so as fellows in the same company. Are we agreed?'

Hibbert gave a reluctant nod but his eyes were smouldering.

It took Nicholas Bracewell the best part of the morning to track down the man. Simeon Howker's name was the last on the list and Nicholas had to work his way through the others before he finally trudged off in the direction of Clerkenwell. The shop was in a narrow lane that twisted between rows of filthy tenements. Few in such a poverty-stricken area of the city could afford a doctor or a surgeon, none could aspire to the services of a physician. The vast majority therefore fell back on their local apothecary, hoping that his herbal remedies would cure the vast range of diseases and disabilities that they took to his door. Nicholas was easily the healthiest man ever to step over the threshold.

'Yes, sir?' asked the apothecary.

'Simeon Howker?'

'The very same.'

'I'm a friend of Doctor Mordrake,' said Nicholas, barely

able to see the man in the dark interior of his shop, 'and I'm hoping that you may be able to help me.'

'If you have dealings with Mordrake, you'll not be needing me. He knows of herbs that I've never even heard of, and can cure anything from smallpox to the standing of the yard.' He stepped out of the shadows. 'Do you have trouble with the standing of *your* yard,' he said with a crude cackle. ''Tis a common problem among men. It either stands when you would have it flaccid, or lies dormant when it needs to rise and bid welcome to a lady. Is that your ailment, sir?'

'No,' said Nicholas. 'I only came for information.'

'Even that has a charge on it.'

Simeon Howker was a short, stringy man in his forties with a lean face that was fringed by a wispy ginger beard. Wearing a black gown and a black skullcap, he peered at his visitor over a pair of glasses. The shop was small, cluttered and musty. Around its shelves, Nicholas could see endless bottles of herbs. Howker named them at speed.

'Aconite, buckthorn, buttercup, cinquefoil, wild cherry, darnel, hellebore, hemlock, laburnum, larkspur, lobelia, mandrake and many more besides,' he said. 'Most are harmless unless mixed with other herbs. Several that are poisonous can yet be used as remedies if sold in the right compounds.'

'And you know how to make those compounds, I daresay.'

'Of course, good sir. I am part apothecary and part magician.'

'You may also be an accessory to a murder.'

'What's that?' said the other, so startled that he retreated into the shadows. 'I'll hear no wild accusations in my shop, sir. I'm a law-abiding man, as any of my customers will witness.'

'It's one of those customers I came to talk to you about,' explained Nicholas. 'Someone recently asked you to make a lethal compound for him that would kill as soon as it was swallowed.'

'Rat poison is all that I sell.'

'This poison was bought by a rat and I'm anxious to catch him. The compound that you mixed for him sent a young friend of mine to an early grave. I want his killer brought to justice.'

'I had no truck with him. Why come to me?'

'Because your name was on the list that Doctor Mordrake gave to me, a list of five apothecaries, who'd sell their souls rather than earn an honest living.' Howker started to bluster. 'Save your breath to tell me what I came to find out and do not try to deceive me,' warned Nicholas, fingering his dagger, 'or I'll cut the truth out of your miserable carcass.'

'I made no poison, sir. It was one of the others.'

'They didn't dare to lie to me and neither must you. Monkshood, belladonna, henbane, a pinch of foxglove and something else to make it more deadly still – those were the ingredients.' He moved forward to confront the apothecary. 'And you mixed them, did you not?'

'No, no,' cried the other. 'I swear that I refused to do it.'

'Then someone did come in search of the poison?'

'Came and went away. I practise no witchcraft. I would never make such an evil potion.'

'You're a craven coward who cannot admit the ugly truth,' said Nicholas, whipping out his dagger and holding it at the man's throat. 'I'll ask you one more time. Lie to me again and I'll send you off to join my friend on a cold slab.' Howker started to quiver. 'Now – who instructed you to make that poison?'

'Nobody.'

The dagger pricked his throat and made him yell. '*Who?*' said Nicholas, knowing that he was at last on the right trail.

'He did not give a name.'

'When did he come?'

'Two days ago.'

'Alone or with someone else?'

'On his own,' said Howker. 'If you please, sir, could you put that dagger away before it hurts me? I'll tell you what I know, I promise you.'

Nicholas sheathed his weapon. 'What did the man ask for?'

'A deadly poison. He said his farm was overrun with rats.'

'Did you believe him?'

'Not for a moment, sir. He was no farmer. And he bought too little of the compound to deal with a plague of vermin. But he paid me well,' he remembered, 'and stood over me while I mixed the compound.'

'Describe him.'

'It's very gloomy in here.'

'Describe the man,' insisted Nicholas. 'You saw him well enough to realise that he was not a farmer, and if you work in this light every day, you must be used to it. How tall was he?'

'About your height, sir.'

'His build?'

'Much slimmer than you.'

'What of his age?'

'Thirty or more, perhaps.'

'Well-favoured?'

'And well-dressed in doublet and hose. A proper gentleman.'

'No gentleman buys poison with intent to murder,' said Nicholas, tartly. 'What else can you tell me about the fellow?'

'Nothing, except that he wore a beard and a jewelled earring.'

'What colour was the beard?'

'As fair as yours and neatly trimmed.'

'A strange customer to come into a shop like yours, then.'

'Very strange.'

'How did he know where to find you?'

'You'll have to ask him that, sir, though I do have a reputation.'

'I can see that you live up to it in this sewer of a shop,' said Nicolas, glancing around. 'Did it never occur to you, when you mixed that poison, that you were serving a man with murder on his mind?'

Howker shook his head. 'I gave him what he asked for. He paid.'

'Did he say where he was staying?'

'Not a word.'

'What about his voice? Low or high?'

'Somewhere in between.'

'Was he a Londoner?'

'Oh, no,' said Howker, confidently. 'He was a visitor to the city. I've heard the tongue before but could not place it. There was a whisper of the country about it yet he did not seem to be a countryman. That's all I can tell you, sir,' he bleated. 'If I'd known that the poison was to kill someone, I'd never have sold it to him.'

'You'd sell anything for money, you rogue.'

'I've a wife and children to support. They come first. Do not blame me, please. I only seek to make my living here.'

'Yes,' said Nicholas, 'as a purveyor of death.'

Resisting an impulse to attack the man, he stormed out of the shop and slammed the door behind him. It had been a long morning but he had finally made some progress. It was a start.

Black Antonio was a tragedy of revenge and thwarted love, written in soaring verse and offering Lawrence Firethorn a title role that allowed him to explore the outer limits of his talent. In his full-blooded portrayal of the ill-starred Antonio, there was not even a tiniest vestige of Lord Loveless, who had tripped across the same boards so entertainingly on the previous afternoon. Firethorn was a different man entirely, a noble savage, honest, upright, fearless in battle yet gentle in his wooing, a tragic hero brought low by the one flaw in his character.

Since the play was a staple part of their repertoire,

Nicholas Bracewell felt able to miss the rehearsal that morning so that he could conduct his search among the apothecaries. George Dart had held the book in his stead, yielding it up for the performance itself. With the death of Hal Bridger still at the forefront of their minds, the actors began with some trepidation but they soon hit their stride. A sizeable audience came to watch them in the bright sunshine. The company gave a sterling account of the play and it went off without incident.

When he had taken as many bows as he felt able to, Firethorn led his troupe gratefully into the tiring-house. Pulling off his helmet, he stared into a mirror and used a cloth to wipe the black pigment from his sweat-covered face. Nicholas went across to him.

'It was like a furnace out there,' said Firethorn. 'I started to melt. Another half-hour in that sunshine and my last bit of blackness would have trickled away. I'd have been White Antonio.'

'That would have made for a very different play.'

'Today I was black on the outside and white on the inside.'

'Master Hibbert is quite the opposite,' remarked Nicholas, quietly. 'A handsome face disguises a very ugly man.'

Most of the actors were so relieved to come through the performance unscathed that they changed quickly out of their costumes and scampered off to the taproom. Firethorn waited until he and Nicholas were alone before he took up the book holder's comment.

'Saul is no villain,' he said, easily. 'He's a proud man with a right to take pride in his talents. I know that it makes for vanity but we all suffer from that disease.' He rubbed the last speck of black from his hands. 'I spoke to him last night, Nick.'

'What did he say?'

'He'll not relent.'

'Neither will I.'

'It's not like you to be so stubborn.'

'I have my pride as well, Lawrence.'

'In the past, you've always put the good of the company first.'

'And I did so again yesterday,' said Nicholas, 'when I clashed with Master Hibbert. During the rehearsals for his play, he sneered and snarled at almost everyone but you and Barnaby. And he had no more concern for Hal's death than he might for a squashed fly.'

'That was shameful of him.'

'I tried to persuade him of that.'

'A little too roughly, it seems. Saul is adamant. He feels aggrieved, Nick. Only an apology from you can mend this rift.'

'Then he'll wait for it in vain.'

Firethorn was worried. 'Do you want to drive him away?'

'No, he's a true dramatist.'

'Well, that's what will happen if this argument between the two of you is not resolved.' He moved in closer. 'I ask you as a friend, Nick. Bend a little, for my sake. Admit to Saul that you were too upset by Hal Bridger's death to know what you were doing.'

'I knew *exactly* what I was doing,' said Nicholas.

'This wound needs a balm. You've always been the healer among Westfield's Men. Act as our apothecary once again.'

'After recent events, I've lost a little faith in apothecaries. They can kill as easily as cure. I did not look for this quarrel, Lawrence. I was provoked beyond measure – and so would you have been. Instead of caring about a playwright we might employ in future,' suggested Nicholas, 'look to the one we already have. Edmund has given us a whole sequence of wonderful comedies but he does not feel obliged to preen himself as a result. Yet, on the strength of one play, Master Hibbert has swaggered like a petty tyrant. We should work to resurrect Edmund. He's a true member of the company.'

'Forget about him,' said Firethorn. 'We have a plan for Edmund.'

'What sort of plan?'

'Never mind.'

'But I do mind,' said Nicholas with suspicion. 'I know Edmund. He needs to be handled with the greatest care.'

'He will be – if Owen and I have our way. But that's for another time. There's room for more than one playwright in our stables, and I'm resolved that Saul Hibbert will join us.'

'Then you may take it for granted.'

'Not if you and he are at each other's throats.'

'I'm no impediment here,' said Nicholas. 'Master Hibbert is clever enough to use the evidence of his own eyes. He knows that Lord Westfield lends his name to the finest company in London.'

'In the whole country!'

'That's why he offered the play to you first. You were Lord Loveless to the life. He must have been thrilled with your performance.'

'And justly so,' said Firethorn, beaming. 'I was at my peak.'

'*That's* the reason a bond has been forged with Master Hibbert,' said Nicholas. 'You accepted his play and the company ensured his fame when we presented it here. There's no way that Saul Hibbert would take his talent elsewhere.'

Intrigued by the invitation, Saul Hibbert had made his way to the Green Man at the appointed time. Having sat alone at a table for some while, however, he was beginning to wonder if he was the victim of a hoax, lured there to satisfy someone's warped sense of humour. After waiting another five minutes, he decided to leave, but, before he could rise from his seat, a voice rang out across the tavern.

'Pray stay where you are, Master Hibbert,' said the newcomer. 'A thousand apologies for my lateness.' He stood beside the table. 'I can see that you that received my letter.'

'It was unsigned. I did not know quite what to expect.'

'Then I hope that you're not disappointed. I like to think that I have a manly hand, so you would not have come here in expectation of meeting a female admirer. After the performance of *The Malevolent Comedy* that I was privileged to witness yesterday, you'll have no shortage of adoring young ladies.'

'Who are you?' asked Hibbert.

'A fellow playwright and friend,' said the other, sitting down.

'Do you have a name?'

'One that has attracted some renown. I am Cyrus Hame.'

'The author of *Lamberto*?'

'Co-author with esteemed partner, John Vavasor. He'll be here soon to join in the discussion. John admired your play as much as me.'

'Thank you.'

Hibbert was still mystified. He looked at his companion and tried to work out why the man had been so eager to meet him. Cyrus Hame smiled back at him. He was a tall, slim, well-featured man in his thirties, wearing a doublet and hose that were striking without being gaudy, and sporting a pearl earring. Hame had an engaging manner.

'Let me be honest with you, Master Hibbert,' he said, stroking his fair beard and displaying a perfect set of teeth. 'I think that your future as a playwright lies with Banbury's Men.'

Chapter Five

During the performance of *Black Antonio*, the inn yard of the Queen's Head had been turned into a rudimentary playhouse. The stage was erected on trestles, benches put into the lower and upper galleries, and the yard itself used as a pit in which those who could only afford a penny stood shoulder to shoulder in the cloying heat. Secure within the world of the play, the audience could shut out the tumult of Gracechurch Street nearby and ignore the other intrusive sounds of a typical afternoon in the capital. Once a performance was over, however, and the spectators had gone, the playhouse was swiftly converted back to its more normal use as an inn. The stage was taken down, the benches removed and the place made fit to receive horses and coaches once more.

Most of the work was done by the lesser lights of Westfield's Men under the control of Nicholas Bracewell.

The only job that was left to one of Alexander Marwood's servants was the onerous one of sweeping a yard that could accumulate the most amazing amount of litter in the course of an afternoon. The man to whom the task was allotted was a hulking giant in a tattered shirt, a pair of ancient breeches and a leather apron. As he swept away with his broom, he sent up a blizzard of dust.

'Hold there, Leonard!' said Nicholas. 'A word with you, please.'

'Any time you wish,' replied the other, grateful for the opportunity to break off. 'The play went well this afternoon.'

'Did you watch it?'

'Bits of it. I always cry at the end of *Black Antonio*.'

'That's a tribute to the actors.'

'I snatched a few minutes here and there, when the landlord was not looking. He hates to see me resting.'

'You wouldn't know how to rest.'

Nicholas and Leonard were old friends. They had met in the unlikely venue of a prison, where Nicholas was falsely incarcerated and where Leonard was facing execution because he had accidentally broken the back of a wrestler who challenged all-comers at a fair. Rescued from his fate, Leonard had been unable to return to his old job at a brewery so Nicholas had found him employment at the Queen's Head. Sweeping the yard, heaving barrels of beer about, cleaning the stables, carrying out simple repairs, helping in the garden and holding horses were only a few of the duties that came his way on a daily basis. Being able to talk to friends like Nicholas Bracewell made such toil more than worthwhile.

'You've heard about Hal Bridger no doubt,' said Nicholas.

'Yes, I felt for the lad. He loved Westfield's Men.'

'His stay with us was all too short, Leonard. What we need to do is to find the man who killed him, and I'm hoping that you can help.'

'How?'

'The fellow was a stranger to the city – that much I know – so he would need to feel his way around the Queen's Head to learn how we stage our plays. Nobody in the company was approached,' Nicholas went on, 'because I asked them. But you are here all the time and you keep your wits about you.'

Leonard grinned. 'What few wits I have, that is.'

'You've a quicker mind than some might think. A stranger could easily make that mistake, accosting you because you'd not suspect them of anything. Think, Leonard. Did anyone talk to you about us?'

'Lots of people pass remarks about Westfield's Men.'

'This was a tall, lean, well-favoured man with a fair beard. Around my own age, I'm told, and dressed like a gentleman. Does that description jog your memory at all?'

'I believe that it does,' said Leonard, furrowing his brow and running a huge palm across his chin. 'There *was* such a man, Nicholas. He spoke to me as I was carrying a pail of milk across the yard.'

'When was this?'

'Three or four days ago.'

'What did he say?'

'He asked about *The Malevolent Comedy* and where it was like to be performed. He was much as you describe, a pleasant man, easy to talk to and interested in your work.'

'But he only asked about one particular play?'

'Yes, Nicholas. He wanted to know where the actors waited until they took their roles onstage. And so I showed him.'

'You let him see into the tiring-house?'

'Only for a second,' said Leonard, fearing disapproval. 'And none of your property was there. I saw no harm in it.'

'Did you recognise the man's voice?'

'Too soft to be a Londoner, yet not as soft and sweet as yours.'

'Thank you,' said Nicholas, proud of his West Country burr. 'But a soft voice hid a cold heart in the case of this man. I think that he may well have poisoned Hal Bridger.'

Leonard flushed with guilt. 'Do you mean that I helped a killer?'

'Not deliberately.'

'I'd have knocked him down, if I'd know that was his ambition.'

'He was here to stop the play for some reason, Leonard, and he chose the most effective method of doing so – he poisoned a member of the cast. I fear he may return.'

'Then I'll look out for him,' said Leonard, grimly. 'He tricked me into helping him murder Hal. That makes me so angry.'

'Control your anger,' advised Nicholas, 'and, when you do see the man again, apprehend him and bring him straight to me. He may, of course, be quite innocent of the charge, but I'd rather take no chances.'

'Nor me.'

They parted company and Leonard went off into the kitchen. Nicholas was about to join the others in the taproom when he saw a woman, hovering at the entrance to the yard. One of the servingmen from the inn was pointing at Nicholas. The man vanished but the woman plucked up the courage to beckon to the book holder. He strode across to her. Nicholas saw the distress in her face when he was ten yards away and guessed who she might be.

'Are you Hal's mother?' he enquired.

'Yes,' she replied in a tremulous voice. 'I want to speak to the man who came to our shop yesterday, one Nicholas Bracewell.'

'That's me, Mrs Bridger. Your husband turned me away.'

'He was too hasty in doing so. Hal was our son.'

'I'm glad that one of his parents acknowledges that. But if you wish to talk with me,' said Nicholas, gently, 'step inside and we'll find some privacy.'

'I'll not come into a tavern,' she said, shrinking back a foot or two. 'Especially one that's used as a playhouse. It's against everything we believe. This place is a sink of immorality.'

'Then we'll move away from it,' volunteered Nicholas, keen to respect her principles. 'If we go into the lane opposite, we might get away from the worst of the din.'

Alice Bridger nodded. A thin woman of middle height, she was wearing a simple black dress with a white collar. Under the brim of her hat was a face that had lost its youthful prettiness without acquiring the hardness that distinguished her husband. Nicholas put her ten years younger than Terence Bridger, and sensed a kinder, more sensitive and more generous person. As they waited for a coach to rumble past before crossing the road, she glanced around nervously.

'Your husband does not know that you're here,' decided Nicholas.

'I came against his will,' she said, apologetically. 'It's the first time I've disobeyed him but I had to know the truth.'

'It will be painful, I fear.'

Nicholas helped her across the road and into the lane. When they found a doorway, they paused beside it to face each other. He was struck by the resemblance that Hal Bridger had shown to his mother. For her part, she seemed surprised that someone who worked in the theatre could be so polite and agreeable. Nicholas smiled.

'We none of us have cloven feet and forked tails, Mrs Bridger.'

'Do not mock me, sir.'

'I was not doing so,' said Nicholas, seriously. 'Before we go any further, let me say that Hal was a credit to the company. I know that you despise the playhouse, but your son was at home with us. He soon made many friends.'

'And you were one of them. Hal told us so.'

'You spoke to him?'

'No,' she explained. 'After he left, my husband would not have him in the house, but Hal wrote to us. His letters were torn up and thrown away before I could read them. But I was curious.'

'So you pieced them together again?'

'They were addressed to both of us.'

'And how did they make you feel?'

'Sad. Very, very sad.'

'For your son?'

'For all of us,' she confessed. 'We were married for over twenty years before we were blessed with a child. That's a long time to wait, a long time to pray. When my son was born, it seemed like a small miracle. We were such a happy family.'

'I'm sorry if that happiness was destroyed. Hal went his own way, as sons are apt to do. I did the same myself at his age. But you did not come to hear about me, Mrs Bridger,' he added quickly, with a self-effacing smile. 'You want to know about your son.'

She clasped her hands tight. 'Tell me what happened, please.'

Nicholas could think of few worse places to pass on sad tidings than a narrow lane only twenty yards away from a busy market, and he wished that she had been sitting down when he spoke. She looked frail and likely to faint but her religion gave her an inner strength that helped her through the ordeal. He tried to make it as swift and painless as possible, suppressing the details about the agony that her son had suffered, and emphasising the many good qualities in the boy's character. All that Alice Bridger had been told was that her son was dead. The news that he had been poisoned made her shudder, but she somehow regained her composure.

'I understand your feelings, Mrs Bridger,' said Nicholas when he had finished. 'Your husband left me in no doubt about your attitude to Hal. I regret it deeply, but I accept it. We'll take full responsibility for his funeral. He'll be buried in his parish church with his many friends there to mourn him.'

'No,' she said, breaking her silence. 'I brought him into the world and I'll see him out of it. We'll take care of the funeral arrangements.'

'Will your husband agree to that, Mrs Bridger?'

'That's our business. As for these friends you talk of,' she went on, fixing him with a stare, 'I'd rather that they stayed away.'

'We'd like to show our respect.'

'Then do so at a later date. You're not wanted at the funeral. Visit his grave, if you must. We cannot stop you doing that.'

'I'll pass that message on,' said Nicholas, quietly. 'And before you go, I wish to do something that your husband prevented me from doing. Hal was a delightful lad and I miss him already. I'd like to offer my sincere condolences.'

'Thank you.'

'If there is anything that we can do . . .'

'No,' she said interrupting him with a wave of her hand. 'There's nothing, sir. You've done more than enough already.'

'Hal came to us of his own accord, Mrs Bridger.'

'And look what happened to him as a result.'

'It was a tragic accident. It could have happened to anybody.'

'You are wrong. What happened to our son was deliberate. It was a judgement from heaven on the sinful life he was leading,' she asserted. 'Hal was punished for his transgression.'

By the time that John Vavasor joined them, Saul Hibbert and Cyrus Hame had drunk the best part of a bottle of wine between them. The two playwrights had got on well, finding much in common and talking about their ambitions in the theatre. Vavasor was delighted to find them in such high spirits. Hame had been instructed to befriend Hibbert and win his confidence. It was John Vavasor, a plump, grinning, red-faced man in his forties, who was primed to offer the bait.

'More wine here, I think,' he said, lowering his bulk onto a seat at the table. A flick of the fingers brought a serving wench. Vavasor tapped the bottle on the table. 'The same again, please, and another cup.'

'Yes, sir,' she said and bobbed away.

'So – this is the celebrated Saul Hibbert, is it?' said the newcomer, eyeing him. 'So young, so handsome and so supremely talented.'

'Thank you,' said Hibbert.

'I envy you, sir. I am old, unsightly and only half-talented.'

'I make up the other half,' said Hame, gaily. 'Apart, we

struggle for recognition, but, together we can produce a play worthy of the name.'

'*Lamberto* is far more than worthy,' said Hibbert. 'I'm honoured to share a table with its authors.'

'The honour is entirely ours,' insisted Vavasor.

A new bottle and a cup soon arrived. After pouring the last of the old bottle into his cup, Vavasor added some wine from the other bottle. Then he lifted his cup in a gesture of congratulation before sipping his drink. Hibbert took a moment to weigh him up. The older man presented a sharp contrast to his friend. While the latter hailed from Lincoln, Vavasor was a Londoner. His suit was expensive but dull, his face decidedly ugly and his voice coarsened by too much tobacco. He looked more like a debauched country lawyer than an eminent playwright. Cyrus Hame poured more wine into Hibbert's cup and his own.

'I told Saul that he would be better off with Banbury's Men.'

'Substantially better,' said Vavasor.

'How much did they pay you?' asked Hame.

'Four pounds,' replied Hibbert, 'with the promise of another pound if the play has more than ten performances within a month.'

'We were paid five pounds for *Lamberto*.'

'But that's divided between the two of you.'

'Cyrus took most of it,' said Vavasor, genially, 'because he has to pay his tailor and his wine merchant. I had the sense to marry wealth so money is immaterial to me. I write for rewards of the heart.'

'Banbury's Men will give us six pounds for our next play,' boasted Hame, 'and they've never paid that much before to anyone. We've set a standard where you could follow, Saul.'

'Are you not afraid that I'd compete with you?' said Hibbert.

'Not at all. The stage at the Curtain will accommodate all three of us with ease. Besides, you write comedies whereas John and I are born tragedians.'

'How do you get on with Lawrence Firethorn?' wondered Vavasor.

'Well enough,' replied Hibbert.

'Then you fared much better than me. When I took a play of mine to him, he sent me away with a flea in my ear. I'd never heard such foul language,' he recalled, grimacing. 'Firethorn threw the play back at me as if it gave off a nasty smell. I'd not work for that monster if the Queen herself commanded it.'

'Yet he's a magnificent actor.'

'In certain roles.'

'I wrote Lord Loveless with him in mind.'

'And he played it well enough,' agreed Hame, 'but I fancy that Giles Randolph could have played it better.'

'Does he have a gift for comedy?'

'For comedy, tragedy, history or any combination of the three,' said Vavasor. 'More to the point, he knows how to nourish new talent like ours – and like yours, Saul.'

'I'm already committed to Westfield's Men.'

'Only for this play. What of your next?'

'Lawrence and I are still discussing terms.'

'Bring them to us before you accept them, and we'll get a far better offer from Giles Randolph for you. Westfield's Men are past their best,' said Vavasor, downing some more wine. 'Apart from Firethorn, there are only three men of consequence in the company.'

'Barnaby Gill is one,' said Hibbert.

'And that testy Welshman, Owen Elias, another. Close your eyes and he's Firethorn with a Celtic lilt. They are the only two actors that Banbury's Men would like to poach.'

'You spoke of three a moment ago.'

'Three people – not three actors.'

'The third person is their book holder,' said Vavasor. 'Nicholas Bracewell is the man at the tiller there. He's steered them safely through every tempest. You must have noticed him.'

'Oh, yes,' replied Hibbert, scowling. 'I noticed him.'

'Was that your device or his?'

'What?'

'I know that he's wont to arrange their fights and invent clever effects for them. Is that what he did in *The Malevolent Comedy*?'

'I do not follow you.'

'During the last act,' explained Vavasor. 'When the servant died.'

'Ah, that.'

'It was a stroke of genius to have him thresh around and knock over all the furniture as if he were felling so many trees. The boy looked to be dying in earnest. Tell me, Saul, was that *your* doing?'

'Yes,' lied Hibbert. 'Everything that you saw was mine.'

When she heard his footsteps outside her front door, Anne Hendrik was doubly grateful. She was not only pleased that Nicholas had returned earlier than she had expected that evening, she was relieved that he had not been killed in a duel. Opening the door to him, she received a kiss and took him into the parlour. Nicholas looked weary.

'A tiring day?' she asked.

'Yes,' he replied, 'but not without its rewards.'

'What of your quarrel with Master Hibbert?'

'Oh, that's behind me Anne.'

'Good.'

'We met to discuss our differences in private and I left him with a dagger through his black heart.'

'Never!' she exclaimed. Then she realised that he was teasing her and beat him playfully on the chest with both fists. 'That was cruel of you, Nick.'

'I'm sorry,' he said, embracing her. 'Forgive me.'

'Then let's have no more jests.'

'As you wish.'

By way of apology, he gave her another kiss. They sat opposite each other and she disposed of her own day in a couple of sentences. Nicholas then told her about the visit to the apothecary in Clerkenwell, and how Simeon Howker's well-dressed customer had sounded very much like the man who had questioned Leonard at the Queen's Head. Anne was more interested to hear about the conversation with Hal Bridger's mother, reassured by the sign of what she took to be pure maternal affection.

'I think that it was a mixture of motherhood and Christian duty,' said Nicholas. 'I can see where Hal got his bravery from. Only a very brave woman could stand up against Mr Bridger.'

'Is that what she was doing?'

'She was expressing grief in her own way, Anne.'

'A peculiar way to me.'

'I admired her. Mrs Bridger was sincere enough in her beliefs to tell me to my face that the Queen's Head was a den of iniquity. It must have rankled that Hal was working so close to home and yet so impossibly far from his parents.'

'At least, they'll be reunited now, albeit briefly.'

'Let's hope so.'

'Meanwhile, you have a killer to track down. How can you possibly find him in a city as large as London? There are so many places to hide.'

'I fancy that we may bring him out into the light.'

'How?'

'By performing Master Hibbert's play again tomorrow.'

'I thought that *A Way to Content All Women* was advertised.'

'It's being set aside, Anne. There's been such a clamour for the new play that we simply must present it again. That will at least assuage its author and, perhaps, entice along the villain who tried to ruin its first performance.'

'Do you think he'll resort to poison again?'

'We'll not give him the opportunity.'

'What makes you think he'll come back?'

'Instinct,' said Nicholas. 'Having failed to stop us the first time, he'll want to try again and *The Malevolent Comedy* is his target. Had the company itself been the mark, he might have aimed at us again today but the performance went unmolested. His grudge seems to be against Saul Hibbert's play. It's stirred up real malevolence.'

'What is there in it that could cause such offence?'

'Nothing in the play itself,' replied Nicholas. 'The playwright is another matter.' He became thoughtful. 'I wonder if I might ask you a favour, Anne?'

'Granted before you even put it into words.'

He smiled gratefully. 'Come to the Queen's Head tomorrow and watch the play from the gallery. I need a keen pair of eyes in the audience. You can see things from up there which are invisible to me.'

'Including this Master Hibbert I've heard so much about.'

'Even in a crowd, you'll have no difficulty picking him out,' said Nicholas with asperity. 'He dresses to be seen and lets everyone know that he's the author. Saul Hibbert is extremely vain.'

'How unlike Edmund Hoode,' she commented. 'He's modest and unassuming about his plays. How has Edmund taken this change of plan for tomorrow? He wrote *A Way to Content All Women*. Does he mind his work being substituted by another comedy?'

'He's bound to, Anne. It must make him feel he's been

cruelly elbowed aside. Lawrence is showing some sympathy for him at last. To make amends, he's taking Edmund to supper this evening.

There were five of them at the table. Edmund Hoode sat beside Lawrence Firethorn while Owen Elias was opposite with the two young ladies in their finest attire. They were in a private room at the Queen's Head and Firethorn was amusing his female guests with anecdotes from his long and tempestuous career as an actor. Bernice and Ursula Opie were sisters, young, bright and nubile. Owen Elias had got to know them during his visits to their house. Linus Opie, their father, was a wealthy mercer with a passion for music and the Welshman had been engaged to appear at his evening concerts on a number of occasions. Neither Opie nor his daughters realised that the man who sang religious songs with such fervour led a private life that would be frowned upon by any church. Elias hoped to maintain the illusion.

Firethorn turned his broadest smile on the two young ladies.

'Have you ever seen Westfield's Men perform?' he asked.

'Once or twice,' replied Bernice. 'Father brought us here for the first time last year. I remember the play well. I loved every second of it.'

'And so do I,' said Ursula. 'It was called *The Faithful Shepherd.*'

'Then you are sitting opposite the man who wrote it,' said Firethorn, indicating Hoode. 'Do you hear that, Edmund? You have two admirers at the table.'

'Admirers?' echoed Hoode with a pallid smile. 'I was beginning to forget that such people ever existed.'

'There are four of us in this very room,' said Elias, heartily. 'Though the two prettiest are sitting opposite you.'

'I endorse that,' said Firethorn with a chuckle of approval.

Bernice Opie smiled but Ursula was slightly embarrassed by the compliment. Though they shared a similarity of feature, the sisters were very different to look at. Both had dark hair, a pale complexion and full red lips. Bernice, however, the younger by two years, had a natural beauty while Ursula was undeniably plain. Their demeanour seemed to match their appearance. Bernice was confident, vivacious and aware, whereas her sister was shy, hesitant and solemn. When Ursula did finally speak at length, it was clear that she was the more intelligent of the two, but the attention of the men was lavished on Bernice.

'You have such a lovely name, Bernice,' said Firethorn.

'Thank you,' she replied.

'Biblical, I take it?'

'Bernice was the daughter of Herod Agrippa.'

'Not to be confused with her great-grandfather, Herod the Great,' put in Ursula, pedantically. 'Agrippa sat in judgement on Paul, with Bernice present at the time, and they both treated him with respect and dignity. Bernice is later thought to have married King Ptolemy of Sicily.'

'And to have been the mistress of the Emperor Titus,' said Bernice, daringly. 'She must have been a remarkable woman.'

The men laughed but Ursula had to hide a blush.

'Bernice is almost as remarkable as her namesake,' observed Firethorn with a flattering smile. 'Do you not agree, Edmund?'

'Yes, yes,' said Hoode, staring in wonder at her. 'I do.'

'Do you intend to marry a king or an emperor, Bernice?'

She gave a brittle laugh. 'I'd never get to meet either, alas.'

'You are meeting both at this very moment,' Elias told her, pointing a finger at Firethorn. 'In his time, Lawrence has played a host of kings and a dozen different emperors.'

'I have ruled the world in its entirety,' said Firethorn.

The next course arrived to interrupt the conversation but it soon resumed. Firethorn and Elias were pleased with the way that things were going. Bernice Opie was angelic yet with a knowing quality that made her even more tempting. Unaware of the fact that she had been brought there to ensnare Edmund Hoode, she enjoyed being the centre of attention and luxuriated in it. Ursula, on the other hand, became more withdrawn but she listened carefully to all that was said. Hoode was as polite as usual, showing an interest in both guests and asking about the concerts organised by their father. Ursula, it transpired, was a talented musician, able to play any keyboard instrument. Bernice was a singer.

Firethorn and Elias were on their best behaviour. Seasoned in the ways of the world, they had both supped with beautiful young ladies in a private room before, always with one object in mind. They were not in pursuit of another conquest this time so they acted with uncharacteristic restraint, treating their guests with avuncular propriety. Both of them tried hard to bring Hoode to the fore so that Bernice could appreciate his talent and versatility.

'Edmund is a complete man of the theatre,' said Firethorn with an arm around his shoulder. 'Poet, playwright, actor, philosopher and artist. Did you know that Edmund designs the scenery for his plays?'

'No,' answered Bernice. 'How clever of you!'

'When I write,' explained Hoode, 'I see clear pictures in my mind.'

'And you act a role as well?'

'If you saw *The Faithful Shepherd*, then you saw me onstage.'

'I believe that we may have seen you in *The Loyal Subject* as well,' said Ursula, making a rare contribution. 'It was a wonderful play.'

'Also from Edmund's magical pen,' said Firethorn.

'We *must* get father to bring us to another play here, Ursula,' said her sister, excitedly. 'Now that we've met Master Firethorn and Master Hoode, I cannot wait to see them on the stage again.' She turned to Elias. 'What could we see at the Queen's Head tomorrow?'

'*The Malevolent Comedy*.'

'What an intriguing title! One of your plays, Master Hoode?'

'Not this time, alas,' said Hoode.

'We'll see it nevertheless if we can persuade our father. Oh, it's been such a lovely evening, hasn't it, Ursula?' Her sister gave an obedient nod. 'We can't thank you enough for inviting us.'

'It's we who are overwhelmed with gratitude,' said Firethorn.

When the meal was over, a coach came to pick the guests up and the three men waved them off in the street. Hoode was transported. He gazed after the vehicle until it disappeared around a corner, his face aglow, his eyes luminous, his mouth agape. Firethorn nudged Elias and they shared a secret smile.

'Did you enjoy your meal, Edmund?' asked Firethorn.

'It was like supping with a goddess,' said Hoode.

'Bernice Opie is truly celestial, is she not?'

'You feasted your eyes on her all evening,' noted Elias.

'And she obviously adored you.'

'I sing at their house on Sunday. I'll take you with me, Edmund.'

'Will you?' said Hoode, eagerly. 'I'd love to meet her again.'

'What man would not?' asked Firethorn with a sly grin. 'I think that Bernice Opie is one of the most gorgeous creatures in London.'

'That may be so, Lawrence, but she was immature and shallow.'

'I thought you liked her.'

'I did,' confirmed Hoode, 'but it was her sister who really caught my eye. Bernice cannot begin to compare with Ursula. *She's* my choice.'

Lawrence Firethorn and Owen Elias goggled in astonishment.

* * *

The decision to stage *The Malevolent Comedy* on the following day was by no means universally popular. Among the actors, only Firethorn and Barnaby Gill were enthusiastically in support of the idea. Most of the others were still haunted by the tragedy that had occurred at the earlier performance, fearing that something equally disastrous might happen. Edmund Hoode had opposed the notion on the grounds that it was too soon after the death of Hal Bridger but his protests were waved aside. To a company so anxious to increase its takings, a revival of the play was essential. Word-of-mouth would guarantee a full audience and the chance to sell so much refreshment to them might even serve to appease the nagging landlord. Horrified that a murder had taken place in his yard, Marwood was too shrewd a businessman to let emotion get the better of commercial gain.

Nicholas Bracewell was opposed in principle to the revival but the decision did not lie with him. Had it done so, he would have opted for *A Way to Content All Women* on that warm Saturday afternoon. Since the company were forbidden to play on the Sabbath, it would have meant that Saul Hibbert's play waited until Monday before being staged again, giving Westfield's Men a longer interval to absorb the blow it had inflicted on them at its first outing. Since the die was cast, Nicholas did all he could to make the revival a success, making sure that someone was in the tiring-house at all times so that no stranger could enter it unseen.

The morning rehearsal was slow and uninspired,

allowing Hibbert to voice his displeasure in the ripest of language. Seated alone in the middle of the lower gallery, he looked like an eastern potentate who had just discovered an outbreak of lethargy in his harem, and who felt deprived of full satisfaction. Only Firethorn and Gill escaped his biting criticism. Hoode was censured and Francis Quilter sharply reprimanded. The playwright reserved his most stinging rebukes for the book holder, however, blaming Nicholas for mistakes that were not his responsibility and trying to shame him in front of his friends. Nicholas was unperturbed. He trusted the judgement of his fellows. The actors knew that he had done his job with customary efficiency.

'Ignore him, Nick,' counselled Hoode when the rehearsal was over. 'He was picking on you needlessly.'

'I'd rather he berate me than the actors. If he wants to bring the best out of his cast, he should treat them with more respect. They're not dray horses, to be forced into a trot with the lash of a whip.'

'Lawrence can be too fond of the whip at times.'

'That's different,' said Nicholas, tolerantly. 'He's one of us. We're used to the feel of his lash.' He looked into Hoode's cheerful face. 'I hear that you supped with him last night.'

'With him and with two charming young ladies, sisters whom Owen knows. He's sung at their father's house.'

'Then they must be the daughters of Linus Opie, a man who loves his music, by all accounts. Owen has mentioned him before. Dick Honeydew has taken part in their concerts as well.'

'When I attend the next one, the only person I'll hear is Ursula.'

'Ursula?'

'The elder of the sisters. She plays upon the virginals.'

Nicholas was amused. 'From the sound of your voice, a virgin has played upon you. Who else was at this supper?'

'None but Lawrence and Owen.'

'Did either of them have designs on these young ladies?'

'No,' said Hoode, 'they stayed their hands for once. Owen was keen that I should meet his two friends, and I thank him from my heart.'

'I thought Lawrence bought your supper because he repented of the unkind things he said about your last play.'

'They were not unkind, Nick, they were all too accurate. And your own objections to it were also just. *How to Choose a Good Wife* was a feeble comedy and I knew it when I was writing it.'

'Your inspiration will soon return,' Nicholas promised. 'We burden you with high expectation, Edmund. All that you need is a long rest.'

'Not any more.'

'What?'

'I've had enough of lying fallow,' said Hoode, joyously. 'When I met Ursula Opie, my creative urge was suddenly fired again. As soon as I got back to my lodging, I started work on a new play.'

Gracechurch Street was even more crowded than usual that afternoon but it was not solely because of the market. So

120

many people converged on the Queen's Head to see the play that, eventually, the gatherers had to turn some away. Every seat was taken in the galleries, every square inch in the yard. Even generous bribes could not get gallants past the door. Disappointed spectators refused to leave until they had been given a guarantee that *The Malevolent Comedy* would be performed again soon. Westfield's Men were the victims of their own success. Their inn yard playhouse was too small to satisfy the demands of their public.

Lawrence Firethorn was cheered by the news that so many people had been eager to see the play. On some of the cast, however, it had a different effect. Like Nicholas, many actors were worried that there might be a second attempt to bring their performance to a halt. It made them nervous and unhappy. Francis Quilter even went so far as to suggest that the play had a curse on it and there were several murmurs of agreement. Firethorn stamped heavily on the dissenters.

'Listen to them, Nick,' he said as they gathered in readiness. 'They have excellent roles in an outstanding play that has brought in the biggest audience we've had all season. This is an actor's dream yet they behave as if it were a kind of nightmare.'

'Their minds are still on Hal Bridger.'

'Well, they should be on *The Malevolent Comedy*.'

'They will be, once we start,' said Nicholas, looking around the tiring-house. 'I understand their qualms. It was only two days ago that Hal lay dead upon that table there. George suffers most. Now that Hal has gone, he has to play the part of the servant himself. I fear that George will collapse *before* the poisoned cup is offered to him.'

'He'd better not,' growled Firethorn, 'or I'll kick him into oblivion.'

Pushing two actors aside, he checked his appearance in the mirror. Nicholas, meanwhile, flicked a glance at George Dart. Eyes closed, the little assistant stagekeeper was obviously praying. Nicholas could guess what entreaties were winging their way up to heaven. While he did not want the performance ruined, the book holder was nevertheless hoping that the killer would show his hand somehow. Nicholas had already warned Leonard to be vigilant and to look for the fair-haired man who had enquired so closely about the company. Anne Hendrik was another spy in the crowd, accompanied by Preben van Loew, her chief hatmaker, a dour, middle-aged Dutchman who was acting as her chaperone against his will. Alone in the yard, he was a reluctant spectator.

There was no rallying speech from Firethorn this time. Instead, he subjected his company to a withering stare. It was a signal for them to shake off their uneasiness and give their best. They responded at once. A minute later, *The Malevolent Comedy* was under way again. It began well and built up a steady momentum, soon turning the inn yard into a veritable sea of laughter. Lord Loveless was pre-eminent yet again, the Clown even more hilarious, and Mistress Malevole a winning blend of impishness and spite. In the role of a comic priest, Edmund Hoode's facial expressions were a source of delight in themselves and nobody realised, when he looked up at the galleries, that he did so in the hope that Ursula Opie might be watching him.

For the first three acts, the play gathered pace and left a trail of uninhibited pleasure in its wake. Notwithstanding the reservations some of them felt, Westfield's Men had somehow improved on their earlier performance, finding a greater conviction and new veins of humour to explore. Nicholas dared to believe that they might come through the afternoon without anything untoward happening. His hopes were soon dashed. During a feast that was held at Lord Loveless's house, the table was laden with wine and food. Lively music was played. There was a mood of merriment. The Clown then somersaulted onto the stage and danced such a spirited jig that the audience clapped him throughout.

Barnaby Gill relished the applause until he discovered that he had a dancing partner. From out of nowhere, a small dog suddenly appeared and jumped up on the boards beside him, doing its best to nip the Clown's heels. Gill was terrified. Unable to kick the animal away, he leapt up on the table, only to be followed by the yapping dog. Between them, they knocked every dish, vessel, candle and piece of fruit from the table, sending it cascading across the stage. Lord Loveless roared with fury, the Clown howled in fright, Mistress Malevole fled into the tiring-house and the comical priest tried in vain to catch the dog.

Thinking that it was all part of the play, the spectators cheered on the animal. Since the women had been turned into a cat, an owl and a monkey, respectively, the arrival of a real animal gave the play additional spice. The dog possessed an actor's instinct. The more they encouraged him, the more chaos he created, eluding the priest, tripping up Lord Loveless and sinking his teeth into the protruding buttocks of the Clown. *The Malevolent Comedy* was suddenly a play about a dog.

Nicholas Bracewell reacted swiftly to the emergency. Grabbing a cloak, he ran onstage and managed to throw it over the dog, snatching it up and holding it tight as it barked and wriggled in his arms. He went through the tiring-house into a passageway that led to a storeroom. Dog and cloak were tossed inside without ceremony and the door quickly locked. Nicholas hurried back to his station behind the scenes to take up the book, hoping that the play could be salvaged. He was in time to hear Lord Loveless deliver a line extempore as he looked around for the absent Mistress Malevole.

'Where has that scheming little bitch gone to now?'

The gale of laughter gave the actors the opportunity to regain their poise. Nicholas pushed Mistress Malevole back onstage and sent Dart with her to pick up all the items that had been knocked from the table. By pretending that the canine interruption had been rehearsed, Lord Loveless and the priest were able to turn it to their advantage, inventing fresh lines to cover the hiatus and finding immense humour in an improvised inspection of the Clown's wounded posterior. In the background, the dog continued to yelp in its new kennel but it went unheard.

Having come safely through the crisis, the actors picked up their speed again and sailed on with renewed confidence. Though they kept one eye open for further unheralded interventions, none came. What the audience heard from that point on came exclusively from the pages of Saul Hibbert's play. If it had been a success at its first performance, it was now a monumental triumph. The spectators whooped, whistled and clapped until the noise was deafening.

Lawrence Firethorn beamed at all and sundry, bowing low to the acclaim then blowing kisses up to the dozens of women who were calling out his name. Lord Loveless was yet one more memorable character to join his already large collection. After giving a final bow, he surged into the tiring-house and tore off his costume in a rage.

'I'll kill that mangy cur if I get my hands on it!' he yelled.

'Do not blame the animal,' advised Nicholas. 'The fault lies with the person who released him onto the stage.'

'And who the devil was that, Nick?'

'The same man who poisoned Hal Bridger.'

Firethorn blinked. 'Are you *sure*?'

'Absolutely sure,' said Nicholas, ruefully. 'He's back.'

Chapter Six

With the performance safely behind them, Westfield's Men were relieved but badly shaken. An atmosphere of quiet terror filled the tiring-house. The death onstage of Hal Bridger had been a more horrifying event but only the furniture had been in danger on that occasion. The dog had preferred human targets, biting at the heels of anyone within reach and sinking its teeth into the Clown's unprotected rear. Barnaby Gill was in despair as he rubbed his sore buttock.

'He tried to eat me alive!' he cried.

'Only because you are such a tasty morsel,' teased Owen Elias.

'I may never be able to walk properly again.'

'Sit in a pail of cold water and you'll be as good as new.'

'I need a doctor.'

'We've always said that,' mocked the other.

'How can you laugh, Owen? I'm in agony.'

'There's no blood to be seen through your hose.'

'That beast of Hades bit me to the bone.'

'He was letting you know what he thought of your performance,' said Firethorn, enjoying Gill's discomfort. 'As soon as you started your jig, the dog decided that it could bear no more.'

'Why did you not come to my rescue?' demanded Gill.

'I did. I was about to run the animal through with my sword when Nick saved me the trouble by throwing that cloak over him.'

'The problem is,' said Elias, pulling a face, 'that everyone in the audience will talk about that dog to their friends. Spectators will come to the next performance, expecting to see the same wanton havoc.'

'We'll never stage this damnable play again!' yelled Gill.

'*You* were the one who insisted that we revive it today, Barnaby.'

'I'd not have done so if I realised that my life would be at risk.'

'Try to remember Hal Bridger,' suggested Firethorn. 'He really *did* lose his life during *The Malevolent Comedy*. All you have to suffer is a blow to your dignity and a bruised bum.'

'I might have known I'd get no sympathy from you, Lawrence.'

'My sympathy goes to the entire company. When that animal was unleashed upon us, the whole performance might have ended in turmoil. Evidently, someone bears us ill will.'

'Only when we perform this play,' said Edmund Hoode, quietly. '*Black Antonio* gave us no trouble. It's only Master

Hibbert's work that brought misfortune upon us.'

'We cannot blame Saul for this.'

'Well, the blame must lie somewhere.'

'Edmund is right,' said Elias, summing up the general feeling. '*The Malevolent Comedy* is cursed. Stage it again and Barnaby's other buttock may serve as dinner for a hungry dog.'

'Never!' wailed Gill, massaging the injured area harder than ever.

'I think that we should forget Saul's play for a while.'

'And so do I,' agreed Hoode.

'That's rank cowardice,' declared Firethorn, raising his voice so that everyone in the room could hear him. 'Nothing will frighten us from doing what we choose. You heard that applause out there. The play is a palpable triumph. We'll stage it on Monday and every other day next week.' There was a loud murmur of protest. 'Would you walk away from certain success?' he challenged. '*The Malevolent Comedy* will line all our pockets. We must be brave enough to seize the opportunity.'

'All next week?' groaned Gill.

'And the week beyond that if interest holds. Yes,' Firethorn went on above the noise of dissent, 'I know that you all have fears and doubts, but there's one sure way to remove them.'

'I do not see it, Lawrence.'

'We've almost forty-eight hours before we stage the play. That's two whole days in which to find the villain who poisoned Hal Bridger and who set that dog upon us. Catch him and our troubles are over.'

'Supposing we do not?' asked Hoode.

'We will,' affirmed Elias. 'We'll find the lousy knave somehow.'

'And if we fail?'

'Then we'll play *The Malevolent Comedy* regardless,' said Firethorn.

'That's suicide,' complained Gill.

'It's courage, Barnaby. Together, we'll face up to anything.'

'You'd not say that if the dog had bitten *you*.'

'I agree with Barnaby for once,' said Hoode. 'Two performances of this play have so far brought two vicious attacks upon us. We've one lad dead and our clown savaged by a dog. Before you commit us to stage the play again, Lawrence,' he urged, 'ask yourself this. What kind of peril awaits us *next* time?'

Nicholas Bracewell took no part in the discussion. There were too many jobs for him to do. The actors were justifiably upset by the unscheduled interference from the dog, but he knew that Saul Hibbert would be even more outraged. For the second time in a row, his play had teetered on the edge of doom. The playwright would demand to know why, and Nicholas accepted that he would be blamed as a matter of course. Confrontation was unavoidable. Before it happened, he had to supervise the dismantling of the stage and the storing of its constituent parts. By the time that task had been completed, the yard was more or less clear and only a few stragglers left in the galleries.

Seeing that he was free at last, two of the spectators came

across to him. They made an incongruous couple. Anne Hendrik was smiling happily but Preben van Loew, in his dark, sober apparel, was as lugubrious as ever. Even the frenzied antics of the dog had failed to convince him that theatre was something from which he might take a degree of pleasure.

'Did you enjoy the play, Preben?' asked Nicholas.

'No. I could not follow it.'

'But your English is excellent.'

'It is not the way they speak,' said the Dutchman, 'but the way they *think*. You would not find anyone like Lord Loveless in my country. We would never search for a wife like he did.'

'I can confirm that,' said Anne, pleasantly. 'My husband certainly did not woo me by making me take a potion in my wine. I loved the play, Nick,' she added. 'I thought it a wild, wonderful, madcap romp. You never told me that there was a dog in the cast.'

'There was not supposed to be one,' said Nicholas. 'He joined us unawares. I still do not know where he came from.'

'Nor me. The animal seemed to pop up out of thin air.'

'No,' said the Dutchman. 'It was from the stable.'

'How do you know?'

'Because I was not always watching the play. Its manners were too strange for a foreigner like me to understand. So I let my eye wander.'

'And you saw the stable open?' asked Nicholas.

'Just a little. Someone tossed the dog out.'

'Did you see the man?'

'No, Nicholas. Only the dog.'

'That's one mystery solved, anyway. The animal all but brought the play to a halt. I simply had to get him off the stage.'

'And you got a round of applause for doing so, Nick,' noted Anne.

'Barnaby Gill did not join in the clapping,' said Nicholas. 'His hands were too busy rubbing his injury. But did you see anything *apart* from the play, Anne?'

'I saw Master Hibbert. He was sitting on a bench in front of us. He was very much as you described – young, handsome, conceited and almost as ostentatious as Barnaby. When the play was over, he was showered with congratulations by everyone.'

'What else did you see?'

'Nothing,' she admitted, 'I was too absorbed in the play.'

'I was not,' said her companion.

'Just as well, Preben. I was supposed to be Nick's pair of eyes in the gallery, but it was you who saw the one thing of real consequence.'

Nicholas chatted with them for a few minutes until he became aware of Saul Hibbert, bearing down on him. Instead of detaching himself from his friends, he introduced them to the playwright, knowing that their presence would force him to moderate his language. The playwright's fury was accordingly suppressed. Ignoring the Dutchman completely, he favoured Anne with a dazzling smile.

'Did you like the play?' he asked, fishing for praise.

'Hugely,' she replied. 'Let me add my congratulations.'

'Thank you.'

'It was truly a marvel.'

'I tried to write a comedy with some depth to it.'

'And you succeeded, Master Hibbert. Behind the laughter, there was much to provoke thought.'

'It's good to know that I had such an appreciative spectator.'

'What I appreciated most,' confessed Anne, 'was the scene with the dog, but Nick tells me that that was entirely unrehearsed.'

Hibbert glowered. 'Unrehearsed, uncontrolled and unwanted.'

'Thanks to Preben here,' said Nicholas, 'we do at least know where the dog came from. It slipped out of the stables, it seems.'

'How could that be allowed to happen? Did you not check the stables before the play began?'

'Of course, Master Hibbert. I make it my business to do so. If there are horses in there, I have the stables locked as a precaution. Finding the stalls were empty today, I simply closed the doors.'

'There was no dog there?'

'Not when I looked.'

'No dog in a manger?' asked the Dutchman, releasing a high-pitched wheeze of a laugh. His face clouded in apology. 'Oh, I am sorry.'

'You should have searched the stables more thoroughly, Nicholas,' chided Hibbert. 'That animal jeopardised my work.'

'Barnaby Gill was the real victim. He was bitten.'

'What's a mere bite to the loss of a whole play?'

'Your play was saved by Nick,' said Anne, coming to his aid.

'Had he not captured the dog when he did, it might have done far more damage. As for searching the stables, no man would have done it more thoroughly. Nick is very conscientious.'

'Thank you, Anne,' said Nicholas.

'Conscientious or not,' Hibbert went on, testily, 'he missed that dog and it was free to bite at my reputation as a dramatist. Be warned, Nicholas. I'll be complaining to Lawrence about you.'

'Do not be surprised if there are complaints against you as well.'

'Against me?'

'From most of the company, I suspect.'

'How could they object to *me*?' asked Hibbert with a look of injured innocence. 'I've given them the finest play they've had in years.'

'But look what it brought in its wake.'

'Yes,' said Anne. 'A death in the first performance and a dog on the loose in this one. Actors have enough problems onstage as it is without having to cope with unforeseen hazards like that.'

Hibbert was taken aback. 'You seem to know a lot about the theatre,' he said, staring at her. 'Have you seen many plays here?'

'Dozens of them over the years.'

'Yes,' explained Nicholas. 'Anne is a close friend of Westfield's Men. You might say that she knows the troupe from the inside.'

'Then she'll accept that you were at fault today,' said Hibbert, 'for not looking carefully enough into the stables.'

'Indeed, I'll not,' rejoined Anne with spirit. 'Nick is no culprit. If anyone should bear the blame Master Hibbert, it must be you.'

'*Me*?'

'For writing a play that clearly offends someone deeply.'

'Yes,' said Nicholas in support, 'it may not be the play that caused resentment but its author. That's the only conclusion I can reach.'

Hibbert was caught on the raw. 'I resent that accusation!'

'Others are starting to make it.'

'Then they are cruelly misled.'

'Are they, Master Hibbert?' asked Nicholas, meeting his glare. 'We have rivals but none that would lower themselves to such shameful devices as we've suffered during *The Malevolent Comedy*. It's not *our* enemies we should look to, therefore, but yours.'

'I have no enemies,' denied the other.

'One of them has followed you to London. He was the man who bought that poison and arranged for the dog to be released during the play. Who would hate you enough to do such things?'

'Nobody.'

'Think hard, Master Hibbert.'

'I do not need to.'

'If we're to catch this rogue,' said Nicholas, earnestly, 'we'll need your help. There must be someone in your past who holds a grudge against you. Tell me his name.'

'How can I, when there is no such person?'

'Are you *certain* of that?'

'Quite certain.'

'Since you've been with us,' said Nicholas, pointedly, 'you've shown little interest in making friends – among the men, that is. Among the ladies, I gather, it's another matter.' Hibbert glowered again. 'Has it never occurred to you that someone who does not make friends is bound to create foes instead?' The playwright shifted his feet uneasily. 'There *is* someone, isn't there?' pressed Nicholas. 'Give me his name. Who is this sworn enemy of yours?'

Hibbert spluttered but no words came out. Wanting to upbraid the book holder, he was inhibited by Anne's presence and by Preben van Loew's mournful expression. Sensing that he had the playwright on the run, Nicholas repeated his demand.

'This man poisoned Hal Bridger,' he reminded. 'Who is he?'

Saul Hibbert did not pause to reply. Pulsing with rage, he swung on his heel and headed for the taproom. He refused to admit that he was the target for the attacks on his play. Only one enemy preoccupied him at that moment and his name was Nicholas Bracewell.

The book holder, meanwhile, was bidding adieu to Anne Hendrik and Preben van Loew, sending them off on the journey back to Bankside. He was grateful that the Dutchman had been there. The hatmaker's indifference to the play had allowed him to see the stable door being opened. It was a valuable piece of evidence. Nicholas was about to go into the building when that evidence was confirmed.

A small boy had been lurking in the shadows, waiting

until Nicholas was on his own. After licking his lips, the boy scuttled over.

'Please, sir,' he asked, nervously, 'are you Nicholas Bracewell?'

'Yes, lad. How can I help you?'

The boy swallowed hard. 'Can I have my dog back, please?'

While Barnaby Gill's wound was being examined in private by a doctor, the rest of the company were in the taproom. Disconcerted by the second mishap with the play, all that most of them wanted to do was to steady their nerves with strong drink. Owen Elias was therefore puzzled when he saw one of the cast trying to leave.

'You are going already, Edmund?' he said in surprise.

'Yes, Owen.'

'The rest of us will carouse for hours.'

'Too much wine only befuddles my brain,' said Edmund Hoode.

'That's the attraction of it, man. Come, join with your fellows.'

'Not today.'

'You're no priest now, Edmund. The play is over.'

'*The Malevolent Comedy* may have finished but another play has already begun.' Elias looked baffled by the remark. Hoode became inquisitive. 'Do you think that she was here today, Owen?'

'Who?'

'Ursula, of course. Ursula Opie.'

'The sisters were both here.'

'How do you know?'

'Because I saw them when we took our bow,' replied Elias. 'They were in the upper gallery with their father, clapping their hands with the rest. They liked the play.'

'What did Ursula think of my performance, I wonder?'

'Ask her when you meet her again tomorrow.'

'Oh, I will.'

'But spare a moment to look at her sister as well,' suggested the Welshman. 'Have you ever seen such a merry twinkle in a woman's eye? And, oh, those ruby lips! Bernice Opie has the lips of a cherub.'

'It's what came out of them that matters to me,' said Hoode, flatly. 'I've never heard anyone talk so much to so little effect. She gurgled like a never-ending stream. Whereas Ursula – God bless her – said little yet spoke volumes.'

'Did she? Neither I nor Lawrence noticed that.'

'You were too busy ogling her sister.'

'Can you blame us? Bernice is divine.'

Hoode smiled wryly. 'Be honest, Owen. Neither of you was attracted to the young lady by her divinity. All that you felt was lust.'

'We are true sons of Adam.'

'Then I must have descended from someone else,' decided the playwright, 'for she aroused scant interest in my breast, let alone in my loins. Besides, respect must always come before desire and Ursula was the only one whom I respected.'

Elias shrugged. 'But she was as plain as a pikestaff.'

'Not to my eye.'

'Then you need spectacles, Edmund.'

'I can see Ursula Opie with perfect clarity.'

'That's something I'd not care to do.'

'Why not?'

'Bernice decorates a room whereas Ursula is that dull piece of furniture you put in the corner. One sparkles, the other does not.' Hoode shook his head. 'It's true, Edmund. But what's this about one play beginning while another ends?'

'Look to the sisters, Owen.'

'What do you mean?'

'Study them both instead of just the pretty one. That's what I did and it was a revelation. Ursula and Bernice Opie are two sides of the same coin. That helped me to see my mistake.'

'What mistake?'

'You'll find out in good time,' said Hoode, waving farewell. 'Enjoy your ale, Owen, and raise a tankard to Ursula for me. You'll have cause to thank her before long.'

'Thank her?' said Elias, perplexed. 'Thank her for *what*?'

The boy's name was David Rutter and he was no more than ten or eleven. Though his clothes were ragged and his face dirty, he had clearly been taught manners by someone. Nicholas found him polite and honest. Before he returned the dog to its young owner, however, he wanted to know all the details.

'You were *paid* to release the dog like that?' he asked.

'Rascal, sir,' replied the boy. 'His name is Rascal.'

'Then he lived up to it this afternoon. Who named him?'

'My father. He came to us as a puppy and was so full of mischief that my father dubbed him Rascal.' Rutter grinned. 'It suits him.'

'Only too well. How much were you paid?'

'A penny beforehand with threepence more to follow if I did as I was told. The gentleman must have thought I let him down because there was no sign of him afterwards.'

'I doubt if he ever intended to pay you anything else. He bought you and Rascal cheaply to inflict some very expensive damage. But how did you get into the stables?' wondered Nicholas. 'When I searched them, they were empty.'

'That's what you thought, sir, but we were there all the time. Rascal and I were hidden under a pile of hay. That was our mistake.'

'Mistake?'

'I was told to let Rascal loose ten minutes after the play had started,' said the boy, 'though I could only guess at the time. But it was so warm and cosy under that hay that we fell asleep.'

'Even with the audience making so much noise?'

'We live beside the river, sir. We're used to noise.'

'So you didn't wake up until the play was two-thirds over?'

'I'd no idea about that. All I could think about was the money we'd earn if Rascal did his job. So I let him out of the stable,' he continued, 'and that was the last I saw of him. What did he do?'

'Let's just say that he made his presence felt.'

The boy was anxious. 'Was he hurt?'

'It was Rascal who did the hurting,' replied Nicholas. 'He bit the Clown and chased everyone else around the stage.'

'The bite was only meant in fun, sir. Rascal does that all the time when we play together. He never bites hard.' He licked his lips once more. 'Can I have him back, please?'

'If you tell me about the man who paid you.'

'Much like you in height but dressed more like a courtier.'

'Have you ever seen a courtier, David?'

'No, sir, but that's how I think they must look – with a fine doublet and a tall hat with an ostrich feather in it. And he was rich,' said the boy. 'When he put a hand in his purse to find me a penny, it came out with a dozen gold coins in it.'

'Was he a fair-haired man with a well trimmed beard?'

'How did you know?'

'And a voice that was not born in London?'

'That was the fellow, sir – you've *met* him.'

'No,' said Nicholas, 'but I've every intention of doing so. Come, David,' he went on, turning away. 'I'll not only show you where I locked Rascal up. I'll give you another penny to take him far away from here.'

When he stormed into the taproom, Saul Hibbert was impeded by members of the audience, who insisted on heaping praise on him. All that he could do was to smile, nod and express his thanks. It was minutes before he could make his way across to Lawrence Firethorn, who was seated at a table with Owen Elias. Hibbert stood over them.

'I need to speak to you, Lawrence,' he declared.

'Then do so sitting down,' replied Firethorn, 'so that we may talk in comfort.' Hibbert lowered himself onto a stool. 'Will you join me in some Canary wine?'

'No, I've come to talk business.'

'And I know what business that is,' joked Elias. 'You wish your play to be known henceforth as *The Malevolent Dog*.'

'I'd boil the creature in oil, if I catch it,' vowed Hibbert. 'Everyone I speak to congratulates me warmly on my play but saves their highest compliment for that yapping animal.'

'I'd save it for Nick Bracewell. He got rid of the dog for us.'

'But he was to blame for it being there in the first place.'

'What makes you think that?' asked Firethorn.

'He admitted as much,' said Hibbert. 'It seems that the dog was hiding in the stables, waiting to be let out. Yet Nicholas claims that the stables were empty when he searched them.'

'Then you can rest assured that they were.'

'In that case, how did the dog suddenly appear?'

'I don't know,' confessed Firethorn, 'but we go to great lengths to make sure there are no animals in the yard before we begin. Someone smuggled in a cockerel one afternoon and let it loose while I was playing a tender love scene.'

'And don't forget that rabbit who once tried to take a role in *The Loyal Subject*,' said Elias. 'He, too, was released by way of a jest.'

'That dog was no jest,' insisted Hibbert, eyes aflame. 'He was brought here in a deliberate attempt to ruin my reputation.'

'What about *our* reputation?'

'That's too well established to be in danger, Owen. Mine, however, is not. If my play had been abandoned because of the dog, *I'd* be the real loser. I'll not stand for it, Lawrence.'

'Calm down,' soothed Firethorn.

'How can I calm down when my livelihood is at stake?'

'You were safely up in the gallery when the attack was made. We were the ones onstage, having to dodge those gnashing teeth. You might begin with a word of thanks for the way we rescued the situation.'

'Yes,' said Elias, 'and for the way that Nick captured the dog.'

'But for him,' argued Hibbert, 'the animal would not have been there in the first place. Your book holder failed miserably in his duty. I'll not have the bungling fool involved in a play of mine again.'

The Welshman bristled. 'Mind your language. Nick is my friend.'

'I'd sooner take his place myself.'

'No man could do that,' warned Firethorn. 'He's far more than a mere book holder. Nick controls the whole performance. He's also in charge of counting our takings, dealing with our churlish landlord, finding any hired men we need and acting as our emissary to Lord Westfield. He has a dozen more responsibilities besides.'

'Most of all,' said Elias, 'he's known and trusted by the company.'

'You are not, Saul.'

'If you want to see Nick's true value, look at the plot he drew up for *The Malevolent Comedy*. It tells the story of each of the five acts, and shows who should be where in every scene. Nick pins it up in the tiring-house before we start. Without it, we'd be lost.'

'Then we keep the plot and get rid of him,' said Hibbert.

'We've had this futile argument before,' recalled Firethorn, 'and our answer's still the same. Nick stays, regardless.'

'Does that mean my play will not be staged again?'

'Far from it. We plan to offer it every day next week.'

'Without my permission?'

'What author would deny permission to have a play performed?'

'I would,' attested Hibbert. 'Look to the contract and you'll see that I'm within my rights to do so.'

Firethorn gaped. 'You'd stop us playing *The Malevolent Comedy?*'

'Unless my terms are met.'

Elias was combative. 'Do you dare to threaten us?' he said.

'I mean to have my way.'

'Then you can take your worm-eaten play and stuff it up your . . .'

'Be quiet, Owen,' said Firethorn, cutting him off. 'We need to haggle here. Saul's comedy could fill our coffers to the brim.'

'I'm glad that you've remembered that,' said Hibbert, smugly.

'What's to prevent it appearing at the Queen's Head on Monday?'

'The presence of Nicholas Bracewell.'

'You demand a terrible price.'

'And I mean to have it.'

'The performance will suffer without Nick's guiding hand.'

'I refuse to believe that, Lawrence. Find a reliable deputy.'

'A moment ago,' noted Elias, 'you were offering to take on the office yourself. Mark my words, you'd not be popular if you did so. And you'd not get the best out of the actors.'

'Nicholas will never touch my play again!'

'Or you'll withdraw it?'

'I'll do far worse than that.'

'Worse?' repeated Firethorn.

'I'll work instead for Banbury's Men,' said Hibbert with conviction. 'I've already received blandishments from them. John Vavasor and Cyrus Hame were sent to whet my appetite. *Lamberto* showed their gift for tragedy. I am wanted at the Curtain for my comic mastery.'

Firethorn was shocked. 'You'd go to Banbury's Men?'

'Only if you deny my request.' He rose quickly to his feet and put his hands on his hips. 'Nicholas Bracewell or Saul Hibbert? Make your choice. Which of us is more important to you?'

Before any reply could be made, Hibbert stalked off dramatically.

'I know which one I'd choose,' said Elias, belligerently.

'Peace, Owen.'

'Nick is worth a dozen Saul Hibberts.'

'I agree,' said Firethorn, 'but Nick does not write plays. If we lose Saul to our rivals, we yield up our best hope of competing with them.'

'Do you believe that Banbury's Men are really after him?'

'Yes, I do.'

'Then why not let him go?' said Elias. 'In return, you can lure away John Vavasor and Cyrus Hame. A fair exchange, I'd say.'

'And so would I, if there were any chance of it taking place. But there's not,' said Firethorn with a sigh of regret. 'When he showed a play to me, I tossed it back in Master Vavasor's face. He'd never join us now, Owen. The fellow has every reason to get his own back at me.'

John Vavasor poured two cups of wine and handed one to Cyrus Hame.

'Do you think he'll come?' he asked.

'I'm certain that he will. Saul Hibbert is an ambitious man.'

'Too ambitious, I fancy. We'd need to watch him, Cyrus.'

'He's no match for us,' said Hame, sipping his drink. 'We played him like a fish at the end of a line yesterday. The promise of more money will be irresistible.'

'Yes, he's as fond of women and fine clothes as you are.'

'Like me, he has good taste in both. That means expense.'

'Ambitious and in need of money – we have him!'

'Unless they bind him by contract to Westfield's Men.'

'They've not done so yet,' said Vavasor. 'He told us as much. And I doubt that Lawrence Firethorn would pay what Banbury's Men will offer. He's a reputation for being tight-fisted – among his other vices.'

'What about his virtues?'

'He has none.'

Hame laughed. 'You really hate the man, John.'

'I loathe him. He said that my play was pure dross.'

'Dross can be turned into gold by the right process.'

'You proved that,' said the other with gratitude. 'You're a true alchemist, Cyrus. My work was base metal until you put it in the roaring furnace of your brain. It came out as new-minted gold.'

'We are partners, John. Each of us needs the other.'

'The question is – do we also need Saul Hibbert?'

'You want to cripple Westfield's Men, do you not?'

'Oh, I do. I want to bring Master Firethorn crashing down.'

They were in a room at Vavasor's house, a spacious mansion that rubbed shoulders with the homes of the high and mighty in the Strand. Having no need to work for a living, Vavasor was nevertheless driven to make his mark in the theatre, even if it meant long hours of unremitting toil. Until he had met Cyrus Hame, all success had eluded him. Suddenly, the two of them were the most celebrated authors in London, and they had all but completed their new play. Vavasor looked wistfully at the manuscript and succumbed to a feeling of doubt.

'Do you think it will be as good as *Lamberto*?' he said.

'No, John.'

'Oh, dear!'

'It will be even better,' Hame said with a grin. '*Pompey* has a nobler hero and a bolder theme. More to the point, the role is even more suited to Giles Randolph's talents than Lamberto.'

'That was not the only reason I chose it for him.'

'No, you wanted him to out-fire Lawrence Firethorn.'

'And so he will,' said Vavasor. 'That will hurt Firethorn more than anything. He's played Pompey the Great many times in a play of that title and thinks the part is his in perpetuity. We'll wrest it from him and show how it should be played. Lawrence Firethorn will squirm in a pit of envy.'

'I begin to feel sorry for him.'

'There's more yet, Cyrus. I want you to write a Prologue that will play upon his name and goad him even more. Harp on the fact that our tragedy will have more fire and sharper thorns than those other versions of the story. Mock him without mercy.'

'The couplets already start to tumble from my brain.'

'Set him down as Pompous the Great.'

'I'll tent him to the quick,' promised Hame. 'He'll wish he never had the gall to turn John Vavasor away.'

'His troupe will slowly crumble. He's lost Edmund Hoode. He's lost his supremacy as an actor. And he's lost his way.'

'He's also set to lose Saul Hibbert.'

'When we can entice him away.'

'That may be sooner than we thought,' said Hame, artlessly. 'From what I hear, Saul was not too happy with the performance of his play this afternoon. I do not blame him. Who wants to be known as the author of a play about a runaway dog?'

They laughed their fill then poured themselves more wine.

* * *

Sunday began, as it always did in the household, with a visit to church. Accompanied by her maidservant, Anne Hendrik walked with Nicholas Bracewell to attend morning service in Bankside, while all the bells of London rang out to call the faithful. When they filed into their pew, Anne knelt in prayer, filling her mind with holy thoughts. By the time they emerged from the church, however, her thoughts had taken a more temporal turn. On the stroll home, she did not mince her words.

'It was utterly shameful of Lawrence!' she said.

'But it was I who made the decision, Anne.'

'That's the most shameful thing of all. Given the choice between you and Master Hibbert, he did not even have the courage to take it. Instead, he shifted the burden to you once again.'

'I had no objection to that,' said Nicholas.

'Well, I do.'

'At least, it allowed me to make the decision.'

'Only because Lawrence knew exactly what that decision would be,' she said, angrily. 'He's such a Machiavel. Because he could not ask you to stand down tomorrow, he tricked you into offering to do so.'

'What else could I do?'

'Defy him and defy Master Hibbert.'

'The company must come first, Anne.'

'For once in your life, stop being so *noble*.'

'There's more to it than that,' he replied. 'I'm not moved entirely by the spirit of self-sacrifice, I can assure you. The simple fact is that *The Malevolent Comedy* will bring in lots of money.'

'It's that malevolent author who worries me. Besides, after the scares they had with the play twice before, none of the actors wants to touch it again.'

'Lawrence does and there's been a request from our patron. Lord Westfield is eager to see it again. That settles the matter, Anne.'

'What of Barnaby? He was bitten by that dog.'

'He swore he'd never go near the play again. But the injury was very minor, and he began to remember all the rounds of applause that the Clown was given for his dances. Barnaby has agreed to go on.'

'Even without you?'

'He's never been my closest friend.'

'But he knows how much they depend on you.'

'I think he'll be reminded of that tomorrow,' said Nicholas. 'I wish them well, of course, but there could be problems behind the scenes. George Dart will hold the book and it may well prove too heavy for him.'

'George Dart?' she said, fondly. 'What would *he* do if someone is poisoned onstage or if a dog is let loose again? George would run away.'

'The play may not be ambushed again tomorrow.'

'What if it is?'

'Then I may be in a better position to do something about it, Anne. Instead of being tied up with the performance, I'll occupy an upstairs room from which I can watch the whole yard. Yes,' he went on, 'and I'll place Leonard where he can receive a signal from me. Between the two of us, we may be able to ward off an attack before it even comes.'

'That's not the point at issue here.'

'It is for me. I want Hal Bridger's killer caught.'

'So do I, but I also want justice for Nicholas Bracewell. You've given them years of loyal service. All that Master Hibbert has given them is one play. Yet he takes precedence over you.'

'I'll admit that I was disappointed by that.'

'You'd every right to feel betrayed. This is akin to treachery.'

'Lawrence was put in an impossible situation,' he said, mildly. 'I do not hold it against him.'

'Well, I do,' she returned with vehemence. 'I'll never forgive him for this – or the others, for that matter. Did nobody speak in your favour?'

'Owen Elias did, so did Frank Quilter. And I'm sure that Edmund would have pleaded my cause, had he still been there. It was all to no avail. Lawrence overruled them.'

'He'd not overrule me.'

Nicholas laughed. 'I think it would take an army to do that, Anne. But do not accept defeat yet,' he warned. 'The situation may still change in our favour.'

'How?'

'Lawrence has to break the news to his wife.'

Until that day, Lawrence Firethorn had been a reluctant churchgoer, attending begrudgingly out of a sense of duty rather than because of any Christian impulse. This time, however, he could not wait to get there because it offered him the sanctuary he desperately sought. Having kept the decision about Nicholas Bracewell to himself, he had made the fatal mistake of confiding in his wife on the Sabbath. Margery's wrath knew no bounds. People six streets away heard her red-blooded condemnation. In full flow, she could even make as strapping a man as her husband quail with fear. Firethorn fled to church with alacrity and prayed that she might forgive him his trespasses.

On the walk back to Old Street, Margery was quiescent but he knew that it was only the presence of their children, and of the apprentices who lived with them, that held her back from a display of public excoriation. She was saving herself until they were behind closed doors again. The fact that her voice penetrated wood, stone and any other intervening material with ease did not hold her back. Neighbours were compelled to listen to the latest piece of marital discord.

'You made Nick Bracewell stand down?' she howled.

'It was his decision.'

'You forced him into making it.'

'I could do little else, my angel.'

'Angel me no more,' warned Margery, 'for you are on the side of the devil. Only a fiend from Hell could treat Nick the way that you did.'

'He upset Saul Hibbert,' said Firethorn.

'By rescuing his play from disaster twice in a row?'

'Saul does not see it like that.'

'But you should, Lawrence. You know the truth of it.'

'Nick did handle him very roughly on Thursday.'

'I'm surprised that he did not tear the fellow apart,' she

yelled. 'Any other man would have done so. One of your lads was murdered and all that Master Hibbert can do is to complain that it spoilt his play. Is human life worth no more than that? God's mercy! In Nick's place, I'd have strangled him with my bare hands.'

'There's no point in arguing over it,' said Firethorn, trying to assert himself. 'The decision is made and we all have to abide by it.'

'Well, I don't.'

'You're not a member of the company.'

'No,' she retorted. 'If I had been, this villainy would never have taken place. Remove your book holder to please this testy playwright? I'd sooner get rid of *you*.'

'Margery!'

'They've managed without Lawrence Firethorn before.'

'And very poorly.'

'How much worse has it been when Nick Bracewell was absent? Your enemies set a proper value on him. Have you forgotten the time they had him put in prison?' she demanded. 'It was not you or Barnaby they sought to impair. They knew they could cause more damage by taking your book holder away from you.'

'Do not remind me,' begged Firethorn, hands to his head.

'Somebody has to, Lawrence. Had I not got him released from the Counter, with the help of your patron, Westfield's Men would surely have foundered. True or false?'

'That was a long time ago, Margery.'

'True or false?' she shrieked.

'True, all true, utterly and completely true.'

'And is this how you repay Nick for his service to the company?'

'It's only while Saul's play holds the stage.'

'That could be a week, perhaps two. What is your book holder supposed to do in the meantime? Sit quietly at home with Anne?' She gave a grim laugh. 'I'll wager that you'd not dare to face *her*. Nobody understands Nick's true worth more than Anne. She'll be disgusted with you, Lawrence, and I share her disgust.'

Firethorn began to sweat. He felt that he was being roasted on the spit of his wife's anger. Having married her for her vitality, he had long ago discovered that there was a severe drawback. Turned against him, the zest and vigour that had made Margery such an appealing woman was a potent weapon. He was tempted to run back to church again to hide.

'Well?' she asked, folding her arms. 'What do you have to say?'

'Nothing, my love.'

'There's no love here for you, sir.'

'Running a theatre company is a difficult business.'

'A nasty, scurvy, double-dealing business in your hands.'

'We'd be fools to turn Saul Hibbert and his play away.'

'And knaves to part with Nick so cruelly.'

'It's only for a time, Margery.'

'Not if this tyrant stays with you,' she said. 'What happens when you coax another play out of him? Master Hibbert will make even more demands then. If you lose Nick now, you'll lose him for good.'

'I couldn't bear that thought.'

'Then why did you force him out?'

'We are merely *resting* him, Margery.'

'In order to please a man you'd never heard of six months ago.'

'All London has heard of him now,' said Firethorn. 'Everyone is demanding to see his play – Lord Westfield among them, and he's seen it twice already. We have the success that we need and we must build on it. Would you have me let Saul take his talent to our rivals?'

'Frankly, yes.'

'That's patent madness.'

'Then you are married to a patent madwoman,' she said. 'From where I stand, *The Malevolent Comedy* is far more trouble than its worth. It's given you too much malevolence and too little comedy. For there's not a man in the company – apart from Barnaby, perhaps – who will laugh at Nick's departure. Yet there are several who'll weep.'

'I'm one of them,' he conceded, sadly. 'Nick is like a son to me.'

'Then behave like an honest father.'

'I dare not, Margery.'

'Renounce this upstart and send him on his way.'

'Saul Hibbert is an important part of our future.'

'Without Nick Bracewell, you'll *have* no future. Call him back.'

'It's too late now. The play has been advertised for tomorrow.'

'Then do not ask me to come and see it.'

'Margery,' he said, slipping an arm around her waist in an attempt to soothe her. 'I would not have this happen for the world. Whatever we decided would involve some loss. I did what I felt was right for the good of the company. Come,' he went on, tightening his hold. 'Bear with me.'

'Take your hand away.'

'You're my wife. You swore to love, honour and obey me.'

'That was before I realised what villainy you'd stoop to,' she said, pushing him off. 'You deserve neither love, honour nor obedience. I cannot honour a man who behaves so treacherously or obey one who issues such unkind commands. As for love,' she added with a harsh laugh, 'you've seen the last of that, Lawrence. There'll be no room in my bed for you while Nick is ousted from his place. You are banished.'

Most of Shoreditch had heard the dread sentence imposed.

Chapter Seven

The house was in a street off Cheapside, close to the Mercers' Hall, where Linus Opie held high office in his guild. It was less palatial than might have been expected of such a wealthy man, with no conspicuous display of gold plate or rich tapestries, and no gilt-framed family portraits on the walls. Instead, the house reflected its owner's love of music. The hall could seat thirty people with ease and still leave room for three keyboard instruments and a dais on which musicians and singers could perform. Edmund Hoode was fascinated to see where Ursula Opie lived. When he arrived that evening with Owen Elias, he was given a cordial welcome and shown to a chair at the back of the hall.

The other guests were largely business acquaintances of their host. They had brought their wives and, in some cases, their children, to hear one of the regular concerts that were put on at the Opie house. Elias had vanished and there was no sign of Bernice or Ursula Opie, so Hoode was left very much on his own. Having nothing whatsoever in common with the obese merchant tailor who sat next to him, he could manage only the most desultory conversation, nodding in agreement to everything that the man said about trade and offering a tentative forecast about the weather on the morrow. Before the concert started, he saw their host conducting the Bishop of London to a privileged position in the front row.

Hoode was amused. Knowing how promiscuous an existence his friend had led, he was tickled by the thought that Owen Elias would perform only feet away from a Prince of the Church. An actor whose private life would never attract an episcopal blessing was now taking a major role in what was, in effect, a religious service. Hoode admired him for it. Elias had a deep, rich singing voice of considerable range and Hoode had often written songs for him in his plays. Like other members of the company – Barnaby Gill and Richard Honeydew, for instance – Elias was keen to develop his singing talent by taking part in concerts, or giving recitals, whenever he could. It was an alternative source of income when the theatres were closed by plague, or when, during winter months, it was impossible to play outdoors at the Queen's Head.

A polite round of applause signalled the arrival of the performers. Bernice and Ursula Opie led the way, followed by Owen Elias and by a callow young man with a lute. They began with a song by Orlando Gibbons, sung by Elias to the accompaniment of the lute. With her sister at the virginals, Bernice Opie then sang one of the three pieces by William Byrd that were in the programme, revealing a pleasing soprano voice with an unexpected power to it. When the lutenist favoured the audience with examples of John Dowland's genius, he turned out to have a high, reedy voice that grated slightly on the ear.

Edmund Hoode barely heard him. His attention was fixed solely on Ursula Opie, moving from one instrument to another as she displayed her command of each keyboard, accompanying both Elias and her sister, individually, and during their occasional duets. Ursula was demure but dignified. She wore a pale blue gown with hanging sleeves of lawn. Her cambric ruff was lace edged and seemed, to Hoode, to set off her features perfectly. A French hood surmounted her head. To one member of the audience at least, she looked, in the candlelight, a picture of quiet beauty. Hoode was entranced.

When the concert was finally over, the guests responded with well-mannered clapping and Hoode was struck by the difference between them and the rowdy spectators who filled the Queen's Head. Drinks and light refreshment were served and people were encouraged to mingle. Hoode tried to ease his way towards Ursula but it was her sister who accosted him, offering her brightest smile to the playwright.

'I was so pleased to see you here, Master Hoode,' she said.

'Thank you. I thought you sang delightfully.'

'Did you prefer the Byrd or the Tomkins?'

'I found the Thomas Tallis most moving.'

'But I did not sing that,' she complained with a frown. 'I was hoping that one of *my* songs would be to your taste.'

'They *all* were,' he reassured her, 'and they could not have been performed better. The duets, too, were a magical experience, greatly helped by your sister's accompaniment.'

'Did you think so? I felt that Ursula was not at her best.'

'Every note she played was a joy to hear.'

'And what about the notes I sang?' she pressed, wanting praise.

'Musical perfection.'

'Were you surprised, Master Hoode?'

'I expected nothing less from you.'

The compliment broadened her smile. Though she was determined to monopolise him, Hoode kept looking around for her sister. When he saw her in a corner, talking earnestly to the lutenist, he felt a flicker of jealousy. Before Hoode could make his way to her, however, Owen Elias descended on him out of the crowd. The Welshman had dressed with care for the occasion, choosing his best doublet and hose, and investing in a new lawn ruff. He spoke as if they were on consecrated ground.

'Did you enjoy the concert, Edmund?' he asked.

'Every moment.'

'What of our duets?'

'I was just saying how much I appreciated them,' said Hoode, 'along with the Byrd and the Tomkins, that is,' he added, turning to Bernice. 'Your voices blended so harmoniously.'

'I simply followed where Bernice led.'

'We loved the play yesterday,' she said, beaming at Hoode. 'You were so comical as the priest. I could not stop laughing, especially when you danced out of the way of that little dog.'

'He was an uninvited member of the cast.'

'So I hear.'

'He livened up the afternoon for all of us,' said Elias. 'But I'm sorry that your sister did not enjoy *The Malevolent Comedy* as much as you. She spoke rather slightingly of it.'

Hoode was alarmed. 'She *disapproved*?'

'Pay no attention to Ursula,' said Bernice. 'She has too solemn a cast of mind. Father and I adored the play but she felt that it bordered on blasphemy to poke fun at the priesthood.'

'Then your sister objected to my performance?'

'Only to the character you played.'

'Ursula is more at ease with the Bishop of London,' said Elias. 'I heard them talking in Latin earlier on. She's a studious young lady.'

'Too much study addles the brain,' said Bernice, happily.

'That's my philosophy as well.'

'What about you, Master Hoode?'

'Oh, I admire your sister's scholarship.'

'Would you wish to waste your time learning a dead language?'

'Probably not.'

'Then you are of the same mind as me. I hoped that you would be.'

Suppressing a giggle, she gazed at Hoode with undisguised fondness. He, meanwhile, was craning his neck to look for Ursula and he was heartbroken to learn that she was no longer in the hall. It was exasperating. Bernice Opie, the sister whom he thought too frivolous and inconsequential, exhibited a clear liking for him while Ursula, the person he had really come to see that evening, would not even speak to him. The irony of the situation was not lost on the sensitive playwright. Bernice's mother came up to spirit her daughter away, leaving Hoode alone with Elias. Nudging his friend, the Welshman spoke in his ear.

'Bernice is there for the taking, Edmund.'

'I'd never dream of doing such a thing.'

'Would you not like her to sing to you in bed afterwards?'

'Shame on you, Owen!'

'Ah, I see,' said the Welshman, chuckling. 'You'd rather make love to her sister in Latin.'

Though he would not be involved with the third performance of the play, Nicholas Bracewell nevertheless turned up at the Queen's Head that morning. The first person he spoke to was Alexander Marwood. The book holder's request was promptly refused.

'No, no,' said the landlord. 'That's out of the question.'

'But I'd have the ideal view from that room.'

'Find another place from which to spy, Master Bracewell. You'll not make use of our bedchamber. My wife would never permit it.'

'I'd only be in there during the play,' said Nicholas.

'No man is allowed into that room.'

Marwood spoke with the cold finality of someone who was only permitted to share the bedchamber himself on sufferance. It was his wife who controlled what happened within those four walls, and that meant a series of lonely nights for the harassed landlord. The joys of marriage had been all too fleeting in his case. Indeed, they now seemed so distant that he began to wonder if they had ever occurred.

'Why did you want to go in that room?' he asked, eyeing Nicholas warily. 'You'll not see much of the play from up there.'

'I'd be looking at the audience.'

'What pleasure is there in that?'

'I do it out of necessity rather than pleasure,' explained Nicholas. '*The Malevolent Comedy* has an enemy and I believe that he may be among the spectators this afternoon.'

Marwood was disturbed. 'To cause more mischief on my property?'

'Not if I can catch him in time.'

'You did not catch him when he poisoned that young lad, or when he had a dog set loose upon you.'

'I'm ready for him now,' said Nicholas, 'and I'll not be hampered by my role as book holder. All I need is a vantage point from which to see the whole yard and watch the spectators.'

'I sense trouble ahead.'

'The play has made you healthy profits so far.'

'What use are they if someone is bent on destroying me?'

'Master Hibbert is the target here. You are quite safe.'

'I'd be safer still if the play was cancelled,' said Marwood, sourly.

'It's been advertised for this afternoon.'

'Then I blame Master Firethorn for putting my yard in danger again. Whenever you play this comedy, you are waving a red rag at a bull. Choose something that will not goad this villain into action.'

'But that's the only way we may be able to ensnare him,' argued Nicholas. 'In staging this play, we're also setting a trap.'

'And *I'm* the one who'll be caught in it.'

'You stand to reap the benefits of a full audience.'

'I stand only to suffer,' moaned the landlord. 'I've done nothing else since I let your accursed troupe into my yard. Westfield's Men have brought murder, mayhem, fire, riot and ruination down upon me. And now you wish to invade our bedchamber! It's too much, sir!'

Wringing his hands, he scurried off across the yard in a state of agitation. Nicholas scanned the windows above him, trying to decide which other room would be suited to his purposes. He was still unable to make up his mind when Leonard ambled over to him, his big, flat, pasty face crumpled with anxiety.

'What's this I hear about you leaving the company?'

'Only for the duration of the play, Leonard.'

'But what if the play should run for a week or more?'

'My task is to make sure that it survives today,' said Nicholas.

'Then you'll be keeping yourself out of work.'

'No, Leonard. I'll be protecting the company.'

'Saving the skin of Master Hibbert more like,' said Leonard with unwonted severity. 'He's upset all of us here at the inn with his high-handed ways, and your fellows do not like him either. George Dart tells me that he had you expelled from your post.'

'Rested only.'

'That rest could last a long time if he writes more plays for you.'

'I've no power to stop him doing that.'

'It's in your interests to let *The Malevolent Comedy* fail,' noted the other, 'and well it may if you do not stand guard over it.'

'I stand guard over the reputation of Westfield's Men,' said Nicholas, proudly, 'and I'd hate them to falter on my account. I'll need your help, too, Leonard. You know where every nook and cranny is. I count on you to search them before the play begins.'

'If you wish, Nicholas.'

'Then stand close to the stage during the performance, ready to help the actors if trouble breaks out. Keep one eye on the room above where I'll maintain my vigil. I'll wave a hand to warn you of danger.'

'What about the stables?'

'Lock them.'

'And the gates to the yard?'

'They'll be chained until the performance is over.'

'You are closing off all the points of attack.'

'We can never do that completely. We must stay alert.'

'At least, the dog will not run wild.'

'We've faced fiercer animals than that,' said Nicholas, smiling as a memory surfaced. 'In Cambridge, a man once set his dancing bear upon us because our play was getting all the attention. In Exeter, some geese decided to wander across the stage in the middle of a performance. Putting on a play is an act of faith, Leonard. We are hostages to fortune.'

'It was ever thus. What else can I do this afternoon?'

'Keep your eyes peeled for that fair-haired gentleman.'

'He's not been near the place since.'

'Has anyone else been asking about Westfield's Men?'

Leonard nodded. 'As a matter of fact, they have.'

'Oh?'

'About one of them, anyway.'

'Who was that?'

'You, Nicholas.'

'Me?'

'The book holder and his duties, anyway.'

'What did you say?'

'That you do far more behind the scenes than ever is seen onstage. That's why it pains me to see that Master Hibbert has ousted you like this. George Dart will be a poor deputy.'

'Tell me about him, Leonard.'

'George?'

'No, the gentleman who was so interested in me. Describe him.'

'That's impossible.'

'Why?'

'Because it was not a gentleman at all,' said Leonard, a slow smile spreading across his face. 'It was a lady, a very beautiful young lady.'

Lawrence Firethorn was in no mood to conduct a rehearsal. After a sleepless night on the floor of his bedchamber, he ached and itched all over. True to her edict, his wife had kept him out of his bed and down on the bare boards in disgrace. Lord Loveless was anything but lordly in the morning but his sense of lovelessness had deepened markedly. With the apprentices trailing behind him, he rode off from Shoreditch in a daze. When his mind finally began to clear, it had to grapple with his dire predicament. Torn between competing claims on him, he knew that he had made an irrevocably bad decision. In trying to keep Saul Hibbert loyal to Westfield's Men, he had been forced to suspend his book holder, scandalise his actors and, worst of all, estrange himself from his wife. He wished that he had never heard of *The Malevolent Comedy*.

The rehearsal was a shambles. Held to refresh the memories of the cast, it only concentrated on key scenes in the play. Since it began without any real commitment on the part of the actors, it quickly descended into farce. Firethorn was the worst offender.

'George!' he bellowed.

'Yes?' replied Dart, acting as prompter.

'Give me the line.'

'Which one, Master Firethorn?'

'The one I'm struggling to remember, you idiot.'

'There've been so many of those this morning.'

'What am I supposed to say to Mistress Malevole?'

'When?'

'Now, George – now, now, now!'

Dart was flustered. 'Which scene are we in?'

'The one we started on ten minutes ago.'

'I've found it. You and Mistress Malevole are in the garden.'

'No, you imbecile!' boomed Firethorn, flinging his hat on to the stage in his fury. 'We did that scene an hour ago. This one takes place in the hall of my house. Are you sure that you have the right play in your hands? A prompter must be prompt and audible. You are neither.'

'Do not hound him, Lawrence,' advised Owen Elias. 'You'll only confuse him further. Try to build his confidence.'

'He's as useless as a Pope's prick.'

'You do him wrong,' said Edmund Hoode, taking pity on Dart. 'It was an act of stupidity to think you could turn him into Nick Bracewell.'

'It would be easier to make a silk purse out of a sow's ear.'

'George will not let us down if you treat him kindly.'

'Kindly!' roared Firethorn. 'If he feeds me the wrong line again, I'll tie him to the flagpole and hoist him to the top.' He snapped his fingers. 'Back to the start of the scene,' he ordered, 'and let's try to get it right this time, shall we?'

'How can we when your memory is like a sieve?' asked Gill.

'Nobody invited your comment, Barnaby.'

'I speak for all of us. You've stumbled badly throughout.'

'Slander!' said Firethorn over the murmurs of agreement. 'I'm feeling for a new interpretation of the character, that's all.'

'And groping for your lines like a blind man.'

'Silence!'

Gill smirked. 'Whatever did Margery give you for breakfast today?'

The remark stung so hard that it set Firethorn off into a violent tirade against the Clown that was only ended when Elias and Hoode stepped in to keep the two men apart. Further rehearsal was impossible. The play was abandoned. The one saving grace was that its author had not been present to witness the general apathy and ceaseless parade of errors. Even the most assured comic moments had been thrown away.

'Take heart, George,' said Hoode, trying to console their little book holder. 'You'll have none of these problems this afternoon.'

'I always lose my place when Master Firethorn shouts at me.'

'He shouted at all of us today.'

Dart was wistful. 'If only Nicholas had been here to bail us out,' he said. 'It's a crime that he's been deprived of his office for me.'

'It's more than a crime, George – it's a vile sin.'

'At the time when we need him most, he's not here to help us.'

'Nick would have been thoroughly ashamed of us this morning.'

'And rightly so,' said Dart. 'Where *is* he?'

During the rehearsal, Nicholas Bracewell had deliberately kept out of the way, not wishing to embarrass his deputy or to subject himself to what was bound to be a painful exercise. He had never been asked to step down before and nursed a grievance that he did his best to keep to himself. On the other hand, he told himself, he could still serve the company by offering it the protection it needed. Much as he might resent Saul Hibbert, he wanted the play to go off without interruption. To that end, he and Leonard searched then sealed off all obvious hiding places for anyone intent on causing disarray. He also spoke to the gatherers on duty at the gate and instructed them to keep a close eye on the spectators as they were admitted. Anyone trying to bring small animals in was to be turned summarily away.

Long before the yard began to fill, Nicholas had retreated to a room that overlooked the stage from behind. Vacated by a traveller earlier that day, it was small, dark and infested with spiders but it was ideal for his purposes. It allowed him to watch unseen from above. Though much of the stage itself was obscured from him, he had a good view of the pit and the galleries. He kept the whole yard under surveillance. His eyesight was exceptionally sharp. During his voyage around the world with Drake, he had done his share of climbing into the crow's nest to act as lookout. Rewards were offered for the first man to descry land and Nicholas made sure that he did not miss any opportunities. That same intense vigilance was now turned on the audience.

The galleries were replete with elegant young gentlemen but none of the dashing gallants fitted the description that Leonard had given of the fair-headed visitor. It was a different matter when it came to beautiful ladies. They were there in such abundance that Nicholas was spoilt for choice. The three aristocratic ladies in Lord Westfield's entourage were quite dazzling and those elsewhere, bedecked with their finery, turned the galleries into a blaze of colour. The reputation of *The Malevolent Comedy* had patently spread, bringing in spectators from every level of society. Its problematical author, flamboyantly attired and seated beside yet another arresting beauty, was in the lower gallery.

The play started well and proceeded without mishap but it had none of the driving thrust of the earlier performances. Studying the reactions of the audience, Nicholas could see that they were not as engrossed as they should have been. They tittered when they should have laughed, laughed when they should have applauded and only came properly to life when Barnaby Gill entertained them with his jigs. Lord Loveless lacked authority, Mistress Malevole was muted and Edmund Hoode, as the comical priest, seemed to forget that he was performing in a comedy. While the play was continuously diverting, it never managed to realise its full potential.

For all that, it provided two fairly exhilarating hours for its audience and was happily free from any of the errors that had littered the rehearsal. Somewhere behind the scenes, George

Dart was entitled to congratulate himself. The most important thing from Nicholas's point of view was that no attempt was made to interrupt the performance. No poison, no dog, no fresh outrage. *The Malevolent Comedy* had finally been staged without attracting any malevolence. As a consequence, it was robbed of some of its tension and hilarity, but its cast had been spared and Nicholas was grateful for that.

The applause that greeted them as they came to take their bow was warm and generous. It did not compare, however, with the ovations that had been received on the two previous occasions. Keenly aware of that, Saul Hibbert looked deeply disappointed and Nicholas could see him apologising to his companion. For the author – as for others who knew the play – the performance had fallen far short of excellence. One man in the upper gallery seemed to relish the fact. Alone of the audience, he was not clapping at all. Instead, he looked on with a smile of satisfaction.

Nicholas recognised him at once as a playwright who had been rudely rejected by Lawrence Firethorn, only to achieve success with a rival company. It was John Vavasor.

Westfield's Men knew only too well that they had let themselves down. Over their drinks in the taproom, they searched for explanations.

'I felt so *tired*,' admitted Edmund Hoode. 'Tired and distracted.'

'My heart was simply not in the play,' said Owen Elias.

Francis Quilter sighed. 'We all know why,' he said. 'We're still in mourning for Nick Bracewell.'

'And for Hal Bridger.'

'Yes, Owen. Even more so for him.'

'Nick will come back but Hal is gone forever.'

'And in his place,' Hoode reminded them, 'we have Saul Hibbert.'

'What will *he* have thought of us today?'

'I daresay that he'll tell us, Frank, and in blunt terms as well.'

'No,' said Elias. 'We've been rescued from that. Lawrence has gone to intercept him and take full responsibility for what happened onstage. It's the one useful thing he's done all day.'

'An act of penitence.'

'He needs to show some of that penitence at home. According to Dick Honeydew, life in Old Street has been even more ear-splitting than usual. Margery took her husband to task for the way he treated Nick.'

'Good for her!' said Hoode.

'I'd love to have been a fly on the wall,' said Quilter.

Elias grinned. 'Every fly within a mile heard the quarrel. Dick tells me that Lawrence was even exiled from his bed. No wonder he was so peevish this morning.'

'It sounds to me as if Margery had the courage that we lacked.'

'Yes,' agreed Hoode. 'She stood up to Lawrence.'

'So did I,' claimed Elias. 'I swore he'd never share my bed again until Nick Bracewell was back with us.'

'Do not jest about it, Owen. It's too serious a matter for that.'

'Where is Nick?' wondered Quilter. 'Is he not here today?'

'I've not seen him, Frank. Nor do I expect to do so.'

'Why not?'

'He'll want to steer well clear of Saul,' said Hoode, 'and, since he was not holding the book this afternoon, Nick may feel out of place.'

'Out of place!' echoed Elias. 'A pox on it! And a pox on Saul Hibbert as well! It's an evil day for us when Nick Bracewell feels out of place among his friends. We need him.'

'He'll not be back while *The Malevolent Comedy* holds the stage.'

'Then we defy Lawrence and refuse to play in it.'

'Yes,' said Quilter. 'I'll back you in that enterprise.'

'Edmund?'

'Let's not act too rashly,' said Hoode, holding up his palms.

Elias was shocked. 'Do you not want Nick back with us?'

'Of course, and as soon may be. But it would be wrong to whip the company into a frenzy over a choice of a play. I've no high opinion of Saul as a man,' he continued, 'but I'm the first to applaud his work. I'm an author myself and know how difficult it is to write a sprightly comedy. There's an important principle at stake here.'

'Yes,' said Elias. 'We want Nick instead of Saul Hibbert.'

'No, Owen. It has a deeper significance than that. Should the company spurn a good play simply because it dislikes the playwright? Look at my case,' Hoode said. 'Everyone loves me yet *How to Choose a Good Wife* was turned down because it was a bad play. That's how it should be. A play must be judged on its merits and not on the personality of its author.'

'I never thought Saul's play *had* any merits,' said Quilter.

'Then you are at variance with hundreds of happy spectators.'

'Edmund is right,' said Elias, grudgingly. 'The play is popular.'

'Not with those of us who have to act in it.'

'I still believe that we should challenge Lawrence.'

'Leave that to Margery,' said Hoode. 'She loves Nick as much as any of us and will do her best to get him back. Margery is our true champion. Let her joust with Lawrence on our behalf.'

Elias nodded. 'It shall be so,' he decided with a smile. 'Margery will knock her husband from his saddle and trample all over him until he begs for mercy. That's where our hope lies – in the arms of a woman.'

Nicholas Bracewell remained in his hiding place until the yard was almost clear. He was pleased that the performance had suffered no disturbance though his relief was tempered with disappointment. He felt that an opportunity had been missed to catch the person who had left such an indelible stain on the two earlier performances. Nicholas showed his customary tact. He did not even think of leaving the room until he saw that Saul Hibbert had disappeared from the gallery. Nothing would be served by another argument with the playwright. At least, Nicholas thought, he would not be blamed for the shortcomings that had come to light that afternoon.

When all but a few stragglers had gone, he left the room and went downstairs. Coming into the yard, he first encountered Leonard.

'What did you see?' asked Nicholas.

'Little beyond the play.'

'You were supposed to be on guard.'

'I was, until the Clown began to dance,' said Leonard. 'I could not take my eyes off him. He made me laugh. I'm sorry, Nicholas.'

'Luckily, we did not need you.'

'I'm always here if you do.'

'Unlock the stables and feed the horses,' said Nicholas, 'or you'll have the landlord shouting at you again. And – thank you!'

'I thank *you* for letting me watch such a wondrous comedy.'

Leonard walked off and Nicholas turned his attention to the stage. Under the direction of Thomas Skillen, the decrepit stagekeeper, George Dart and the others were removing the boards and folding the trestles. After bearing the weighty responsibility of holding the book, Dart had now reverted to his more usual role as an underling, and Skillen kept reminding him of it. To spare the old man effort, Nicholas took over many of the stagekeeper's duties himself but Skillen was proving that he was still capable of doing them, even though now in his seventies.

Nicholas gave him a cheerful wave and waited patiently until the stage had been put away. George Dart then ran eagerly back into the yard to speak to him, looking up at Nicholas like a dog that expects a pat of approval from its master.

'You did well, George,' said Nicholas.

'Thank you.'

'The play went off without any misadventure.'

'I was too frightened to make a mistake,' replied Dart.

'We'll make a book holder of you yet.'

'Coming from you, that's real praise.'

'I never doubted you, George.'

'Master Firethorn did. After the rehearsal this morning, he was ready to nail me to the wall of the tiring-house.'

'I hope that he had the grace to congratulate you this afternoon.'

'Yes, he did.'

'Good,' said Nicholas. 'Fetch me the play and I'll be off.'

'Will you not stay to join us in the taproom?'

'Not today.'

'But everyone will expect you there.'

'I'd feel a little uneasy,' confessed Nicholas, 'because I was not really part of the company this afternoon. I'd be an outsider. Besides, there's always the chance that Master Hibbert will be there as well to soak up praise from any spectators. For a number of reasons, I prefer to keep out of his way.'

'So do the rest of us,' said Dart, sharply.

Nicholas clicked his tongue. 'Now then, George.'

'We hate the man.'

'Show a proper respect for a talented author.'

'I do that for Edmund Hoode. He truly deserves it.'

'I agree with you there.'

'Master Hibbert does not. He bullies us. In any case,' Dart went on, 'you should not dare to talk of respect. You showed him little of it yourself when you set about him the other day.'

'I'll not deny it,' said Nicholas. 'My temper was frayed and I hit out. But that's all in the past.'

'Not if he stays. Master Hibbert will never forgive you.'

'That's his business.'

'He wants you out of Westfield's Men for good.'

'I mean to remain,' declared Nicholas.

'That's the best news I've heard all day.'

'Thank you, George. Now get the book so that I can take it home and lock it up securely.'

'I'll about it straight.'

Dart raced off and Nicholas smiled. As a result of his success as book holder, there was a spring in Dart's step and confidence that oozed out of his spare frame. In the course of the afternoon, he had come through a time of trial. Nicholas was glad for him, hoping that it might liberate him from the mockery that was his usual lot. The new-found confidence did not last long, however. When he reappeared minutes later, Dart was the same worried, woebegone, timorous little creature he had always been. Nicholas felt sudden alarm.

'Where is it?' he asked.

'It's not there. I've searched high and low.'

'Where did you leave it?'

'On a bench in the corner.'

'Could one of the actors have taken it?'

'No,' said Dart. 'As soon as the play was over, they rushed off to the taproom. The book was there when we took the stage to pieces. I saw it before I came out to speak to you.'

'That's the only complete copy of *The Malevolent Comedy*,' said Nicholas. 'Without it, the play cannot be staged. Think, George. Are you *sure* that you left it on the bench?'

'I'd swear to it on the Holy Bible.'

'Then there's only one conclusion – it's been stolen.'

Lawrence Firethorn was in despair. Battered by circumstance and bruised by marital confrontation, he had led his company with less than his accustomed gusto that afternoon. To his utter chagrin he had been compelled to give Saul Hibbert an abject apology then stand there while the author denounced the performance in forthright language and had especial words of censure for Lord Loveless. Reeling from the encounter, all that Firethorn wanted to do was to drink himself into a stupor. Instead, he found Nicholas Bracewell waiting for him at the door to the taproom with bad tidings. The actor was apoplectic.

'The book was *stolen*?' he cried.

'So it appears,' replied Nicholas.

'Are you certain that nobody took it in jest?'

'This is no jest, Lawrence. Everyone knows how

sacrosanct the book of a play is. That's why I guard it so carefully.'

'But you were not there this afternoon, Nick. In my folly, I let George Dart take your place. He's to blame for all this. I'll crucify him!'

'George served you well this afternoon,' said Nicholas, coming to his defence, 'and worked just as hard after the play was over. He could not watch the book every second. The real fault lies with the thief, not with George.'

'What am I to do?' groaned Firethorn, clutching at his hair. 'I've already worn sackcloth and ashes for Saul Hibbert once. Am I to don the robe of shame again?'

'Send me in your stead.'

'Oh, no.'

'I'll try to reason with our author.'

'You'd find a charging elephant more inclined to reason. No, Nick,' said Firethorn, 'it falls to me to face his ire again. I'll tell Saul what's befallen us. Stay here to learn the outcome.'

'I will,' said Nicholas. 'We need a quick decision on the matter.'

Leaving his book holder at the bottom of the staircase, Firethorn ascended the steps again and went along the passageway. He tapped on the door of Hibbert's but elicited no response. He knocked harder.

'Go away!' yelled Hibbert from inside the room.

'This is Lawrence again.'

'I don't care if it's the King of Mesopotamia – go away!'

'But I need to speak to you on urgent business.'

'I've urgent business of my own!' rejoined Hibbert, angrily.

Firethorn heard the rhythmical creaking of the bed and understood what that business might be. He waited until the sound reached its peak then faded slowly away. The actor-manager banged on the door again.

'I'm still here, Saul,' he called out.

'Then you can stay there all night.'

'I came to warn you that we may not be able to stage your play tomorrow. Or any other day this week, for that matter.'

'Why not?'

'When you are ready to listen, I'll tell you.'

A long pause was followed by the sound of movement. When the door was finally inched open, a sullen Hibbert peered out. But for the shirt he had hurriedly put on, the author was naked.

'Your timing was poor enough onstage today,' he said, nastily, 'but it's deserted you altogether now. You knew that I was entertaining a lady and should have kept your distance.'

'This news will brook no delay.'

'What news?'

'The book has been stolen.'

'What book?'

'The prompt copy of your play,' explained Firethorn. 'When George Dart's back was turned, someone sneaked into the tiring-house and took it. *The Malevolent Comedy* has vanished.'

'Damnation!'

'There may yet be a remedy.'

'Yes,' snarled Hibbert. 'I'll hire a brace of lawyers to sue you for the wilful loss of my property. This is a disaster.'

'Do you still have your foul papers?'

'What?'

'Your early draught of the play,' said Firethorn. 'The one from which the fair copy was made by the scrivener.'

'No, it was covered in blots and scribbles. I threw it away.'

'Then we are lost.'

'What of your own copies?' asked Hibbert. 'Sides were written out for the actors. Put them all together and we have a complete play.'

'Only if we had all kept our roles. Most of us have not. When we commit a part to memory, it stays lodged in the brain. We toss the written record of it away.'

'That's idiocy.'

'It's practicality. I've played thirty-six different roles this season, dozens more in the past. By my troth, if I kept a copy of every part I played, the house would be filled to the rooftops with paper.'

'Nicholas Bracewell is behind all this,' said Hibbert, vindictively. 'I'll wager that he stole the play in order to get revenge.'

'He'd never dream of hurting the company in any way.'

'His quarrel is with me.'

'Then he'll settle it in his own way,' said Firethorn, 'but not like this. Nick is the only person who can save us from this sorry plight.'

'I'll not have him involved.'

'Then resign yourself to seeing another play at the Queen's Head tomorrow. And hire as many lawyers as you like,' he went on. 'Look to our contract and you'll find that the book is the legal property of Westfield's Men. We bought it from you.'

'I still have moral ownership.'

'That's a poor argument in a court of law.'

'The book must be found forthwith,' ordered Hibbert. 'Instead of bickering with me, you should be out looking for it.'

'And where would you suggest we start?' asked Firethorn. 'We're still trying to find the man who poisoned Hal Bridger then paid for a dog to be unleashed upon us.'

'I'll warrant he's behind this latest crime as well.'

'A moment ago, you accused Nick Bracewell.'

'He'll be gloating over this terrible loss of mine.'

'You mistake him badly. Nick is more upset than anyone. The book of any play is like a precious jewel to him. He'd defend it with his life.'

'Pah!'

'It's true, Saul,' said Firethorn. 'Had he been in his place today, a whole army would not have been able to wrest the prompt book from him. In pushing Nick aside, you took away your play's protection.'

'I still abide by that decision.'

'Even though you saw the effect upon us? That was the main reason we lacked any spirit today. We missed our book holder.'

'Can one man make such a difference?'

'Judge for yourself.'

'Saul,' purred a woman's voice in the background.

'One moment,' Hibbert said to her.

'Come back to bed now.'

'Go to her,' encouraged Firethorn, waving him away. 'I can see you'd rather sport with your mistress than save your reputation.'

'My reputation is everything to me, Lawrence.'

'Then watch it wither on the vine. It rests on three performances of a play that no longer exists. Success entails keeping yourself in the public eye, Saul. A month off the stage and you'll be forgotten.'

Hibbert was rocked. 'Is there no way we can redeem ourselves?'

'Only one.'

'What's that?'

'Turn to Nick Bracewell. Let him work his magic.'

'How could he come to our rescue?'

'The way he did once before,' said Firethorn, 'when a play of Edmund Hoode's went astray, stolen by a disaffected actor. Within the space of twelve hours, Nick had conjured another copy out of the air.'

'I don't believe it.'

'Then ask Edmund. The play was called *Gloriana Triumphant*. We played it to celebrate the victory over the Spanish Armada.'

Hibbert's resolve weakened. 'Is there no other solution here?'

'None.'

'Could nobody else do what Nicholas would do?'

'They would not have the knack of it, Saul.'

'I'd rather it be *any* man but him.'

'Nick may say the same about you, I fear.'

'What do you mean?'

'He'd come to the aid of other playwrights without hesitation. With you, alas, he's more likely to drag his feet.'

'He'd dare to refuse?' asked Hibbert, aghast.

'I've no means to compel him.'

'Hold him to his contract.'

'You abrogated that, Saul. He was contracted to stay in place for every play we staged but you disbarred him from yours.' Seizing the advantage, Firethorn twisted the knife gently. 'It might be the one way to win him back,' he suggested, floating the idea. 'The one way to soothe his injured pride.'

'The one way?'

'Let him occupy his rightful position again.'

'He'll not touch my play!'

'Without him, you may *have* no play.'

'Saul,' cooed the woman. 'How long are you going to be?'

'Just wait!' he snapped at her.

'Is that how you treat a lady?' she complained.

'Be quiet, please. I need to think.'

'You've already made your feelings clear,' said Firethorn, pretending to withdraw. 'I'll tell the company we play *Black Antonio* again tomorrow and send George off to the printer for some new playbills.'

'Wait, Lawrence!'

'Go to the lady. She sounds impatient.'

'I'll need time to meditate on this.'

'Time is not on our side, Saul. The whole five acts of your play will have to be copied out again. Can you imagine how long *that* will take?'

'It took me months to write it.'

'Then why throw all that effort away in a fit of pique?'

'I need to have my work back on the stage.'

'Then make your peace with Nicholas.'

'You talk of a man who assaulted me.'

'Let him make amends by snatching your career from the fire.'

'You are sure he'll do it?'

'Only at the price I named,' said Firethorn, exploiting the other's uncertainty. 'Even then, I'll have to use all the persuasion at my command. Which is it to be?' he asked, adjusting his position so that he got a tantalising glimpse of the naked woman on the bed. 'Will you swallow your pride and call Nick back? Or would you rather watch your star fall down from the sky after only three performances?'

Hibbert pondered. 'Seek his help,' he said at length.

'Wisdom at last.'

'Be sure to put *The Malevolent Comedy* back onstage tomorrow, but do something else for me. Find me the man who stole it in the first place,' he demanded. 'Who on earth can the rogue be?'

John Vavasor let himself into his house and received a token kiss from his wife. He went straight to the room where Cyrus Hame was poring over a manuscript on the table. His co-author looked up.

'I've been working on that Prologue you requested,' he said.

'Does it roast Lawrence Firethorn?'

'Like a chestnut in hot coals.'

'I long to see it,' said Vavasor, taking the sheet of parchment from him. 'The more poniards it inserts into his carcass, the more I'll like it.'

'How did you fare at the Queen's Head?'

'The play was good, the performance rather tepid.'

'Saul Hibbert would not have liked that.'

'He'll soon be ripe for more conference with us.'

Hame smirked. 'Have we so soon won him over?'

'No, Cyrus,' said the other, complacently. 'Our silver tongues have helped but I fancy the real damage was done at the Queen's Head. Saul will not be running towards Banbury's Men as much as running away from the troupe that let him down.' He burst out laughing. 'Oh, my word!' he said, waving the Prologue in the air. 'This is worth its weight in rubies. First, we rob him of his playwright. Then we steal his vaunted role as Pompey the Great and finally – best of all – we take away his reputation with this buzzing swarm of rhyming couplets. We are *made*, Cyrus,' he exclaimed, 'and Westfield's Men are doomed at last.'

Chapter Eight

Margery Firethorn had an iron determination that the passage of time only served to reinforce. Enraged by her husband when he was in the house, she was even more furious with him now that he was absent. While she did her daily chores, she turned over in her mind the many kindnesses that Nicholas Bracewell had shown to her and the countless favours he had done for Westfield's Men. Money could not repay the efforts and sacrifices he had made on the company's behalf. And yet Lawrence Firethorn, her once beloved husband, the actor-manager of the troupe and its commanding presence, had humiliated his book holder by making him step down on the whim of a tetchy playwright. In Margery's eyes, it was a hideous betrayal of someone she cherished. She could not have been more appalled if the cruelty had been meted out to one of her own children.

Sensing her mood, the servants kept out of her way in

the house in Shoreditch. When they heard her talking to herself, they knew that Margery was working herself up into frenzy that would be released when her husband dared to return home. As befitted an actor's wife, she was rehearsing her lines, but they were far too raw and unchristian to be allowed on a public stage without incurring protest. The day wore on and her temper glowed redder with every minute. When she chopped meat in the kitchen, she did so with such force and viciousness that she might have been beheading her spouse. Margery was primed for action.

Expecting her husband to come home late, drunk and with his tail between his legs, she was surprised to hear the familiar gait of his horse, trotting up Old Street early that evening. When she watched him through the window as he dismounted, she saw no sign of remorse in his face. It made her simmer even more. Having stabled his mount, Firethorn came into the house with something of his old swagger and braggadocio.

'All is well, my dove,' he announced. 'I've moved mountains.'

'You can move yourself back out that door if you try to woo me with pet names,' she warned him. 'I'm no dove, angel, pigeon, peacock, bear, honeycomb, sweet chuck, little rabbit or light of your life.'

'No, my dearest darling. You are all of them rolled into one. You are my apple of desire, Margery.'

'Dare to bite me and I'll choke you to death.'

Firethorn laughed. 'You know so well how to court your husband.'

'No husband of mine would play false with Nick Bracewell.'

'That's why I have set all right,' he boasted. 'I not only insisted that he be brought back, I put Saul Hibbert in his place and won the applause of the whole company. You see before you a conqueror.'

Margery was suspicious. 'Is this some trick of yours, Lawrence?'

'Since when have I descended to trickery?'

'Whenever it suits the occasion.'

'Well, this is an occasion for honesty and atonement.'

'You wish to apologise to me?' she said, slightly mollified.

'No,' he replied with a grand gesture, 'but I'm prepared to accept *your* apology.'

'For what?'

'Misjudging your husband. Calling me names that should never have been uttered on the Sabbath, and raising your voice to such a pitch that my disgrace was spread far and wide.'

'You deserved every vile syllable.'

'Did I deserve to be made a stranger to your bed?'

'Yes,' said Margery, 'and you'll remain so.'

'But I've made amends. Nick is back and Saul chastised.'

'So you say.'

Firethorn was dismayed. 'Do you doubt your husband's word?'

'Frankly, I do.'

'Then you'll hear it from Nick's own mouth. He's on his way here with other members of company. I galloped ahead to warn you, Margery, and to bury our differences.'

'Coming here?' she said. 'Why?'

'Thus it stands. The performance this afternoon was jaded but at least we suffered no setback. Until, that is, we had all moved off to the taproom. George Dart, who acted as Nick's deputy, did not, alas, have Nick's common sense. In short,' he said, 'he let his attention wander and the book of *The Malevolent Comedy* was stolen.'

'By whom?' she gasped.

'The villain who has dogged this play from the start.'

'How can you perform again without the prompt copy?'

'That's why they are all heading for Shoreditch. If our memories are good enough, we can recall the words and have them set down by our scrivener. Westfield's Men will create a new play.'

'It's a pity you cannot create a new author as well.'

'Saul has been duly humbled by me.'

'Not before time.'

'When I told him of the theft,' said Firethorn, 'he ranted wildly and threatened to set a pack of lawyers on us. But I soon imposed my authority on him when I pointed out that only Nick Bracewell could save us and brought him – by my own cunning, Margery – as close to begging for Nick's help as could be expected. All is therefore well.'

'You've still got five acts of a play to pluck out of your memories.'

'We'll do it somehow.'

'And this is all due to you, Lawrence?'

'You would have been proud of your husband.'

'I always am,' she said, fondly.

'Does that mean I'll not sleep on the floor tonight?'

'I'll join you there, if you do.'

'Come here, my songbird!' he said, throwing his arms around her and planting a kiss of reconciliation on her lips. 'As I rode out of the city, I thought so much about this moment.'

'How much time have we got?' she asked, wickedly.

'Enough.'

And sweeping her up in his arms, he carried her swiftly to their bedchamber and flung her down on the pillows like an eager bridegroom.

Nicholas Bracewell had been to Hoode's lodging so many times that he did not need the landlady to conduct him to the room. Instead, he knocked on the door, waited for the summons then went in. Edmund Hoode was surprised to see him. He stood up from his table.

'Nick,' he said, 'what are you doing here?'

'I've come to collect you.'

'Where are you taking me?'

'All the way to Old Street,' replied Nicholas, 'and we must pick up Matthew Lipton on the way.'

'Our scrivener?'

'We've work that needs his flowing hand.'

Anxious to get back to his lodging, Hoode had left the Queen's Head before the theft of the prompt copy had been discovered. Nicholas therefore gave him a brief account of what had taken place. Hoode was dumbfounded. A playwright himself, he knew that nothing could distress an author as much as the theft of his work. Plagiarism was one thing, but the removal of the one complete copy of a drama was a heinous crime. On the occasion when it had happened to him, Hoode had been mortified. Fortunately, he had been able to retrieve the situation with the help of Nicholas and the company's regular scrivener. Other heads would be used to reconstruct a missing play this time.

'How did Saul Hibbert receive the news?' asked Hoode.

'Badly.'

'At least he could not lay the blame on you this time.'

'He tried hard to do so,' said Nicholas. 'From what I can gather, he first pointed the finger at me as the thief. Lawrence spoke up for me.'

'His show of loyalty is long overdue.'

'But no less appreciated for that.'

'And you're back with us?'

'Happily, yes. That was the concession that Lawrence demanded of him,' said Nicholas, 'though I daresay it was made with reluctance.'

'Some good has yet come out of this reversal, then.'

'We still face a problem, Edmund.'

'Do we?'

'The man who stole the book thinks that he's made it impossible for us to perform the play again. When he sees *The Malevolent Comedy* back onstage tomorrow, he'll be very angry.'

'We'll have confounded him.'

'Only for a while,' Nicholas pointed out. 'He's still free

to maim us in some other way. Next time, his measures may be more desperate.'

'What do you mean?'

'I'll tell you on the way.'

'Then let's go to Matthew's Lipton's house.'

Nicholas glanced at the table. 'I'm sorry to drag you away from your work, Edmund,' he said. 'Is this the new play you've mentioned?'

'I'd have moved on to that in due course.'

'What were you penning when I came in?'

Hoode gave a wan smile. 'A sonnet.'

'Ah, you've felt the warm glow of passion again.'

'What I feel are the pangs of unrequited love. And the worst of it is, they seem to have dulled my brain. Tell me, Nick,' he said, opening the door, 'can you think of a clever rhyme for Ursula?'

Ursula Opie believed in the dictum that practice makes perfect. Seated at the keyboard, she studied the music in front of her and tapped out the notes with care and precision. She was so absorbed in her work that she did not hear the sound of her sister's footsteps, coming up behind her in the hall. Bernice recognised the solemn music at once.

'Why are you so attached to William Byrd?' she asked with a note of complaint. 'The house is filled with him all day long.'

'Master Byrd is the finest composer alive,' said Ursula, serenely.

'Father tells me that he's a devout Roman Catholic.'

'Music is above denomination, Bernice.'

'How can it be?'

'You only have to listen.'

'I'd rather hear something more lively,' said Bernice, clapping her hands together. 'Play a galliard so that I may dance.'

'I'd never do anything so vulgar.'

'Then let me hear a stately pavane. Anything is better than church music all the time. Oh, if only we had a house in the country!'

'Why?'

'Because there is so much more merriment there, Ursula. Country people know how to enjoy themselves. Do you remember that first play we saw at the Queen's Head?'

'It was *The Faithful Shepherd*, written by Edmund Hoode.'

'It contained a whole host of dances,' recalled Bernice. 'The names alone were a delight to hear. There was Mopsy's Tune, Dusty My Dear and the Bishop of Chester's Jig.'

'They were amusing enough in their place,' said Ursula, primly.

'When I saw the actors dance and frolic with such gaiety, I wanted to leap onstage and join them.' Bernice twirled around a few times. '*The Faithful Shepherd* was a delight. I never thought we'd be allowed to meet the author.'

'Master Hoode was a proper gentleman.'

'And a handsome at that. Is it not so, Ursula?'

'I did not notice.'

'Come, even you must observe if a man is well or ill favoured.'

'I admire Master Hoode for his intellect, not his appearance.'

'I take pleasure in both. He looked so fine at the concert.'

'The concert?' said Ursula, glancing up. 'I did not even know that he was here. I hope that he did not think it rude of me to ignore him.'

'I paid him enough attention for both of us.'

'As long as he did not feel neglected in our house.'

'No, Ursula,' said her sister, dreamily. 'There was no danger of that. When I could not speak to him, I watched him every moment. Such a noble countenance, such a modest manner.'

'True enough.'

'Such a kind and thoughtful being.'

'I liked him more than Master Firethorn.'

'Oh, he was too fond of himself – not so Edmund.'

'I liked him more than Owen Elias as well.'

'I like him more than *any* man.'

'Bernice!'

'Why try to hide it from you?' She gave a brittle laugh and hugged her sister. 'Oh, Ursula, I think that I'm in love!'

And she pirouetted around the hall by way of celebration.

Basking once more in the love of his wife, Lawrence Firethorn was a portrait of contentment. Nobody would have guessed that his company was assailed from within by a demanding playwright and attacked from without by a mysterious enemy. As a result of the latest exigency, he was forced to participate in an act of collective repair. *The Malevolent Comedy* had to be forged anew. Firethorn sat in the middle of his parlour as if he did not have a care in the world, beaming at his friends and showing excessive courtesy to Matthew Lipton, their scrivener. Twenty minutes in Margery's capacious arms had transformed him. Reading the telltale signs, the other members of Westfield's Men were grateful to her.

'Let's move on to the second act,' decided Firethorn.

'But we haven't mentioned my jig yet,' said Barnaby Gill.

'We can take that for granted.'

'Indeed, you will not.'

'*Here the Clown dances* – that's all that it said in the play.'

'Then let that be set down,' said Gill, nodding to the scrivener. 'The first act is not complete until I've brought it to a conclusion.'

Gill's argumentative streak was slowing them up. Everyone else was resolved to bring the play back to life as quickly and painlessly as possible, but Gill's pedantry hampered them. Not content with recalling his own lines, he was disputing the accuracy of those remembered by others. There were seven co-authors. Firethorn had invited Edmund Hoode, Frank Quilter, Owen Elias, Barnaby Gill, Richard Honeydew and the book holder to join him. While their host was nominally in charge, it was, in fact, Nicholas Bracewell who controlled the exercise. The actors knew their own lines and cues, but he was the only one who was familiar with the play in its totality and his prodigious memory came into its own.

'What do I say next?' asked Quilter, groping for his line.

'Nothing,' said Elias, 'for the speech is mine.'

'Mine, surely,' contended Hoode, 'for the priest must speak first.'

'Wait your turn, Edmund.'

'I could say the same to you.'

'Nick,' invited Firethorn with a smile, 'give us instruction here.'

'You are all wrong,' said Nicholas, patiently. 'The speech falls to Mistress Malevole.'

'I thought so,' agreed Richard Honeydew.

'Why did you not say so?' asked Gill, irritably.

'I was not given the chance.'

Honeydew was the only one of the boy apprentices there but the other three were in the kitchen, being fed and mothered by Margery. From time to time, she brought drink and refreshment into the parlour, always pausing to give Nicholas a warm hug and her husband a kiss. The busiest person there was Matthew Lipton, a rangy individual of middle years with a habit of sucking his few remaining teeth. Copying out the words as they were dictated to him, he had difficulty in keeping up with Firethorn, who insisted on giving a performance rather than a simple, slow recitation.

What simplified the whole business and gave it a firm structure was the fact that Nicholas had brought the plot of the play. He had drawn it up as a guide to the cast, dividing each act up into its scenes and listing who and what was needed in them. In a comedy that relied on its pace, it was vital to have such a detailed record of entrances and exits. Changes of scenery were also marked as were the cues for the musicians. During a pause for refreshment, Nicholas studied the plot.

'Our thief was a stranger to a tiring-house,' he said, 'or he would have taken the plot as well. Without that, our task would have been ten times more laborious.'

'I find it laborious enough as it is,' opined Quilter.

'So do I,' said Lipton, flexing his hand. 'I begin to feel cramp.'

'Fight it off,' ordered Firethorn. 'We need that neat calligraphy of yours until the bitter end.' He turned to Nicholas. 'So the villain we seek is not a man of the theatre.'

'He may not be a man at all,' replied Nicholas.

'An eunuch, then? Or a half-man like Barnaby?'

'I'm no half-man!' protested Gill. 'Nor an eunuch either.'

'The thief may well have been a woman,' said Nicholas. 'A young and beautiful one at that, according to Leonard. She asked him about the work of the book holder.'

'What does that lumbering oaf know about it?' said Firethorn.

'Enough to understand the importance of the prompt book.'

'And you think this woman may have taken it?'

'It's a possibility.'

'Would she have committed the other outrages?'

'No,' said Elias. 'What woman would stoop to using poison?'

198

'Margery, for one,' replied Firethorn with a hearty cackle. 'Had there been any in the house yesterday, she'd have poured it down my throat then danced on my dead body.'

'So much for the joys of marriage!' remarked Gill.

'They'll be forever beyond your reach, Barnaby. You'll have to get your pleasure from being bitten on the bum by a rabid dog. Yes,' he went on, looking at the scrivener. 'Set that down as well. *The Clown is bitten*.'

'Do not listen to him Matthew!'

'And you may add – *on the right buttock*.'

'No!'

'Change that, Matthew. Barnaby prefers the left.'

'To come back to the matter in hand,' said Nicholas when Gill's protests had died down, 'I believe that the man we seek may have a confederate. He certainly bought the poison from the apothecary and paid that lad to set Rascal on us. But I fancy that this woman is part of the conspiracy,' he went on, 'and I wonder if the reason may not be right in front of us.'

'How so?' asked Hoode.

'While we have been going over every single line of the play, I've seen things that did not strike me so much in performance. Look at the three women whom Lord Loveless sets up as rivals for his hand.'

'Rosamund, Chloe and Eleanor.'

'The characters are excellently well drawn.'

'That's so throughout the play, Nick.'

'Not always,' said Nicholas. 'There's real flesh and bone

on all three ladies, and it brings them to life.' He glanced at Honeydew. 'The same goes for Mistress Malevole. There's a depth and definition to her that several of the men lack.'

'What do you read into that?'

'I'm not sure, Edmund. But I do begin to wonder if Saul Hibbert's women may be based on real people. They behave as if they do. And if that's the case,' Nicholas speculated, 'none of them would be pleased to see the play for it pillories all four unmercifully.'

'That's where the comedy lies,' said Gill, fussily.

'Would you want to be shown as a cat, an owl or a monkey? For that's what happens to the three women. Nor does Mistress Malevole come out of it with any credit. She's portrayed as a malevolent snake, who schemes her way into Lord Loveless's affections. No,' Nicholas concluded, 'Saul Hibbert has little affection for his ladies.'

'Then the play does not have the ring of truth at all,' said Firethorn, 'for Saul has far too much affection for the fairer sex. When I spoke to him earlier, I had to prise him from a hot bed of passion. The fellow adores women.'

'He uses them, surely,' said Hoode, 'but I sense no adoration in the man except for himself. Passion, once past, can leave only scorn in some men. I side with Nick. The ladies in the play are poorly treated.'

'Everyone takes a knock in *The Malevolent Comedy*,' said Gill.

'But those most hurt are Rosamund, Chloe and Eleanor. They are swinged soundly throughout. I wonder what their real names are.'

'What does it matter? Let's get back to our work.'

'All in good time,' said Firethorn, musing on what he had heard. 'Nick may have seen something that eluded our gaze. Women can become frothing demons in an instant, as I learnt to my cost only yesterday. If one of them *was* turned into a laughing stock onstage, she'd seek revenge. Could *that* be the reason our prompt book was stolen?'

'It all comes back to one question,' said Nicholas.

'Go on.'

'What do we really know of Saul Hibbert?'

'We know him for a playwright of exceptional talent.'

'And exceptional vanity,' added Quilter. 'We also know him for his spite and malice. Nick was the victim of that. Master Hibbert will never be a true member of a company because he despises us.'

Gill preened himself. 'He does not despise me or my work.'

'But where did he come from?' asked Nicholas. 'How did he get here and what did he do before he came? Where did he learn to turn a line and shape a scene? In brief – who *is* Saul Hibbert?'

Cyrus Hame was just about to leave when his landlady showed in the visitor. He was taken aback to see Saul Hibbert standing there. The newcomer had lost some of his overweening confidence.

'I hope that I'm not intruding on your time, Cyrus,' he said.

'No, no. Come in.'

'You said that I might call upon you.'

'Upon me or upon John. Though should you go to the Vavasor residence,' said Hame, indicating his untidy little room, 'you'll find it more commodious than my humble lodging.'

'I'd rather talk to you.'

'Then take a seat and let's converse.'

'Not if I'm holding you up, Cyrus.'

'The lady will wait,' said Hame with a confiding grin. They sat either side of a little table. 'How may I help you?'

'I wished to ask about contracts.'

'That's something you'll have to discuss with Giles Randolph. Only he can sign on behalf of Banbury's Men.'

'But is he a fair man? Do his terms favour the playwright?'

'We made sure that they did.'

'You have control over your work?'

'Why do you ask?'

'Lawrence Firethorn slipped terms into the contract that I barely noticed in my readiness to sign. I've lived to regret that.'

'Other authors have said the same of him. Master Firethorn is slippery. Does he want another play?'

'More than one.'

'But you've not committed yourself?'

'No,' said Hibbert, 'I wanted to speak to you or John first. You claim that Banbury's Men will pay me more and treat me better.'

'We can only talk from our own experience.'

'It's much happier than mine.'

'A playwright should go where he's most esteemed,' said Hame. 'Look at John Vavasor. He was reviled by one company and welcomed by another. Lawrence Firethorn was brutal to him.'

'I'm less than satisfied with Master Firethorn myself.'

'Then you have a remedy within your grasp.'

'Do I?'

'John and I have told you as much.'

'But the power of decision lies with Master Randolph.'

'Naturally,' said the other, 'but we came to you with his authority. He trusts our judgement and knows that we would not offer praise lightly. For reasons too obvious to relate, Giles is unable to attend a performance at the Queen's Head. Even if he were not onstage every afternoon,' he went on with a sly grin, 'I doubt that he'd ever find his way to Gracechurch Street, any more than Lawrence Firethorn would go to the Curtain.'

'So you've delivered good reports of me to Banbury's Men?'

'Giles cannot wait to embrace you.'

'How much would he give me in advance?'

'In advance?'

'Against my next play,' said Hibbert. 'The truth is that I've spent too freely since I've been here, and need the funds to keep me while I work on my new play.'

'Giles will not buy a pig in a poke,' cautioned Hame.

'That's not what he'll be doing. I'll be able to show him a first act and tell him the plot of the whole play. *The Malevolent Comedy* has attested my merit. Its successor will have even tastier pork on it.'

'Let me talk to Giles.'

'Soon, please. My purse grows slacker by the day.'

'Then we are two of a kind,' said Hame, companionably. 'We sail before the wind of our creditors. John had the good fortune to marry money. I can only seem to spend it.'

'I share that fault, Cyrus. I'm a man of extravagant tastes.'

'There's no disgrace in that. But what of Westfield's Men?'

'What of them?'

'No ties of loyalty to bind you?'

'None,' said Hibbert, bitterly. 'After all that's happened, I'd break with them at the drop of a hat.'

Cyrus Hame lifted his hat in the air and let it fall to the floor. Saul Hibbert laughed. Having come for help and advice, he was going away reassured. A profitable future seemed to open up before him. They left the room and stepped out into the street. Hibbert went his way. His spirits were lifted and his arrogant strut restored but, long after the two of them had parted, it was Cyrus Hame who was still laughing.

Midnight bells were chiming when Nicholas Bracewell finally got back to Bankside. Forsaking the bridge, he had been rowed across the river by a talkative waterman with an interest in the stars. Nicholas was given a lecture on astrology that owed more to the ale the man had drunk than to any serious study of the subject. Arriving back at his lodging, he was pleased to see a light burning in Anne's bedchamber. He let himself into the house and tiptoed upstairs, opening her door as silently as possible.

'I'm still awake,' she said, drowsily.

'Did you get my message?'

'Yes, Nick. It was kind of you to send it.'

'George Dart blamed himself for the loss of the book,' he said. 'He was so keen to atone in some way that I took advantage of him. I felt that you ought to know what was afoot.'

'Was the play reconstructed?'

'To the last letter.'

'You've always had an amazing memory.'

'It does not compare with Lawrence's. He holds over thirty parts in his head. When we go on tour,' said Nicholas, 'he can play any one of them after a mere glance at the prompt book.'

'And where is the book for *The Malevolent Comedy*?'

'Right here, Anne.' He patted the manuscript under his arm. 'I'll lock it away before I come into bed. May I get you anything?'

'Yes, please,' she whispered. 'Nick Bracewell.'

He kissed her gently on the forehead then went along the passageway to the room that he had rented when he first moved in. Since he now shared a bed with Anne, he used the room for storage. The most important item there was a large oaken chest, ribbed with iron and fitted with two locks. When he used his keys to unlock the chest, he opened the lid to reveal the history of Westfield's Men, a collection of prompt books that went back over the years and that had been carefully annotated by the man in charge of them. It was a theatrical treasure trove. After adding the new play to the collection, he closed the lid and locked the chest again. Shortly afterwards, he was blowing out the candle beside the bed and snuggling up to Anne.

'Will you be in danger tomorrow?' she said.

'I hope not.'

'Every time you've played the piece, there's been misfortune.'

'The actors are all too aware of that, Anne. Most of them would love to see the back of *The Malevolent Comedy*. They think it brings bad luck. Frank Quilter said that it has the mark of the devil upon it.'

'What do you think?'

'That the mark is more likely to be upon the author.'

'Then more trouble lies ahead.'

'We'll be ready for it.'

'Good.' She pulled him close. 'At least, you'll be back where you belong. What brought Lawrence to his senses?'

'Necessity.'

'He deserved to be severely scolded for what he did.'

'Margery took on that task,' he said, smiling. 'She's more skilled in the black arts of torture than Master Topcliffe at the Tower. I've her to thank for putting her husband on the rack. Margery defended me.'

'She should not have needed to do so.'

'I'll waste no sleep, worrying on that score,' he said. 'It's been a long day. Tomorrow, we face another trial.'

'Would you like my eyes in the gallery again?'

'No thank you. I can spare you this time. Besides, it

would be cruelty to make Preben sit through a second performance.'

'He's not recovered from the first visit yet.'

'Are all Dutchman so gloomy and severe?'

'Jacob was not,' she replied, 'or I'd never have married him. He could be very jolly at times. Preben is more serious. He's been in England for years yet still bears the stigma of being a stranger. But,' she added, 'I did not stay awake simply to talk about him. I want to hear the gossip.'

'There's little enough of that, Anne.'

'No quarrels, no scandal among the actors?'

'All I can tell you is that Edmund is in love.'

'That's to say the Thames is full of water. Give me news.'

'This is news,' said Nicholas. 'I had it from Owen. He brought two sisters to sup with Edmund and one of them enchanted him. Our lovelorn poet is already writing a sonnet to her.'

'Is that good or bad?'

'Good for us but bad for Edmund.'

'Bad for him?'

'According to Owen, he's fallen in love with the wrong sister. Her name is Ursula and she's no interest in men unless they compose religious music. Edmund is doomed to worship from afar.'

'You said that it was good for Westfield's Men.'

'Very good, Anne.'

'Why?'

'It's made him start writing again.'

* * *

Edmund Hoode lay on his bed fully clothed and stared at the ceiling. Enough moonlight was spilling in through the shutters to dapple the walls. Tired but unable to sleep, he wrestled with the fourteen lines he hoped would win the heart of Ursula Opie, arranging and rearranging them constantly in his mind until he reached a degree of satisfaction. There was a secondary problem to be addressed. Did he send the poem to her anonymously or disclose his identity? If she was touched by it, then she should be told the name of its author. If, on the other hand, she was offended in some way, it was better that she should not know its origin or grave embarrassment could ensue.

After long cogitation, he settled on a compromise. Hoode decided to append the letter 'E' to his sonnet, both admitting and denying that it was his work. 'E' could just as well stand for Edward, Eustace, Edgar or a number of other names, allowing him to disclaim authorship if any discomfort threatened. To a woman susceptible to noble sentiments expressed in high-flown language, however, it could represent only one poet and she would respond accordingly. Hoode had recovered from the disappointment of the concert. Shy in public, Ursula had not lingered in the hall. Like him, she was a private person, a creature of thought and deep feeling, a young woman, as the concert had shown, with a strong spiritual dimension to her life. Bernice had sung her songs prettily but Ursula had played with a commitment that revealed how much more the music meant to her. Hoode yearned for her.

With the sonnet bursting to come out of him, he leapt

off the bed, lit a candle and reached for his quill. There was no hesitation. The words over which he had pondered so long now came streaming out of his brain in the perfect order. After reading the poem through, he felt a surge of creative power. It needed no correction. Instead, he set it aside, pulled another sheet of parchment in front of him and started to work again on his play. Sustained by the knowledge that it had been inspired by Ursula Opie, he laboured long into the night. When the first cock began to crow, Hoode, impervious to fatigue, was still crouched low over his table.

Nicholas Bracewell set out very early the next morning with the prompt copy of *The Malevolent Comedy* in a satchel slung over his shoulder. By the time he had crossed the bridge and entered Gracechurch Street, the market was already under way, its booths, stalls and carts narrowing the thoroughfare, its customers thronging noisily, its vendors extolling the virtues of their produce aloud and its poultry squawking rebelliously in their wooden cages. Nicholas's broad shoulders soon found a way through the press but he did not turn in to the Queen's Head. Walking past it, he went on to the parish church of St Martin Outwich on the corner of Bishopsgate and Threadneedle Street. Built over a century earlier, the church stood beside a well that was served in earlier times by a device that allowed one bucket to descend the shaft as the other was pulled up. A pump had now been installed and, when Nicholas went past, housewives were queuing with buckets to draw water.

The funeral of Hal Bridger had taken place the previous day. Out of deference to the wishes of the parents, Nicholas and the others had stayed away but he wanted to pay his respects to his young friend. It did not take him long to find the grave in the churchyard. A fresh mound of earth rose up through the grass, a simple cross was standing over it. Nicholas came forward and removed his cap. Looking down at the grave, he tried to recall happier times in the boy's short life. He remembered the smile of astonished joy on Bridger's face when he first hired him to work for Westfield's Men, and the fierce pride he took in performing even the most menial duties for them.

Apart from Nicholas, the lad's closest friends in the company had been George Dart and Richard Honeydew. They had spent many pleasant hours together. Cast adrift by his father, it had meant so much to Bridger to be accepted by his new family. He had repaid them with his love and dedication. Nicholas felt the sharp stab of bereavement. It made him even more determined to find the killer. Until that happened, Hal Bridger could never fully rest in peace. Closing his eyes, Nicholas offered up a prayer. He then put on his cap and turned to walk away, realising, for the first time, that he had been watched. A woman was standing by the church porch, so still and silent that she might have been a marble statue. It was Alice Bridger.

There was a long and very awkward pause. Nicholas was made to feel like an interloper, guilty of trespass, intruding upon private grief. He did not know whether to stay or leave. In the event, it was the woman who made the first move, walking slowly towards him and looking much more frail and vulnerable than at their first meeting. Clearing his throat, Nicholas held his ground and prepared his apology. Alice Bridger needed a moment to find her voice.

'Thank you,' she said, softly.

'For what?'

'Showing that you cared.'

'We all cared about Hal.'

'Yes, but yours was the name he mentioned most.'

He glanced down at the grave. 'We kept away from the funeral.'

'I was grateful for that.'

'What about Mr Bridger?'

'My husband will give you no thanks, sir,' she said, brusquely. 'He believes that we lost our son twice. Hal died when he left us, then he was murdered because of you.'

'Simply because he joined a theatre troupe?'

'It's an ungodly profession.'

'Then why are we not all struck down, Mrs Bridger?' asked Nicholas, gently. 'If our sin is so unforgivable, how have we and the other theatre companies in the city escaped retribution?'

'You are trying to mock me again.'

'No, I respect anyone who lives by the tenets of their faith.'

'Even though you do not have a faith yourself?'

Nicholas hunched his shoulders. 'It was wrong of me to come so soon,' he said, 'and I apologise for that. I should have let more time elapse so that feelings were not so fresh and raw. Think what you wish of us, Mrs Bridger, but be sure of one thing. The prayer I said over Hal's grave came with Christian humility. God save his soul!'

'Wait!' she said, touching his arm as he turned to go.

'Yes?'

'You told me how Hal died but you did not tell me in what pain he must have been. The coroner was more honest.'

'I wanted to spare you such details.'

'I understand that now. It was a kindness on your part.' Her lips began to quiver. 'Will they catch the man who poisoned him?'

'That's a task we've set ourselves, Mrs Bridger.'

'What can you do?'

'Much more than any officers,' he replied. 'I've already found the apothecary who sold the poison. The customer he described was seen at the Queen's Head, talking to one of the servants. If he dares to come again, he's certain to be recognised.'

'He'll not return, surely.'

'He already has, I fear.'

'When?'

'On Saturday last. He paid a boy to set loose his dog during our performance so that it would harry the actors. And yesterday,' said Nicholas, patting his satchel, 'the same man – or his confederate – stole our prompt book.'

'Why did he do that?'

'To stop the play being staged.'

'I do not understand how.'

'That's because you've never ventured into a playhouse,

Mrs Bridger. There's only one complete copy of any play and it's used to prompt the actors if they lose their lines. It's also the only way that the book holder can follow the progress of a performance.' He patted his satchel again. 'I've a new copy of our play right here.'

'Which one?'

'*The Malevolent Comedy.*'

'Was that not the play that cost Hal his life?'

'Unhappily, it was.'

She was rueful. 'So his murder was part of a comedy?'

'His murder was part of an attempt to stop this play from being seen. It's happened three times in a row now. Someone had such a violent grudge against the piece that he's determined to sweep it forever from the stage.'

'Oh dear!' she cried, tears coursing down her cheeks.

'I'm sorry, Mrs Bridger. I did not mean to upset you.'

'It's so cruel, so very cruel!'

'What is?'

'You say that this man wants to wipe a play from the stage?'

'By any means.'

'Then I find myself in sympathy with him, for I'd stop *every* play from being performed and spreading its corruption. Can you not see the awful cruelty of that?' she went on, tears still flowing. 'I am at one with the man who murdered my only child?'

There was no rehearsal that morning. After three recent performances, it was felt that the cast were sufficiently confident to need no extra time spent on their lines. In any case, the hasty conference that had taken place at Lawrence Firethorn's house the previous day had involved all the leading actors and been in the nature of an intensive rehearsal. They now knew *The Malevolent Comedy* better than ever before. Instead of working on the play again, therefore, they were deployed to search the premises to make sure that no danger was lurking at the Queen's Head. Keeping the satchel with him, Nicholas Bracewell took care that he never once lost sight of the prompt book.

Richard Honeydew was curious. When the actors were starting to gather in the tiring-house that afternoon, he went over to Nicholas.

'Where did you keep the book last night?' he asked.

'Under lock and key.'

'How many plays do you have in your chest?'

'Fifty or sixty at least, Dick.'

'What would happen if they were all stolen?'

'Do not even conceive of such a tragedy,' said Nicholas. 'We would be bereft. There's no way that we could rebuild each play, brick by brick, as we did with Master Hibbert's comedy. Most would be lost forever. The company would wither for lack of anything to play.'

'I'd hate to lose *The Loyal Subject*.'

'Is that your favourite?'

'Along with *The Merchant of Calais*.'

'Both plays by Edmund Hoode.'

'Hal Bridger thought our best play was *Cupid's Folly*.'

'That will please Barnaby for he steals all the laughs in it.'

'Hal giggled whenever he thought of the play.' Honeydew's face darkened. 'He'll not see it ever again, Nick.'

'I know.'

'When they buried him yesterday, I wanted to be there.'

'So did we all,' said Nicholas. 'Hal's stay with us was short but he made many friends among Westfield's Men. The pity of it is that his parents bear us such ill will.'

'He rarely spoke of them. They cast him out.'

'Yet they grieve for him now, Dick – at least, his mother does.'

'How do you know?'

'I met her in the churchyard this morning when I went to pay my respects at the grave. Mrs Bridger was there.'

'Does she still blame us for what happened?'

'She blames the whole notion of theatre. It's abhorrent to her.'

'We do no harm,' said Honeydew, innocently.

'We do, in her eyes, Dick, and you are one of the chief culprits.'

'Me?'

'Boys dressing up as women, painting their faces, flaunting themselves on stage. Making lewd gestures and exciting improper feelings in the spectators. That's how Hal's parents view us,' said Nicholas, sadly. 'We are purveyors of sin.'

'All that we strive to do is to entertain people.'

'Puritans do not believe in entertainment, Dick.'

'Then I'm glad we do not have any of them in our

audiences,' said the boy. 'But, since the church is so close, I'll try to say a prayer for Hal myself as I go past.'

'Do that.'

Honeydew went off to put on his costume and Nicholas cajoled two of the other apprentices who had arrived late. There was a distinct tension in the tiring-house. Superstition had taken its hold. About to embark on a fourth performance of a play, the actors all felt in their hearts that it would be prey to some mishap again. The general unease was even shared by Lawrence Firethorn.

'Is all well, Nick?' he asked.

'I think so. We've taken every precaution.'

'We did that last time.'

'The book will not go astray this afternoon, I warrant you.'

'There are other ways to damage us.'

'We'll be ready for them, whatever they are,' said Nicholas.

'I hope so. Margery is in the audience today.'

'After last night, I'd have thought she'd heard enough of *The Malevolent Comedy*. It invaded your house for hours.'

'That only served to increase her interest,' said Firethorn. 'For her sake, I want the performance to go well. If we get safely through the play today, it may even cheer Saul up.'

'Is he still surly?'

'Surly and critical. He's not forgiven me for making him accept you as book holder again. That festers with him.'

'Did he thank you for our efforts to rewrite his play?'

'No, Nick. He still wants George Dart dismissed for losing it.'

'Since when can a playwright pick and choose hired men?'

'I made that point to him.'

'Good. Master Hibbert is still very new to the playhouse.'

'His novelty is wearing off for me,' confided Firethorn. 'When he first appeared, I thought he'd come to lead us to the Promised Land. I did not realise that it would be beset with cups of poison and renegade dogs. I'm not so ready to commission a second play from Saul Hibbert now.'

Nicholas was relieved but he said nothing. Time was running out and, from the commotion he could hear in the yard, it sounded as if another large audience was waiting for them. The flag had been hoisted above the Queen's Head to show that a play would be performed and the musicians had taken up their places in the gallery above the stage. Owen Elias, in a black cloak, was running a tongue over his lips as he rehearsed the opening lines of the Prologue. Everything was ready. The strain on the actors was almost tangible. Nicholas tried to lift it.

After warning everyone in the tiring-house with a wave, he sent a signal up to the musicians. When the trumpets blared and the drum boomed, an anticipatory hush fell on the audience. On a cue from the book holder, Owen Elias strode out onstage to deliver the Prologue.

Malevolence, my friends, is here to stay.
It works with spite and cunning every day
And night to gain its ends. Employ it well
When you would seek to wed and only sell

Your precious freedom at the highest price,
Or live in sad regret. Take my advice.
A man can marry anyone he choose
But women know a marriage bed can bruise.
So, ladies, stalk your prey behind a smile,
And bring him down with malice and with guile.

It was not so much the lines as his vivid gestures that garnered the first laughs. The Welshman gesticulated to such comic effect that he received a round of applause at the end of his speech. It was all that the other actors needed. Approval was their life-blood. They went in search of it with a confidence that had seemed impossible minutes ago. No sooner did Lord Loveless appear in his ridiculously garish apparel than he got a rousing cheer and the Clown, too, was given a special welcome. Firethorn and Gill were known and admired by all. Moved by the warmth of their reception, the two of them blossomed and gave performances that were somehow enhanced in every particular. The loveless lord was more absurd than ever and the Clown's antics were more hilarious. In one short opening scene, the audience was conquered.

Nicholas was enthralled. It was a new play. With everyone bringing an extra vigour and subtlety to their performance, the nuances and shades of colour in *The Malevolent Comedy* were brought out clearly for the first time. Richard Honeydew was renowned for his portrayal of noble queens and beautiful princesses, but he revelled in a different role now, finding a deeper malevolence in his character than had ever been there before. It was almost as if he were trying to prove what Nicholas had observed when they met to recreate the play from memory.

Mistress Malevole was a cunning serpent, subjecting the other three women to repeated humiliation so that she could entwine herself around Lord Loveless and lick him with her forked tongue. Rosamund, Chloe and Eleanor were not mere characters in a play. They sounded like real women, voicing real complaints, stripped of any dignity and derided in public to satisfy the author's malice. All that the audience saw was a riotous comedy that bowled along with effortless speed. What the book holder heard, however, was a wicked satire on the weaker sex. In front of howling spectators, the women were really suffering.

While not losing his concentration, Nicholas kept one ear pricked for the sound of any impending attack. The rest of the company had clearly forgotten that the piece was synonymous with misfortune, and that it had taken the life of Hal Bridger less than a week earlier. Shaking off their fears, they played with a zest that gave a sharper edge to the comedy. The laughter and applause throughout was so generous that it added several minutes to the performance. When they saw that the play was over, there was a massive sigh of disappointment, followed by an explosion of clapping hands, stamping feet and deafening cheers.

It was by far their best performance of the play and it augured well for any revival. Nicholas was relieved. All the precautions that he had set in place seemed to have worked. While the actors took their bows in the reverberating cauldron of noise, he was simply grateful that they had come through without assault or interruption. The play's curse had been lifted. They had finally been spared.

Even the sceptical Francis Quilter was impressed. Coming off stage with the others, he tapped the prompt book in Nicholas's hands.

'It's a better play than I thought,' he admitted.

'You were always too censorious, Frank.'

'I let my dislike of the author obscure my judgement.'

'So you admire the play now?' said Nicholas.

'Yes, but I hate Saul Hibbert even more.'

'Why?'

'His work exceeded all expectations today,' replied Quilter. 'That means Lawrence will bind him hand and foot by contract, and we'll have him writing more comedies for us.'

'Why, so I will!' said Firethorn, joining them. 'Did you hear that happy pandemonium out there, Nick? We were supreme. And as for Saul, I'll chain him to a desk and make him write for us forever.'

'Make no hurried decisions,' urged Nicholas.

'We need him.'

'It's what *he* needs that concerns me.'

'Your place is safe, Nick. He'll not shift you again.'

'I care not for myself. My anxiety is for others.'

'Why?'

'Master Hibbert treats most of them as if they were mere servants to his genius. After this afternoon, I fear that he'll be worse than ever.'

'He'll learn to love us all in time.'

'Not unless he has the power he craves,' said Nicholas.

'Leave off,' said Firethorn, genially. 'This is a time for celebration rather than anxiety. We've set fire to an audience as never before this year and we should warm our hands at the blaze. Be happy for us, Nick.'

'I am – truly delighted.'

'Then come and join us in the taproom. I was worried, I confess. In view of what happened before with this play, I was as nervous as a kitten when I was waiting to go onstage. Once there, I knew that my fears were groundless. I felt the triumph coming,' said Firethorn, putting a hand to his heart. 'Nothing can take the pleasure of it away, Nick. We gave them a magnificent play this afternoon and nobody tried to stop us.'

Richard Honeydew was troubled. Old enough to play the part of Mistress Malevole extremely well, he was still too young to appreciate the full import of the character. Though the performance had been his best yet, it had left him confused and apprehensive. There were times when he lost all control, when he felt that Mistress Malevole took him over and made him explore aspects of her character that he did not even know were there. He had been forced to be more savage, more ruthless, more calculating. The audience might have loved his portrayal but it almost frightened him. When he came to take off his wig and dress, his fingers were trembling.

Amid the swirl of bodies and the noise of banter, nobody

paid any attention to him in the tiring-house. That suited Honeydew. He had a sudden desire to be alone. Living at Firethorn's house, he would be returning there with the other apprentices in time but there was no hurry. They would have to wait for Margery, who would surely want to celebrate with her husband before she took them back home. Honeydew had plenty of leeway. Changing quickly into his own clothing, therefore, he gave his costume to the tireman and darted out of the room.

His footsteps took him in the direction of Bishopsgate. When he reached the corner of Threadneedle Street, he realised why. Something was impelling him to visit Hal Bridger's grave. He was humbled. Instead of thinking of himself, he should be paying his respects to someone who was no longer able to act upon a stage. Honeydew had to make his own small act of remembrance. He went into the churchyard and searched for the grave. Like Nicholas, he soon found it and smacked his palms together to scare away the two ravens who had perched on the mound of earth. Richard Honeydew removed his cap and stood in silence.

His own cares seem to float away and he went into a kind of trance. He felt close to Hal Bridger. He could almost hear his laughter and see the excitement in his face. Honeydew tried to talk to him but got no reply. When he reached out to touch him, the boy was not there. Yet he was still nearby and grateful for the visit of a friend. Honeydew could sense his gratitude. There was contact.

The rustle of light feet through grass made him turn round. Walking towards him was an attractive young woman, holding a handkerchief to her eyes. She stopped a yard away from him.

'Who are you?' she asked.

'My name is Dick Honeydew.'

'I see.'

'I was Hal's friend.'

She lowered her head. 'Then you'll know how he died.'

'I was there at the time,' he said. 'It was dreadful.'

'Yes. Yes, it must have been.'

'I . . . came to bid farewell to him.'

'So did I,' she said, dabbing her eyes as she looked at him. 'Hal was my nephew. I loved him so much.'

'Were you at the funeral yesterday?'

'No, we only arrived in London this afternoon. I've just come from his parents. They told me where to find the grave so that I could pay my respects. I'm honoured to share the moment with you, Dick.'

'Thank you.'

'Will you step into the church with me and say a prayer for him?'

'Gladly.'

Honeydew was unguarded. It never occurred to him that the beautiful, elegant woman in front of him might have worn something more suitable to a churchyard than the striking red and green dress with a matching hat. From the little that Hal Bridger had told him about them, Honeydew had gathered the impression that his parents were earnest, austere, dedicated Puritans. When he had joined Westfield's Men, they had disowned him, behaviour that Honeydew simply could not understand. In his trusting way, the apprentice was pleased that at least one member of Hal's family seemed to show genuine grief.

They did not even reach the porch. As soon as the boy's back was turned, a man came around the angle of the church and crept up behind him. When the moment was ripe, the sobbing aunt tossed away her handkerchief and used both hands to grab Honeydew by the shoulders and push him towards her accomplice. Before he knew what was happening, a cloak had been thrown over him and strong arms lifted him from the ground. Honeydew was terrified. He was unable to struggle free and his cries for help went unheard beneath the thick woollen cloak.

There was no escape. He had been kidnapped.

Chapter Nine

John Vavasor had been visiting his brother in Richmond that day and did not return to the city until early evening. Instead of going home, he rode straight to the Green Man, where he could be certain of finding his co-author. Cyrus Hame was in high spirits. He was carousing at the tavern with two of the actors from the Curtain, sharers with Banbury's Men, who had enjoyed the success of *Lamberto* and who looked forward to repeating it with *Pompey the Great*. Vavasor joined them and revelled in the jollity until the actors took their leave.

'They cannot stop thanking us for *Lamberto*,' said Hame. 'It was so far above the level of their other plays that it is set to remain a favourite with them for a long while.'

'Every time it's performed, our names will be voiced abroad.'

'John Vavasor and Cyrus Hame.'

'By rights, it should be Cyrus Hame and John Vavasor.'

'Why?'

'You should take first place.'

'I'd not hear of it.'

'You made the play acceptable to Banbury's Men,' said Vavasor.

'I'll own that I do have that knack,' said Hame, affably. 'I've always been able to improve a play but, first, I need a good play on which to work. In *Lamberto*, you provided that.'

'You changed it completely, Cyrus.'

'I merely brought out its full power. You are the master craftsman, John, and I, a simple journeyman. Your name should take precedence.'

'You are so gracious.'

'And you are so generous. Though we toiled side by side on the play, you let me have the lion's share of the fee.'

'You could have had it all, Cyrus.'

'Your benevolence is overwhelming.'

'I write for fame. All that I wanted was to see my work on a stage.'

'Whereas I prefer to write for money,' said Hame, feeling his purse. 'Fame is simply a dream, a fantasy, an illusion, something that only exists in the minds of others. Money is *real*. You can hold it in your hands, toss it in the air, bite it with your teeth and, best of all, spend it. That's where my ambition lies.' He sipped his drink and became reflective. 'Yet I sometimes wonder if it could have been played better.'

'What?'

'The role of Lamberto.'

'Giles Randolph surpassed himself.'

'Yes, but would he have surpassed Lawrence Firethorn?'

'Do not mention that foul name!' rasped Vavasor.

'We are bound to compare the two titans of the stage.'

'I'd not let Firethorn say a single word that I wrote.'

'Nor me, John, but I'll not deny his monstrous talent.'

'It's his monstrous character that I object to. He's a colossus of conceit. But, no, to answer your question, I do not think that he could have matched Giles as Lamberto.'

'Could Giles have matched him as Lord Loveless?'

'Matched him and beaten him,' said Vavasor. 'On the strength of what I saw at yesterday's performance of *The Malevolent Comedy*, many actors could have outdone Firethorn. He simply walked through the part, Cyrus. I've never seen him put so little effort into a role, and the rest of them were no better. They were lacklustre.'

'That does not sound like Westfield's Men.'

'They let Saul Hibbert down badly.'

'He'll not have liked that.'

'It will have brought him one step closer to Banbury's Men.'

'Our main task is to drive a wedge between him and Firethorn,' Hame reminded him. 'That's all that Giles urged upon us. Saul has written a fine comedy but there's no certainty that he can do it again. If he fails to fulfil his promise, he'll fall by the wayside.'

'I'll not weep for him. He's as big a monster as Firethorn.'

'There's not room for two of them in Westfield's Men.'

'Three – you forget Barnaby Gill.'

Hame laughed. 'The worst of them, in some respects.'

'We've done what was asked of us,' said Vavasor. 'We poured our poison into Saul's ear. We dangled the prospect of more money in front of him, stroked him, flattered him, fawned upon him and led him to believe that he'll be welcomed with open arms at the Curtain.'

'Only if his mind is fertile enough, and I begin to doubt it.'

'Why?'

'All that he has to offer is one act of a new play.'

'Does he work so slowly?'

'Saul is lazy and too easily distracted.'

'I'd written six plays before *Lamberto*,' recalled Vavasor, 'and the moment that it was sold, we began work on *Pompey the Great*.'

'You are chased by demons, John.'

'I have this nagging compulsion to write.'

'Saul's only compulsion is to boast about what he *will* write,' said Hame, 'but there's little evidence of any serious labour. He had the nerve to ask for money in advance when the play is still locked in his brain.'

'Giles Randolph would never countenance that.'

'I told him so.'

'Let him sink or swim as a playwright,' said Vavasor, callously. 'I care not. All that I wish to do is to drag him away from the Queen's Head and give Firethorn a slap in the face.'

'We'll give him far more than a slap, John.'

'God willing!'

'Oh, there's nothing godly about it. It relies solely on the malevolence that Saul describes so well in his comedy.'

'I do not follow you, Cyrus.'

'We have to be malign and merciless,' said Hame, icily. 'We have to shake Westfield's Men to the very core by stealing their new playwright. Let me turn prophet and make this one prediction. By the end of the week, Saul Hibbert will be ours.' He smirked. 'Whether we keep him or not, of course, is another matter.'

The disappearance of Richard Honeydew did not come to light for an hour. It was Margery Firethorn who first noticed that he was not there. When she rounded up the other apprentices to take them back home with her, they had no idea where Honeydew had gone. The alarm was raised and Nicholas Bracewell instituted an immediate search. It was fruitless. Nicholas was disturbed. Had it been one of the other boys missing, he would not have worried so much. Inclined to waywardness, they had been known to wander off or play games in odd corners of the inn. Honeydew, by contrast, always stayed close to the adult members of the company. He was far too responsible to get lost.

Leonard was rolling an empty barrel across the yard with practised ease. When he saw his friend, Nicholas rushed over to him.

'Dick Honeydew has vanished,' he said.

'Is he not back, then?'

'Back from where?'

'Wherever he went,' said Leonard. 'I saw him leave.'

'When was this?'

'Earlier on – when I was sweeping the yard.'

'Was he alone?'

'Yes, Nicholas.'

'Which way did he go?'

'Straight out through the gate and into Gracechurch Street.'

'But why?' asked Nicholas. 'He should have stayed here.'

'He was in a dream.'

'A dream?'

'Yes,' said Leonard. 'When I called out to him, he did not even wave back. He could not have heard me. The lad was miles away.'

'Did you see which way he turned?'

'Left, towards Bishopsgate.'

'Bishopsgate? Surely he did not intend to walk back to Shoreditch on his own.' The answer dawned on Nicholas. 'The church!'

'What church?'

'St Martin Outwich. It's where Hal Bridger was buried.'

Leonard was relieved. 'Ah, that's where he is, then. No need to trouble ourselves any more.'

'Except that he should have got back by now. Thanks, Leonard,' said the book holder, moving away. 'I'll go in search of him.'

'Would you like me to come with you?'

'No, just tell the others where I've gone. I'll not be long.'

Nicholas went out into Gracechurch Street and swung left, striding purposefully through the crowd and keeping his eyes peeled for a sign of Honeydew. Reassured by the thought that he might have gone to pay his respects to his friend, Nicholas was also quietly alarmed that he had not yet returned. London was a dangerous place for anyone. A small, trusting, defenceless boy like Honeydew was especially vulnerable. He could have been the victim of a footpad or been set on for fun by one of the gangs of ragged children who inhabited the area. Nicholas quickened his pace. The boy might be in need of help.

When he approached the churchyard, he caught a glimpse of a figure near one of the graves and thought for a moment that it was Honeydew. It was only when he got closer that he realised it was an old man, standing in silence beside a gravestone with his hat in his hands. There was nobody else in the churchyard. Nicholas went into the church but it, too, was empty. He took the opportunity to drop to his knees before the altar in order to pray for the boy's safe return.

Going back outside, he intended to speak to the old man but he was no longer there. The churchyard was deserted. He began to wonder if Honeydew had, in fact, been there at all yet he could think of no other destination. It seemed unlikely that he would have gone to Bridger's home to offer his condolences to the parents. Had he done so, he would have been ejected without ceremony by the leather-seller. If that had been the case, Honeydew would have been back at the Queen's Head a half an hour ago.

Nicholas was distressed. The apprentice was a special friend of his, looking to the book holder for protection against the repeated teasing of the other boys. Because he was the most talented of them, Honeydew was always given the leading female roles and this aroused great envy. The others invariably tried to play tricks on him and, most of the time, they were thwarted by Nicholas Bracewell. The book holder took the disappearance personally. It hurt him almost as much as the death of Hal Bridger. He had a duty of care to both boys and he had failed them.

Richard Honeydew, hopefully, was still alive and it was imperative that he was found quickly. The problem for Nicholas was that he had no idea where to start. Vexed and preoccupied, he walked slowly towards the gate. Before he got there, he saw Alice Bridger enter the churchyard. She blinked in surprise.

'What are you doing here again?' she asked.

'Looking for one of the apprentices.'

'Why?'

'I believe that he came here to say a last farewell to Hal.'

'When was this?'

'Within the last hour.'

'A small, slight, fair-haired boy with a red cap?'

'Yes,' said Nicholas, eagerly. 'Did you see him?'

'I think so.'

'*When*, Mrs Bridger? What did he do? Where did he go?'

'I cannot say where they took him.'

'They?'

'There were two of them,' she replied. 'I was in the porch

when the boy walked towards the church with the young lady. Then suddenly, a gentleman came up behind them. He threw a cloak over the boy and carried him off.'

'Where?' demanded Nicholas, anxiously. 'In which direction?'

'I did not see.'

'Could you not have come and warned us?'

'How did I know that the boy belonged to you?' she said.

'No,' he conceded, 'you could not have done. I see that now.'

'In truth, even if I had realised who he was, I could never have entered that abominable tavern of yours.'

'Why not?'

'I would have felt unclean.'

'You could have sent someone in for me.'

'No, sir. I could not.'

'A boy's life may be at stake. Does that mean nothing to you?'

'It means everything,' she replied, looking helplessly towards her son's grave. 'Our son's life was at stake in that dreadful place where you put on those plays. I hope that there's not a second tragedy but evil must be punished, as it was in Hal's case.' She reached into her pocket and drew out a handkerchief. Turning back to Nicholas, she offered it to him. 'The young lady dropped this.'

Saul Hibbert was in a more cheerful mood. The afternoon performance had been a revelation to him, showing just what the company could do when they were fully committed and reinforcing his belief in the supreme quality of his play. Congratulations flooded in from all sides. When the spectators had gone, he could still hear their paeans of praise and feel the endless pats of approval on his back. His self-esteem burgeoned even more. After a celebratory drink with Lawrence Firethorn in the taproom, he made his way back to his chamber to luxuriate in his increasing renown and to change his attire before he went out that evening.

He was on the point of departing when there was a knock on the door. Expecting it to be one of the servants, he opened the door and was instead confronted by a glowering Alexander Marwood. The landlord had a determined glint in his eye and a sheaf of bills in his hand.

'What do you want?' asked Hibbert, haughtily.

'Payment, sir.'

'I paid you last week.'

'There have been several other charges since,' said Marwood, holding up the bills. 'On Sunday, for instance, you dined in your room with a young lady.' He read from the first piece of paper. 'Item, a dish of anchovies. Item, a bottle of Canary wine. Item—'

'Yes, yes,' said Hibbert, nastily. 'I know what we ate and drank.'

'Then perhaps you'll settle the bill.'

'All in good time, my man.'

'No more credit can be extended to you.'

Hibbert stiffened. 'Are you deaf as well as demented?' he said. 'Surely, the applause out there reached even your ears. It went on for an eternity. Anyone who was in the yard today will tell you that I'm the finest playwright in the whole of London. I bring fame and honour to the Queen's Head. You should be paying me to stay here.'

'That's what I *am* doing.'

'Be off with you!'

'Not until this business is resolved.'

'Do you dare to hound me with these petty amounts?'

'In total, the bills amount to almost two pounds.'

'Then I've been ruinously overcharged.'

'Every item has been recorded with care,' said Marwood, wounded by the accusation of fraud. 'My wife keeps the accounts and Sybil does not make mistakes.'

'Well, she made one when she married you! I've never seen such an ugly visage. How can your wife bear to look at someone who belongs in a menagerie with the other animals?'

Marwood was indignant. 'I'll stand for no insults, Master Hibbert.'

'Then you'd best get out of my way or you'll hear a hundred of them. Begone, you pestilence!' shouted Hibbert. 'Go back to your kennel before I reach for my sword.'

'What about these bills?'

'A pox on them!'

Grabbing the bills from Marwood, he tossed them into the air to create a minor blizzard. He picked up his hat then walked out of the room. The landlord dropped to his knees and gathered up the bills before pursuing Hibbert quickly down the steps. At the bottom of the staircase, Lawrence Firethorn was talking to Nicholas Bracewell. They looked up as the two men descended, guessing at once why Marwood was on the heels of his guest. Hibbert adopted a lofty tone.

'Ah, Lawrence,' he said, 'I crave a boon. Remove this leech of a landlord from me before he sucks my blood.'

'I've more important concerns than that,' said Firethorn.

'What's more important than indulging *me*? I've brought laughter back to the Queen's Head with my play. That deserves a reward.'

'It would if laughter was *all* that you brought,' said Nicholas, trenchantly. 'But disaster has come in its wake.'

'Yes,' retorted Hibbert, indicating the landlord. 'Here he is.'

'I'm no disaster,' protested Marwood.

'You're a sly, wrangling, squirrel-faced, cheese-eating knave!'

'Do you hear that, sirs?'

'You're a green-sickness carrion!'

'Enough of this, Master Hibbert!' said Nicholas, forcefully. 'You've no cause to abuse the landlord. Before he speaks to you, we must have private conference.'

'You will have to wait,' said Hibbert, 'for I'm going out.'

'Not until we've said our piece,' warned Firethorn.

'What about these bills?' said Marwood, waving them in the air.

'They'll be paid in time,' Nicholas told him, moving the landlord gently aside. 'There's another account to be settled first.' He fixed his eye on Hibbert. 'Shall we return to your room?'

'No,' retorted Hibbert, trying to leave.

'Then we'll have to insist,' said Firethorn, blocking his way.

'I'll not be treated like this, Lawrence.'

'You'll be treated as you deserve.'

'Do you not *recognise* me?' demanded Hibbert. 'I'm your saviour. I'm the difference between success and failure. Thanks to my play, the yard was filled and Westfield's Men have been made famous.'

'We were famous long before you came, Saul, and will be so long after you leave us. Before that happens,' said Firethorn with quiet menace, 'we need a word alone with you.'

'It's not a convenient time.'

'Then we'll *make* it convenient,' said Nicholas, taking him by the scruff of his neck and pushing him back upstairs. 'You'll not leave this inn until we've heard the truth.'

Spluttering with rage, Hibbert tried to break free but Nicholas had the superior strength. The playwright was forced back into his room and pushed towards the bed. Following them in, Firethorn closed the door behind him. Saul Hibbert's face was red and the veins on his temples were standing out like whipcord.

'What is going on?' he yelled at Firethorn.

'We are hoping that you'll tell us,' said Nicholas.

'I was talking to Lawrence.'

'Then I'll give you the same reply,' said Firethorn. 'We are hoping that you'll tell us, Saul. In fact, we'll not leave this room until you do.'

'Are you threatening me?'

'Yes.'

'Then you'd best beware,' said Hibbert. 'Bear in mind that I have the power to withdraw *The Malevolent Comedy*. Browbeat me and you'll not put on my play tomorrow or any other day.'

'It's already been cancelled,' said Nicholas.

'And may never be performed by us again,' added Firethorn.

Hibbert was shaken. 'Why not?'

'Because we have no Mistress Malevole, and the play is impossible without her. Dick Honeydew has been kidnapped.'

'Kidnapped?'

'Earlier on,' explained Nicholas. 'When he was visiting a churchyard to pay his respects at the grave of Hal Bridger – another victim of your play, Master Hibbert. One murder, one dog, one stolen prompt book, a lost apprentice. You may be proud of your play but it's brought us nothing but misery.'

'That's not my fault.'

'We believe that it is.'

'And we want to know why,' said Firethorn, clenching his fists. '*The Malevolent Comedy* is nothing more than a malevolent tragedy to us. It's aroused someone's ire and we've suffered badly as a result. Tell us why or – by Jupiter – we'll beat the truth out of you.'

Instead of staying at the Queen's Head with the others, Edmund Hoode had left early so that he could pay a visit to the home of Ursula Opie. She had not been out of his thoughts since he had first met her, and, as time had passed, she had assumed an even greater magnitude in his life. In his hand was the scroll on which his sonnet was written. The moment had come to deliver it to the woman to whom it was dedicated, but Hoode could not be seen to do that himself. Anonymity had to be preserved.

When he got to the house, therefore, he lurked in a lane opposite and kept watch on the building, hoping against hope that Ursula might make a providential appearance. Since she did not, he looked around for someone to carry his poem to her, confident that its honeyed lines and uninhibited passion would find a positive response. A stringy youth strolled towards the lane. Hoode stepped out to intercept him and offered him money to deliver the scroll to the house. The youth was only too ready to accept the commission.

'Shall I say who it's from, sir?' he asked.

'No, no,' replied Hoode. 'Simply give it to the servant who answers the door and ask him to set it on the keyboard of the virginals.'

The youth sniggered. 'Virginals?'

'Do as I tell you or I'll find someone else.'

'I'll do it, sir, if you pay me.'

'Here, then.' Hoode slipped some coins into his palm.

'Thank you.'

'Obey my instructions and the young lady will receive it.'

'Does she have a name?'

'The most beautiful name in Creation. Away with you.'

'Yes, sir.'

The youth nodded and ran off. Concealing himself in the lane once more, Hoode watched until he saw that his orders had been carried out then he headed for his lodging. The sonnet had been safely delivered. It would soon be winging its way into Ursula's heart. He felt elated. Keen to resume work on the new play that she had unwittingly spurred him to write, he broke into a trot and laughed all the way back to his lodging.

Saul Hibbert's protests were long and loud but they did not convince his visitors. Nicholas Bracewell and Lawrence Firethorn stood either side of him, eyes never leaving his face. Their presence was intimidating.

'For the last time,' said Hibbert, vehemently, 'I'm not responsible for what's happened. I regret it, naturally, but I'll not take the blame on my shoulders. Nobody I know could have inflicted all this on us. I have no enemies.'

'You'll have two standing before you, if you do not tell the truth,' said Firethorn. 'Somebody bears a grudge against you or the play.'

'Or both at once,' added Nicholas. 'What's his name?'

Hibbert shrugged. 'I cannot even hazard a guess.'

'Then what's *her* name?'

'Her name?' The playwright was suddenly uneasy. 'Whose name do you mean?'

'Two people took Dick away from that churchyard. One was a man but the other was a young lady. A witness saw them. She picked up this when the lady left it behind her.'

He held up the handkerchief. 'So it seems that you do have enemies after all, Master Hibbert. Who is she?'

'How should I know?'

'Because your play has clearly upset her or her companion.'

'Not with intent.'

'I wonder,' said Firethorn. 'Nick believes that some of the characters in *The Malevolent Comedy* may have been inspired by real people, put on stage so that they can be reviled and ridiculed.'

'Is that what you did with Rosamund, Chloe and Eleanor?' pressed Nicholas. 'And was Mistress Malevole a real woman?'

'Every author draws from life,' said Hibbert, evasively.

'But he does not always turn his acquaintances into victims.'

'I had a little, gentle, harmless fun at someone's expense, that is all. The ladies concerned live far away from London so there's no chance that any of them would see the play and be offended.'

'Then why was a young woman involved in the kidnap of Dick Honeydew?' said Firethorn. 'And it's not the first time we've heard of her, is it, Nick?'

'No,' replied Nicholas. 'One of the servants here, Leonard, was accosted in the yard by a young lady who showed a great interest in the work of the book holder. That same afternoon, our prompt book was stolen. It was no coincidence. I believe that the same person was in that churchyard earlier on. She was there to distract Dick so that he could be set upon by her accomplice.'

'What sort of woman is capable of that, Saul?'

'None that I know,' said Hibbert.

'Well, she appears to know you,' accused Firethorn, angrily. 'So does the man. Who are they?'

'Truly, I can put no names to them.'

'Perhaps a description of the man may help,' said Nicholas. 'I had it from the apothecary who sold the poison that killed Hal Bridger. What he told me tallies with what Leonard said. He, too, as I believe, met him. The fellow had more than a passing interest in your play.'

'Go on'

'He was tall, slim, fair-haired, bearded and well-dressed. He was also well spoken but he was not a Londoner. The apothecary said that the fellow had a country accent yet a townsman's look to him.'

Hibbert shook his head. 'I do not recognise him at all.'

'Think, man,' urged Firethorn.

'I know nobody who fits that description.'

'No creditor, perhaps? No vengeful landlord whom you bilked?'

'No, Lawrence.'

'Could he be some irate husband you once cuckolded?'

'There are one or two of those in my past,' admitted Hibbert with a smile, 'but none with courage enough to pursue me. Besides, how would they know where to find me? I've kept constantly on the move.'

'To escape from your enemies?' said Nicholas.

'I told you. I have none to speak of.'

'You've just confessed to a couple of them. A man whose wife has been seduced could well hire people to come after you.'

'Only if they knew where I was.'

'Perhaps they picked up your trail,' said Firethorn.

'I've been careful to leave none.'

'What about your family?'

'They live in York,' said Hibbert. 'I've not seen them for years.'

'Do you not let them know where you are?'

'No, Lawrence. I'm a rolling stone.'

'One who gathers no enemies, according to you,' said Nicholas, tiring of his prevarication. 'We are being misled, Master Hibbert, and we do not like it. Dick Honeydew may mean nothing to you but we love him dearly. Lawrence has brought the boy up under his own roof.'

'Dick is like a son to me,' said Firethorn, sorrowfully. 'You'll not find a more likeable lad, nor one with more talent on a stage. Margery and I are shocked that anyone should even consider snatching him away from us. That being so,' he went on, putting a growl into his voice, 'we'll be very upset if anyone hampers our search for Dick, if anyone – like you, for instance – holds back information that could save his life.'

'So tell us the truth,' insisted Nicholas, taking a step forward.

Hibbert backed away. 'That's what I have done.'

'You are hiding something from us.'

'Why should I do that?'

'Because your only concern is yourself,' said Nicholas. 'It does not matter to you if people are hurt because of your play. All you can think of is the applause it will bring you. We do no trust a word you've told us.'

'It's the truth.'

'It's your version of the truth and that's not quite the same. You are a man who keeps on the move, hides his tracks, ignores his parents and refuses to honour his debts but who nevertheless expects people to respect him.'

'Every time we perform your play,' said Firethorn, 'catastrophe follows. Yet you claim that Saul Hibbert has no enemies.'

'I swear it!' attested Hibbert.

'Then the puzzled is solved,' said Nicholas, 'because that may not be your name. Nobody hates Saul Hibbert because he did not exist until you came to London. The name is just another mask for you to wear, is it not?' He seized him by the doublet. 'Who exactly *are* you?'

For the first time, the playwright looked genuinely afraid.

Bernice Opie was bored. Her father was out of the house on business, her mother was visiting a friend and Ursula was so engrossed in her book that she refused to put it aside. Bernice was on her own. Wanting to return to the Queen's Head that afternoon, she had been balked by the fact that she could not go unaccompanied. She was desperate to see Edmund Hoode once more but was unable to do so. The only way that she might meet him again was at the next music concert to be held at the house but that was weeks away, and, in any case, Bernice could not be certain that he would be there. She missed him badly.

Irked and frustrated, she wandered around the house in search of something to distract her but nothing could hold her attention for more than a few minutes. At length, she went into the hall and stood on the dais, recalling that it was from that particular spot that she had seen Hoode the previous Sunday. Pretending that he was still there, seated at the back of the room, Bernice waved to him then blew him a fond kiss. In her imagination, he returned the kiss. She giggled.

She then noticed something lying on the keyboard of the virginals. Crossing over to the object, she saw that it was a scroll, tied up with pink ribbon. It did not appear to be addressed to anyone. Bernice unrolled it with curiosity and scanned the opening lines with heady excitement.

> *I spied an opal in the Opie hall,*
> *Hope's jewel, fit to lie against my heart,*
> *An opiate opal, glittering yet small,*
> *To lull me in love's sleep with loving art.*

She was so profoundly moved that she had to sit down before she could read any more. It was extraordinary. Couched in the sonnet was a clear message to her and she did not have the slightest doubt about the identity of its author. Appended to the poem was the letter 'E'. It simply had to stand for Edmund Hoode. The clues were too numerous to be ignored. Hoode had visited the hall only days earlier and watched Bernice while she took part in the concert. One of the songs she had sung was called *Hope of Heaven*. Her father had commissioned it. The song had been written for her by a young composer named Reginald Jewell. The reference to 'Hope's jewel' could not be more explicit.

It never crossed her mind for a second that the sonnet had actually been intended for her sister. Nobody could ever describe Ursula Opie as 'glittering yet small'. It was Bernice who had glittered in the candlelight and outshone every other woman in the room. And how had Edmund Hoode ever guessed that an opal was her favourite gemstone? It was the decisive piece of evidence and proved that they were true soul mates. His declaration of love filled her with joy. At the very moment when she was on the edge of despair, Edmund Hoode had come to her rescue and changed her whole life with fourteen lines of poetry. It was heaven-sent.

Bernice glowed with delight. His love for her had to be requited.

Saul Hibbert was cornered. Had he been up against the book holder alone, he would have reached for his dagger and struck back, but there was Lawrence Firethorn to contend with as well. Though not as tall and broad-shouldered as Nicholas Bracewell, the actor-manager was the son of a blacksmith with a blacksmith's solid build. Together, the two men posed a daunting physical threat and they stood between Hibbert and the door. It was time to make a few concessions.

'My real name is Paul Hatfield,' he admitted, 'but I changed it for reasons that are private.'

'I think that we can guess what they are,' said Nicholas.

'Then you would be right. Paul Hatfield *did* have enemies. There were certain ladies in my life with a grudge against me that made it necessary for Paul Hatfield to disappear.'

'And where did this change from Paul to Saul occur?' asked Firethorn, sarcastically. 'On the road back from Damascus?'

'It was on the road to Norwich, as it happens.'

'Where had you been before that?'

'Oxford.'

And before that?'

'I'd need to give you a geography of England to tell you that.'

'You say that certain ladies might bear a grudge,' observed Nicholas. 'What about gentlemen?'

'No,' said the other, firmly.

'Why not?'

'Because I prefer the company of ladies.'

'Who does not?' said Firethorn. 'Yet a man and a woman are in league against you here. Who are they?'

'I wish I knew, Lawrence.'

'You must have some notion.'

'None at all. Nicholas was right about the play,' he went on. 'The ladies were real enough. I even kept their names – Rosamund, Chloe and Eleanor. That was perhaps unwise.'

'What about Mistress Malevole?' asked Nicholas.

'She, too, was plucked from my memory.'

'Then she would find your portrait of her offensive.'

'Only if she saw it and that's impossible. The lady is two hundred miles away and has never been to a playhouse in her life. Let me be frank,' said Hibbert. 'When the first attacks were made, I could not believe they were against me. I thought that Westfield's Men had upset someone and that you were the target.'

'We are,' said Nicholas, 'but only because of you.'

'We need to find Dick Honeydew fast,' said Firethorn. 'Help us.'

'I wish that I could,' replied Hibbert. 'I can give you the names of Rosamund Fletcher, Chloe Blackstock and Eleanor Dyce, but what use would they be to you? None of them would do this to me. When I knew them, they were dear, sweet, kind young ladies.'

'So you repay them with cruel satires,' said Nicholas.

'They'll not be hurt by something they'll never see.'

'Someone has seen the play and raised the strongest objection.'

'I'm as anxious as you to find out who it is.'

'I doubt that.'

'Someone in your past is prepared to *kill* to get their revenge. What terrible thing did you do to provoke such anger? What crime did you commit against someone?'

'No crime at all.'

'Running away,' said Nicholas. 'Changing your name. Hiding in the capital city. That's not the action of an honest man.'

'I'll confess to the crime of dishonesty but no more.'

'Your dishonesty is obvious enough,' said Firethorn. 'It's brought fearsome retribution down upon us. If it was an assault on your person, I could understand it but it's *The Malevolent Comedy* that's under attack and we pay a heavy toll as a result.'

'Yes,' agreed Nicholas. 'Because of your play, Hal Bridger is already dead and buried. And now, Dick Honeydew has been kidnapped. Be warned of this,' he went on, fire pulsing in his veins, 'if anything happens to Dick, I'll come looking for you with a sword.'

Richard Honeydew was terrified. Bound and gagged, he was locked in a disused stable, lying on the vestigial remains of straw and watching a rat emerge inquisitively from a drain. The place was dank and fetid. Fingers of light poked in through the holes in the timber. Cobwebs abounded. The irony was that he was so close to a main thoroughfare. He could hear many people nearby and pick out the sound of passing horses and the occasional cart. Yet it was impossible for him to cry for help. When he had been attacked in the churchyard, he had been taken completely by surprise. All that he could do was to wriggle and protest. Honeydew's resistance had been short-lived. The man carrying him had let the boy feel the point of his dagger, threatening to stab him if he struggled or shouted any more. Honeydew had obeyed so his kidnap aroused no suspicion in the street. It looked as if the man were carrying a bundle of clothing over his shoulder.

They had not gone far so were still within the city walls.

But their location was a mystery because Honeydew had no idea in which direction he had been taken. Covered by the cloak, he had seen nothing and heard very little. All that he knew for certain was the beautiful young lady with the warm smile had deceived him, and that his kidnapper was strong and determined. He also suspected that he was the man responsible for Hal Bridger's death during the play. That added an extra dimension of horror to his predicament.

He schooled himself to stay calm so that he could think clearly. The disappearance of the rat was a relief. Unable to defend himself, the boy had been in fear of an attack but the animal had merely sniffed at his feet before scurrying off. Westfield's Men would look for him. He knew that. As soon as they became aware of his absence, Nicholas Bracewell would organise a thorough search but Honeydew did not have much hope of being found. His kidnappers had chosen his prison with care. He could be kept there indefinitely.

Honeydew began to tremble all over. Fear for his own safety was uppermost in his mind but he was also worried about the company. He was letting them down. Without him, *The Malevolent Comedy* could not possibly be performed at the Queen's Head and he felt sure that that was why he had been seized. It meant that they intended to hold him there all night and all of the following day. Why release him then, if they wanted to keep the play off the stage? Honeydew could be there all week.

There was one way to ensure that Saul Hibbert's play

was never again presented, and that was to kill the boy apprentice who played the part of Mistress Malevole. A replacement could be found but Firethorn would not even consider it. The taint of a second murder would be too much for him and the superstitious actors. The play would vanish from the stage. Honeydew wondered if his kidnappers realised that. He trembled more violently. The rat poked its head out of the drain again. The boy closed his eyes in prayer.

Every available man was involved in the search. Nicholas Bracewell took control and sent them off in small groups. The first quartet was dispatched to the churchyard itself and told to stop passers-by, asking them if they had seen someone being carried away earlier on. Others combed all the side streets in the vicinity of the church, looking for clues, questioning anybody they met. George Dart was sent off to fetch Edmund Hoode, who would be deeply upset if he was excluded from the hunt. Lawrence Firethorn, Barnaby Gill and Francis Quilter all had horses so they could conduct their search from the saddle.

At his own insistence, Leonard was also involved, risking the landlord's wrath to help in tracking down the missing boy. Nicholas went with him because Leonard was the only person who had met the man and woman presumed to have been the kidnappers. He could identify them. Owen Elias made up the trio, wearing his sword and yearning for a chance to use it against the kidnappers.

'Saul Hibbert should be here as well,' said Elias.

'Hatfield,' corrected Nicholas. 'His name is Paul Hatfield.'

'I don't care if his name is Nebuchadnezzar, King of Babylon. He should be here to help.'

'He'd be more of a hindrance, Owen.'

'Do you think he told you the truth?'

'Part of it.'

'What did he leave out?'

'Far too much.'

'He has sworn enemies, after all,' said the Welshman, 'that's clear. What puzzles me is why they attack his play and not him. If they'll go to the lengths of poisoning someone, why not pour it down *his* throat?'

'Because that would let him escape too easily.'

'Easily? I'd hardly call Hal's death throes easy.'

'They want to keep him alive to suffer,' said Nicholas. 'We know how much this play means to its author. He's pinned everything on its success. Somebody is set on taking that success away from him.'

'Why?'

'I don't know and I'm not sure that *he* knows.'

'In his position, I'd know at once who the culprits were.'

'That's because you have many friends and few enemies, Owen. It's the other way round with Master Hibbert, or Hatfield, or whatever his real name is. Few friends and so many enemies to choose from that it's impossible to know where to start.'

'I'd start with Rosamund, Chloe and Eleanor.'

'He swears it must be someone else.'

'A woman scorned can become a wild virago,' said Elias, soulfully. 'I can tell you that. Even the softest of them can turn termagant in a second. Last year, one such meek and mild lady tried to deprive me of something I hold most dear and send my singing voice much higher.'

'Lead a more wholesome life.'

'And lose all the excitement? That I'll never do, Nick.'

They walked on up Gracechurch Street until they saw Edmund Hoode, running towards them with George Dart beside him. The two newcomers were panting for breath.

'Have you found him yet?' asked Hoode.

'No,' said Nicholas. 'There's no sign.'

'This play will be the death of us.'

'As long as it's not the death of Dick Honeydew.'

'I think we should burn the prompt book,' Elias put in. 'The sooner *The Malevolent Comedy* goes up in smoke, the better.'

'I'd rather put the torch to its author,' said Hoode. 'I hate to say it of a fellow playwright but he must go. He's like the seven plagues of Egypt all in one.'

'Forget him for the time being,' urged Nicholas. 'The only person we need to think about now is Dick Honeydew. He's the youngest of us and the one least able to look after himself.'

Elias nodded. 'We've been hit at our weakest point,' he said. Putting back his head, he roared his question to the bustling street. 'Where *are* you, Dick?'

Richard Honeydew did not hear him. There were so many competing noises filling his ears and he was, in any case, too far away from Owen Elias to catch the slightest sound of his question. The gag around his mouth prevented him from giving an answer to anyone and the ropes were starting to dig into his wrists, arms and legs. Honeydew was in great discomfort. Propped up against a wall, he was aching in every limb. When he heard footsteps approaching, he tensed himself, afraid that his kidnapper was returning to kill him.

A rusty bolt was drawn back on the top half of the door and it was opened a few inches. Someone looked in to check that he was still there. Minutes seemed to pass before the lower half of the stable door was unbolted. Honeydew swallowed hard and tried not to show the dread that was gnawing away at his stomach. The door opened and the young woman he had met in the churchyard stepped inside with a cup of water. She looked sternly down at him.

'If I give you this to drink,' she cautioned, 'you must promise not to cry out. Do you understand?' He nodded obediently. 'Nobody would hear you but we'd have to punish you hard. Do you want to be punished?' He shook his head. 'Sit still while I undo this.'

Putting the cup down, she used both hands to untie the gag and remove it. Honeydew gave a gasp of relief and coughed. She held the cup to his mouth. The water was cold and refreshing. He sipped it greedily. When he had drunk it all, she used the gag to wipe away the moisture around his mouth. It was a gesture of almost maternal kindness. Yet the woman seemed far from kind. He could not believe that someone so beautiful could also look so hard-faced and forbidding.

'Where am I?' he asked.

'Where your friends cannot find you.'

'How long will you keep me here?'

'We shall see.'

'Who are you?'

'The important thing is who *you* are,' she said, coldly. 'Mistress Malevole. You do not look so cruel and cunning now, do you?'

'Why do you hate me so?'

'I only hate what you represent, Richard.'

He was surprised. 'You know my name?'

'Your name and your significance to Westfield's Men.'

'They'll come after you for this,' he said, bravely. 'Let me go or Nick Bracewell and the others will follow you to the ends of the earth until they catch you.'

'Yes, I've heard of this book holder of yours.'

'He'll find you somehow.'

'He will not get the chance.'

'Will you hurt me?'

'Not if you do as we tell you.'

'Must I stay here all night?' he bleated.

'You'll do what we decide.'

'Who was that man in the churchyard?'

'You ask too many questions, Richard Honeydew.'

'Why did he say that he'd kill me?'

She gave no reply. Instead, she tied the gag back in position and picked up the cup. After glancing round, she went out again and bolted both halves of the door after her. Honeydew was alone again. He was to be imprisoned all night, far away from the house he knew and the friends he loved. It was getting colder. He fought back tears.

Bernice Opie was unable to keep the news to herself. After reading the sonnet dozens of times, she felt such an upsurge of love inside her that it could not be contained. Her joy had to be shared. She found her sister in the parlour, still reading a book and lost in a world of contemplation. Bernice came up behind her and snatched the book from her hands. Ursula was outraged. She jumped up from her chair.

'Give that back to me, Bernice,' she demanded.

'Not until you hear what I've been reading.'

'That book is mine.'

'You shall have it in a moment,' said Bernice. 'First, listen to my tidings. I've received a declaration of love, Ursula.'

'What?'

'A poem was delivered to the house earlier. It's a sonnet in praise of me and it has made my head spin.'

'I can see that,' said Ursula. 'Who wrote this poem?'

'Master Hoode. There's no name given but it has to be him.'

'Are you sure of this, Bernice?'

'Who else could it be?' She handed the scroll to her sister. 'Read it for yourself. He calls me his opal and plays upon my name.'

Frowning with concentration, Ursula read the sonnet, taking more notice of its artful construction than of anything else. There were clear hints that it was, in fact, addressed to her but she discerned none of them, thinking it inconceivable that any man would dedicate such a poem to her. The depth of feeling that was revealed brought a tinge of colour to her cheeks. She gave the scroll back to her sister.

'Is it not the most wonderful thing you ever read?' asked Bernice.

'I do not care for some of the rhymes.'

'Ursula!'

'And the final couplet is a trifle clumsy.'

'I'll not have a word said against it.' She handed back the book. 'Be happy for me. Your sister is loved and loves the man in return. Does that not please you?'

'It might if I could be sure that Master Hoode was the poet.'

'Look to "Hope's jewel" and you'll see it must be him.'

'It could equally well be Master Jewell,' warned Ursula. 'You saw from his song that he has a gift for language.'

'Master Jewell is far too religious,' said Bernice with mild disgust. 'His breast could never harbour such love and devotion. Besides, I gave him no encouragement. "E" must stand for Edmund.' She gave a short laugh. 'I've written a letter to him.'

'Is that wise, Bernice?'

'It's only polite.'

'You must not be too impulsive. That's ever your failing.'

'What would you do, then, in my position?'

'Nothing at all. I'd simply wait and watch.'

'Edmund has declared himself. He deserves an answer.'

'You must at all costs preserve your dignity,' said Ursula. 'Our parents brought us up to be honest and open in all our dealings. You should not have a secret correspondence with a man.'

'Why not? It makes my blood race.'

'Bernice!'

'I could never show this poem to Mother or Father. They would both disapprove strongly. I'd not be allowed to see Edmund again.'

'That would only be for your own good.'

'How can you say that?' protested Bernice. 'I love him.'

'You hardly know the man.'

'I know enough to realise that I adore him. When he wrote this,' she said, holding up the poem, 'he was reaching out to me. I felt that I had to respond.'

'No,' said Ursula. 'You are too hasty and unguarded. I can see how much this has affected you, but you must restrain yourself. Whatever happens, Bernice, do not send that letter.'

'That advice comes too late.'

'Why?'

Her sister smiled dreamily. 'It's already on its way.'

The search for the missing apprentice went on for hours but to no avail. Nicholas Bracewell adjourned to the Queen's Head with Edmund Hoode and Owen Elias so that they could review the situation. They sat around a table in the taproom with a jug of ale to help their deliberations. Their concern for Richard Honeydew was growing.

'I pray that Dick is still alive,' sighed Hoode.

'I feel sure that he is,' said Nicholas.

'They did not stop short of murder before, Nick.'

'No,' said Elias, anxiously. 'Look what happened to Hal Bridger. If the same people kidnapped Dick, then he's in mortal danger.'

'I prefer to think not, Owen,' said Nicholas. 'Had they meant to kill him, they could have done so in the churchyard. The young woman must have won his confidence so that he could be seized unawares by her accomplice. Mrs Bridger saw it happen. Why carry the boy off like that if murder was their intention?'

'They'd not have struck him there on consecrated ground.'

'Then we'd have found the body in some alley by now.'

'How did they know he would visit Hal's grave?'

'I think he was followed from here, Owen. The street was far too crowded for them to pounce on him there. They bided their time until he turned into the graveyard.'

'Villains!' cried Hoode. 'And one of them, a young lady.'

'The two of them deserve hanging.'

'The three of them,' said Elias, sourly. 'Add the name of our new playwright to the list. But for him, none of this would have happened.'

'They've finally found a way to keep his play off the stage,' said Nicholas. 'My fear is that they'll try to take Dick far away from London to make sure that *The Malevolent Comedy* is truly finished. That's why I've posted someone at every gate out of the city. If we keep them there, we've a chance of finding the boy.'

'We've not had much luck so far, Nick.'

'No, but we've only searched the streets. Now we turn to the inns.'

'Why?' asked Hoode.

'Because that's where they might be, Edmund. These are strangers to London, remember. Leonard spoke to them both and each had a voice that came a long way from the city. That means they would have found somewhere to stay.'

'Then it's probably somewhere close enough to the Queen's Head to keep an eye on us. '

'Yet no common tavern,' decided Nicholas. 'They were well dressed and educated. I fancy that they'll be used to comfort. They'll have chosen their accommodation with care.'

'Then let's visit every inn that might attract them.'

'You go with Owen. I'll partner Leonard. He, at least, has seen the pair. If we divide our strength, we can cover more establishments. Drink up,' he said. 'It will grow dark soon.'

'Teach us the way to go, Nick.'

'We'll search all night, if need be,' vowed Elias.

'So will I,' said Nicholas.

'When Anne is waiting for you in a warm bed?'

'I've sent George Dart to tell her I'll not be home tonight, and to explain why. Dick Honeydew's safety obliterates all else.'

'Then let's get out there,' said Elias, rising to his feet.

'Yes,' said Hoode, getting up and stroking the hilt of his

sword. 'I'm armed and ready for action. We've many crimes to avenge.'

'We have to find the malefactors first,' Nicholas told them, 'and I'll not rest until that's done. Dick is here in London somewhere – I *feel* it. And he's relying on us to rescue him.'

He got up and glanced across the taproom. Leonard was talking by the counter to one of the servingmen, who handed him a letter. Leonard brought it across to them.

'It's for you, Master Hoode,' he said.

'Me?' asked Hoode, taking the letter.

'It has the sweetest smell. I think it's from a lady.'

'An answer *already*?'

Nicholas was crisp. 'Read it later, Edmund, whoever she may be. This is no time for letters,' he said, leading them out into the street. 'We have something far more important to do. Dick Honeydew needs us.'

He had never watched the evening shadows fall with such attention before. Still locked in the stable, Richard Honeydew saw the fingers of light grow paler and paler until they vanished altogether. In their place came a darkness that crept slowly under the door before searching out every corner of the stable. He was at length enveloped in a blackness that was deep and impenetrable. Honeydew could still hear voices in the street but they were far fewer in number. The crowds had gone. Horses passed with less frequency. The breeze had stiffened, making him shiver and blowing wisps of straw across the floor. Though he could no longer see the rat, he could still hear him, scampering to and fro.

Fear kept him awake but fatigue nibbled steadily away at him. Sleep eventually came as a blessed release. He slumped to the floor. No sooner had he dozed off, however, than he was awakened again. The sound of the bolts and the creaking of the doors brought him out of his slumber. A candle glowed in the dark. It was set down beside Honeydew then blown out. Firm hands grabbed the boy.

'Hold still,' ordered a man, 'or it will be the worse for you.'

Richard Honeydew had heard the voice before in the churchyard. For the second time that day, he was lifted up and thrown uncaringly over the man's shoulder.

London was full of inns but some were so ramshackle, or catered for such low company, that they could be discounted at once. Nicholas Bracewell was looking for a place where a lady and gentleman might stay in some degree of comfort. Accompanied by Leonard, he was searching the area to the south of the Queen's Head while Hoode and Elias went off in the opposite direction. It was painstaking work. Some landlords were helpful, others loath to give away any information about their guests. They encountered several people who were visiting London from the country but none that looked remotely like those they sought. Leonard began to lose heart. Pessimism set in.

'They are not here, Nick,' he said.

'They must be.'

'Then perhaps they went over the bridge to Bankside.'

'They'd be less likely to find a good lodging there,' said Nicholas, 'and they would not have carried Dick Honeydew all that way.'

'What if they had a coach?'

'They followed the boy on foot. That much we can guess.'

'Then where did they take him?'

'Where would *you* take him?'

'Down to the river,' said Leonard after a moment's thought. 'Put him in a boat moored away from the bank and we'd never find him.'

'These people are newcomers. They do not know the city.'

'Then they'd find a room at a respectable inn.'

'That's where we have to run them to earth.'

They went into more inns and talked to more landlords. Another hour slipped past but it yielded no result. As they came out of yet another tavern, Leonard's hopes had virtually disappeared.

'This will take an age, Nicholas. What can two of us do?'

'Edmund and Owen take part in the search as well.'

'It needs a small army,' said Leonard. 'One of them should be Master Hibbert. It's his bounden duty to be of help.'

'He's not inclined to discharge such a duty,' said Nicholas.

'He should be. Dick was only kidnapped because of his play.'

'Our author had somewhere else to go.'

Leonard was worried. 'You do not think he has fled, do you?' he asked. 'That's what the landlord fears. He thinks that Master Hibbert will run up huge bills then steal away without paying them.'

'He'll not leave,' said Nicholas, confidently. 'He came to London to make his name and will not quit so easily. In any case, Leonard, I've made sure that he stays.'

'How?'

'By bringing this.' He tapped his satchel. 'I have the only copy of *The Malevolent Comedy* here with me. He'd never leave without that. It's worth its weight in gold to him because it proves his worth as an author. As long as I have it, our spendthrift playwright is bound to us.'

They were in Tower Street and the night was dark. Though their eyes were used to the gloom, they could not see far ahead of them. Leonard had drunk his share of ale earlier in the evening and needed to relieve himself. When they came to an alleyway, he stepped into it.

'Go on ahead, Nicholas. I'll catch you up.'

'Meet me in the White Hart.'

'Where's that?'

'On the left, no more than a minute away.'

'I'll see you there,' said Leonard, vanishing into the dark.

Nicholas walked on alone, glad of his friend's company but pleased to be alone, if only briefly, so that he could reflect on what had happened. He felt partly to blame for Honeydew's disappearance, recalling that it was he who told the boy where Hal Bridger was buried. If he had made no mention of the fact, the apprentice might not have left the Queen's Head. Another worry lay at the back of his mind. Honeydew's performance that afternoon had been remarkable for its bite and savagery. It did not sound like Dick Honeydew at all. It was almost as if the boy had been in someone's grip, forced to take on a personality that was so at odds with his natural tenderness. Honeydew could be regal and even peremptory onstage, but, in Mistress Malevole, he had revealed a spitting hatred and rancour that had always been beyond him before. It was yet another charge to bring against the author. His play was having a corrupting effect on its leading lady.

His thoughts were rudely interrupted. Nicholas had gone no more than twenty or thirty yards when he heard quick footsteps behind him. Before he could even turn round, he received a sharp blow on the back of the head from a cudgel. It sent him pitching forward onto the ground.

Chapter Ten

Nicholas Bracewell reacted instinctively. He had been taken completely by surprise but the blow had been partially softened by his cap, so that he was hurt rather than stunned. As soon as he hit the ground, he rolled over and reached for his dagger, ready to defend himself against his assailant. But there were two of them, brawny figures, both armed with cudgels, intent on beating him senseless. Nicholas needed help.

'Leonard!' he yelled. 'Ho, there!'

'Close his mouth!' snarled one man.

They tried to belabour him but Nicholas was no harmless victim. Rolling rapidly from side to side, he used one arm to ward off the cudgels and the other hand to wield his dagger. As a blow glanced off his shoulder, he stabbed hard with his blade and opened up a deep wound in a wrist. Shrieking with pain, one of the men dropped his cudgel. The other continued to flail away with his weapon, bruising Nicholas's arm and knocking the dagger from his grasp. He aimed a vicious strike at the book holder's eyes but Nicholas jerked back his head just in time. Grazing his temple with searing pain, the cudgel drew blood.

When he tried to kick the fallen man, however, his attacker lost his advantage. Seizing his foot, Nicholas twisted the ankle hard then pulled. His adversary came tumbling down on top of him. Nicholas grappled with him and managed to roll over on top of him, only to feel a hard stamp in the back from the other man. Bent on revenge, and with blood dripping from his injured wrist, he lashed out with his foot at Nicholas. At the same time, the man beneath the book holder tried to bite him on the face. Rage gave Nicholas an upsurge of strength. Subduing the man on the ground with a fierce relay of punches, he rolled over, leapt to his feet and faced the other attacker. He saw a dagger in his hand. Leonard was at last lumbering up the street towards him but would not get there in time to save his friend.

Nicholas used the only weapon available. He lifted the satchel quickly from around his neck. Before the man could lunge at him with the dagger, Nicholas swung the satchel by its strap with as much force as he could, catching the other across the cheek and making him reel.

'I'm coming, Nick,' shouted Leonard. 'Leave him to me.'

But the attackers had had enough. Seeing that the odds had turned against them, they opted for retreat. The man with the wounded wrist helped his dazed companion to his feet and the two of them limped off into the darkness. Panting heavily, Leonard finally reached his friend.

'You called at an awkward time,' he said, apologetically.

'I managed on my own, Leonard.'

'Let's go after them.'

'No,' said Nicholas, breathing hard and rubbing his bruised arm. 'I'm in no condition to give chase. They'll be well away by now.'

'Did they get your purse?'

'They were not after money.'

'Then why attack you?'

'They were here to give me a beating. We were stalked.'

'I heard nobody behind us.'

'They knew their trade. As soon as I was alone, they struck.'

Blood was trickling down the side of his face from the cut on his temple. Nicholas pulled out the handkerchief that had been dropped in the churchyard and used it to stem the flow. With his other hand, he rubbed the back of his head gingerly.

'Are you hurt, Nick?'

'I've lost some blood and gained some painful bruises in return, but nothing is broken.' He retrieved his dagger and slipped it back in its sheath. 'I was lucky. I survived.'

'Why did they pick on you?'

'Because that's what they were paid to do.'

Leonard was aghast. 'Someone *hired* them?'

'I think so, Leonard.'

'To kill you?'

'To give me a beating I'd remember. That's why they used cudgels. When I stabbed one of them in the wrist, he lost his temper and pulled his dagger on me. He meant to use it.'

'I should have been here to help you.'

'They'd not have shown their hand with you here, Leonard.'

'I'll not leave your side again, Nick.'

'Thank you.'

'Who set these bullies on to you?'

'I mean to find out,' said Nicholas, slinging the satchel around his neck again. 'This is what saved me,' he went on, patting the leather. 'After bringing so much misery, *The Malevolent Comedy* has finally done us some good. I told you that it was worth its weight in gold.'

Owen Elias and Edmund Hoode fared no better in their search. After futile visits to a whole variety of inns, they ended up halfway down Cheapside. By mutual agreement, they decided to abandon the hunt for the night. Elias was full of remorse.

'This has been like a penance to me, Edmund,' he said.

'A penance?'

'Yes. We've been to over thirty alehouses and I've not been able to take a drink in any of them. I'm like a sultan in a harem, who looks upon his array of gorgeous wives but is unable to touch any of them.'

'Searching for Dick Honeydew has kept both of us sober.'

'If we could get him back safe, I'd not drink for a month.'

'I may remind you of that,' said Hoode with a weary smile. 'I hope that Nick and Leonard have had more success. If not, we'll search again in the morning.'

'I'll go back to the Queen's Head. I said I'd meet Nick there.'

'Then I'll off to my lodging.'

'One moment,' said Elias, detaining him with a hand. 'You've not told me who sent that letter yet. I know that you've been dying to read it all night, but held off doing so.'

'That was *my* penance.'

'It must be from a lady, then.'

'I'm indebted to you for that, Owen. Until you brought her into my life, I did not know that such a paragon existed.' He clapped Elias on the shoulder. 'Farewell – and a thousand thanks.'

They parted company and Hoode hurried back to his lodging. It was too dark to read the letter in the street and, in any case, he felt that it deserved the utmost privacy. Hoode was convinced that it was a response to his sonnet and would therefore offer encouragement. Had his declaration been rejected, he would have been met by a stony silence yet he been favoured with an instant reply. Ursula had spoken. It was more than he had dared to expect.

When he got back to his room, he lit the candle on the table and sat down to read his letter, first inhaling the bewitching aroma that the paper gave off. Breaking the seal, he unfolded the missive and studied the contents, written in a neat, modest, feminine hand that, to him, symbolised the character of the young lady who had sent it. The message was short and unsigned but it was enough to make him let out a cry of joy. Hoode was not only thanked for the gift of his sonnet, he was invited to meet its recipient. Time and place were specified. His heart began to pound. He had never dreamt that Ursula would be so bold and so ready to meet him alone. Her letter was a poem in its own right. He kissed the paper softly then read the words again. Hoode almost swooned.

A tryst had been arranged.

'God's mercy!' exclaimed Lawrence Firethorn. 'What happened to you?'

'I met with trouble.'

'Serious trouble, by the look of you.'

'They came off worse than me, Lawrence.'

'They?' said Owen Elias

'There were two of them,' explained Nicholas Bracewell. 'Both armed with cudgels. They surprised me in the dark.'

'Then where was Leonard? He kept you company. Two against two puts the matter beyond doubt. You and Leonard could see off half a dozen ruffians between you.'

'Leonard was busy elsewhere.'

Nicholas had got back to the Queen's Head to find both his friends awaiting him. They were alarmed to see the extent of his injuries. By the light of the candles, they saw the bruised face, the swollen lips and the dried blood on his temple. His buff jerkin had been badly scuffed in the course of the fight and his hose torn. Both sets of knuckles were raw. Nicholas gave them a shortened account of what had befallen him, not wishing to let his problems deflect them from the fate of the missing boy.

Firethorn's sympathies, however, were with his book holder.

'These are grim tidings, Nick. You might have been killed.'

'I think their orders were to break a few bones.'

'And they'd have done so if you'd not fought back,' said Firethorn. 'And where was Leonard all this while – pissing against a wall!'

Nicholas was tolerant. 'The call of nature had to be answered.'

'My concern is with the wants of Westfield's Men.'

'So are mine,' said Elias, bitterly. 'We've lost Dick Honeydew. We could not bear to lose you as well, Nick.'

'I'll make sure that it never happens,' said Nicholas.

He was disappointed that Elias had returned empty-handed, but he resolved to widen the hunt on the following day. After helping in the early stages of the search, Firethorn had turned his mind to the question of what the company could stage in place of *The Malevolent Comedy*. An audience needed entertainment and, whatever straits the troupe was in, the actor-manager would never consider turning spectators away. After going through the available costumes and scenery in their storeroom at the inn, he had reached a decision.

'We play *Cupid's Folly* tomorrow,' he announced.

'Why not *Black Antonio* again?' asked Elias. 'I have a leading role in that. In *Cupid's Folly*, all eyes will be on Barnaby.'

'This is no time to put yourself first, Owen. For my own part, I'd sooner play the tragedy but I feel that we should substitute a comedy for a comedy. All that we lack is a maypole.'

'That's easily made,' said Nicholas. 'You've chosen well, Lawrence. It's not only a rustic caper for a hot afternoon, it's a play we've done so often that it needs no rehearsal. George Dart can hold the book and I'll be free to carry on the search.'

'That was my reasoning.'

'Good.'

'I've spoken to the printer, George will collect the playbills first thing in the morning. Those anxious to see *The Malevolent Comedy* will be displeased but at least we have something to set before them.'

'And at least we know the real name of the author,' said Elias. 'We cannot say that of Saul Hibbert or Paul Hatfield or whatever he chooses to call himself today.'

'His name no longer matters,' said Firethorn, harshly. 'His play has done for us. We'll never perform it again.'

'Then he'll want it back,' said Nicholas, 'to take elsewhere.'

'It's our property now, Nick. We have a contract.'

'No, you only have a contract with Saul Hibbert and

he, it appears, did not write the play. Paul Hatfield is the author. The contract is void. On the other hand,' he said with a grin of satisfaction, 'it was signed in the presence of a lawyer so the playwright committed a crime. We were the victims of wilful deception. That entitles us to keep the play.'

'Possession is everything in law,' said Firethorn, 'and it will stay in our possession to stop anyone else from gaining profit from it. There is no way that the author can get his hands on it.'

A thought struck Nicholas. 'Yes, there is,' he said.

'What do you mean?' asked Elias.

'Those men were not simply there to give me a beating tonight.'

'Why else?'

'They were after our copy of the play.'

Saul Hibbert, as he still preferred to be known, had enjoyed his meal at the Green Man, all the more so since John Vavasor had paid for it. What worried Hibbert, however, was that neither Vavasor nor Cyrus Hame were as lavish in their praise of him as they had been earlier, and, whenever he raised the subject of Banbury's Men, his companions hinted at possible doubts. When they ended the supper with a glass of brandy, Hibbert probed for reassurance.

'What exactly did you tell Master Randolph about me?'

'Everything good, nothing bad,' said Hame, blithely.

'You told him every last detail of my play?'

'Of course. But Giles is more interested in the next one you write.'

'*That's* the one Banbury's Men would like,' said Vavasor. 'You do have a second play ready, do you not?'

'I will do,' replied Hibbert. 'Very soon.'

'I hope so. Giles is not a patient man.'

'How many other playwrights can he call upon?'

'He does not need to call on any,' said Hame. 'They come to him in droves. John and I are fortunate in that few of his supplicants write tragedy. Most favour comedy so you have many rivals, Saul.'

Hibbert was hurt. 'You said that my play was far above all else.'

'In some senses, it is.'

'In what sense is it not?'

'Well,' said Vavasor, lighting a clay pipe from the candle, 'to begin with, it lacks a natural part for Giles Randolph. There's no doubt that he could play Lord Loveless – Cyrus and I discussed that very point – but it would not make best use of his talents. Change the name of your heroine and you might have something to tempt him.'

'Change the name?'

'Yes, Saul. If a *Master* Malevole created all the mischief, instead of a woman, he would be untouchable in the role. Dark, brooding, sinister characters are what Giles relishes.'

'Do you have such a character in your next play?' said Hame.

'Not at the moment,' admitted Hibbert.

'Oh dear!'

'But that can soon be remedied.'

'It must be. Giles is to his company what Firethorn is to Westfield's Men. Both must shine in a leading role or a play has no appeal.'

'You gave me the impression that Banbury's Men would buy anything and everything I wrote.'

'Subject to certain conditions.'

'You mentioned no conditions, Cyrus.'

Hame beamed at him. 'They must have slipped my mind.'

'All that we were empowered to do,' said Vavasor, taking over, 'was to sound you out. To see if you were ready to shake the dust of the Queen's Head from your feet.'

'I'm more than ready!' growled Hibbert.

'Break with them and we can talk further.'

'I've already done so and I need employment.'

'Can you so soon have used up so much good will?' taunted Hame. 'That does not bode well. Actors need to be flattered to keep them in the right humour. John and I take it in turns to stroke Giles's feathers.'

'Well, I'll not do so,' said Hibbert with a flash of anger.

'Then bid farewell to your hopes.'

'Since when have certainties become hopes? When we first talked, you said that I was assured of a cordial welcome.'

'And so you are – if your next play pleases.'

'The same holds for us,' said Vavasor, exhaling a cloud of tobacco smoke. 'Everything rests on the quality of our work. *Lamberto* gave us our moment at the pinnacle. We can only hope that *Pompey the Great* does likewise. First, however, it must win over Giles Randolph.'

'If it fails,' added Hame, 'then John and I must take it elsewhere.'

'How can it fail if it has the same attributes as *Lamberto*?'

'How can any play of yours fail if it has the virtues that were seen in such abundance in *The Malevolent Comedy*? Do not wear such a gloomy face, Saul,' he went on, reaching out to pat Hibbert gently on the shoulder. 'You are among friends. We share your ambitions. We want you to join us at the Curtain.'

'Meanwhile,' said Vavasor, 'you are building your reputation at the Queen's Head. As long as your play draws in large audiences, you will always be sought after.'

'Success breeds success.'

'Cyrus has summed up the life of a playwright in three words. Success is everything and you've achieved it. Tomorrow, I daresay, the name of Saul Hibbert will fill that inn yard again.'

Hibbert was decidedly unsettled. He took a long sip of brandy. Hame traded a glance with Vavasor. The two men were patently enjoying their guest's obvious discomfort.

'What did John say to upset you so much?' asked Hame, casually. 'There's no reason why your work will not delight an audience again tomorrow, is there?'

At least, he was in the warm now. Rescued from the stable, Richard Honeydew had been carried into a building, up some stairs and along a passageway. The room into which he was taken had a large cupboard in the corner and the boy was thrust into it with a series of dire warnings. The woman had then taken over, untying his legs so that he had some freedom of movement and giving him a pillow for his head. The cupboard door was then locked. Honeydew felt warmer, safer and more comfortable but he was still a prisoner.

He tried hard to hear what was being said in the bedchamber, hoping that it might give him some clue as to the identity and purpose of his captors. But their conversation was too short and muted. He had seen enough of the young woman to be able to recognise her again but the man had been careful to hide his face from the boy. All that Honeydew had caught was a glimpse of fair hair and beard, and of a blue doublet.

The man had not stayed long in the room. After telling the woman to watch their prisoner with care, he let himself out. The woman fell silent for a long while but Honeydew sensed that she was still the other side of the cupboard door. Had he been left alone, escape was at last a possibility. The boy could have kicked his way out of the cupboard, hauled himself up to his feet then tried to break the lock on the door of the bedchamber by hurling himself at the timber. Even if he had failed, he would have made enough noise to summon help.

As it was, he could do nothing but lie there in the dark and listen to the floorboards creaking whenever the woman moved. Honeydew kept shifting his position to ease the pain.

The ache in his back and arms was constant. The gag was hurting his mouth. He was also very hungry. Instead of being given his usual healthy supper by Margery Firethorn, he was deprived of food and water. It was another source of pain.

Yet there were compensations. He did not fear for his life so much now. The fact that they had taken him indoors suggested that they would look after him, albeit still as their prisoner. Honeydew was not so much a murder victim as a hostage. He was being held so that his captors could get what they wanted, and that was to stop a play from being performed again. The boy could only guess at their reasons for doing so.

When the cupboard was suddenly unlocked and thrown open, he blinked in the candlelight. The young woman was holding a piece of bread and a cup of water. Her expression was still stern but there was a faint hint of softness in her voice.

'Are you more comfortable here?' He nodded. 'I'm going to take the gag away again but be warned. Call out and I'll tie it back again. Then you'll spend the whole night in the stable.' His eyes widened in horror and he shook his head. 'Make sure that you behave yourself, Mistress Malevole, and say nothing at all.'

She removed his gag and fed him some bread. He chewed it gratefully. Another mouthful followed then he was allowed to sip the water. The meal was over in minutes and she wiped the crumbs from his lips before replacing the gag more gently than before. Honeydew was touched by what he perceived as her kindness. She looked at him for a long time as if weighing something in her mind. At length, she blurted out her statement.

'Nobody was meant to die onstage like that boy,' she said with regret. 'It was a mistake.'

The door was promptly closed. Honeydew was in the dark again.

Alexander Marwood needed no persuasion to yield up the spare key. He was so affronted by his guest's behaviour that he had thought of searching the bedchamber himself for money to pay the outstanding bills. In the event, it was Nicholas Bracewell who let himself into the room belonging to the man he knew as Saul Hibbert. He took no chances. In case the playwright returned to the inn, Nicholas had stationed Owen Elias near the gate. A warning whistle from the Welshman would give the book holder ample time to get clear.

Nicholas worked quickly. Entering with a lighted candle, he scoured the room in one sweep, noting how many suits Hibbert owned and how many empty bottles of wine stood beside the bed. On the table lay a few pages of a new play but it was clear, from the number of lines that were crossed out then changed, that the author was struggling to make any progress with it. The play was called *A Woman Killed with Tenderness*. It was another comedy.

A leather bag then caught Nicholas's attention. When he undid the strap, he found that it was filled with letters, documents and bills that seemed to relate to a number of different towns. The playwright had been ubiquitous. In addition to Norwich and Oxford, he had spent time in Lincoln, Nottingham, Chester, Lichfield, Worcester, Bristol and even in Nicholas's hometown of Barnstaple in Devon. The most valuable item in the collection, however, was a letter written in Hibbert's own looping hand. Nicholas was astonished at what he read:

> *Sweet wife,*
> *As ever there was any good will or friendship between me and thee, see this bearer (my host) satisfied of his debt, I owe him twenty pound, and but for him I had perished in the streets. Forget and forgive my wrongs done unto thee, and Almighty God have mercy on my soul. Farewell till we meet in heaven, for on earth thou shalt never see me more. This 2nd of September, 1595.*
> *Written by thy dying husband*
> *Saul Hibbert*

Nicholas put everything back in the leather bag and strapped it up again. He went around the room once more, making sure that everything was exactly where he had found it. The letter answered many questions about its author but it posed even more. It set Nicholas's mind racing. He stepped outside the door and locked it behind him. When he turned to leave, he almost walked into Alexander Marwood. The landlord thrust his face close enough for Nicholas to smell his foul breath.

'Did you find any money?' asked the landlord.

'No,' replied Nicholas.

'Well, when you do, it's *mine*.'

Saul Hibbert was disturbed. Though he had eaten well and drunk deeply, he had not enjoyed the supper with his friends as much as he had anticipated. Their manner towards him had subtly changed and he could not understand why. While John Vavasor had been as bland and generous as before, he was not as encouraging to the new playwright as he had been. And, while Cyrus Hame was his usual jocund self, there were moments when he seemed to be teasing Hibbert. It was as if the two men knew something that their guest did not. Since they were not prepared to share it with him, Hibbert was bound to conclude that it was something to his disadvantage.

His position had become precarious. Estranged from one company, he simply had to find a home for his talent or his hopes of earning renown as a playwright in London would vanish. His two earlier plays had enjoyed only a few performances each with minor theatre companies, whose limited resources and lack of repute doomed them to an incessant tour of the country. Now that he had finally reached the capital, Hibbert had to find a way to stay there. *The Malevolent Comedy* was not the passport he had assumed it would be. Its undoubted quality was not enough to commend it. Repeated attempts to keep it off the stage had left Westfield's Men in uproar against the play, and no other London company would touch it.

At the same time, it was the only clear evidence of his genius, of the spark of magic that set him apart from the general run of authors. It had to be repossessed. If all else failed, it could be offered to one of the companies that toured the provinces and at least bring in some much-needed funds for Hibbert. Though the play was contracted to Westfield's Men, he would have no compunction about letting it be performed elsewhere, far away from London and from the beady eyes of Lawrence Firethorn and his lawyer.

Hope of being taken up by Banbury's Men had weakened slightly but had not been relinquished. All that Hibbert had to do was to complete *A Woman Killed with Tenderness* and offer it to Giles Randoph. Work on the play had been extremely slow because its author had been too preoccupied with enjoying the trappings of success. As he strolled back to the Queen's Head, he vowed that he would return to the play in earnest on the following day. In prospect, it was an ever better comedy than one that had introduced his name to the city. All that he had to do was to convert the ideas that buzzed in his brain into words on a page.

It was dark when he turned into Gracechurch Street then a blaze of light appeared on the opposite side of the road as two watchmen came towards him with lanterns. They plodded on past Hibbert and the light soon faded away. Immersed in thought, he hurried on until he could see candles burning in the windows of the Queen's Head. A hooded figure stepped out of the shadows and thrust something into his hands.

'This is what you wanted, sir,' said a gruff voice.

'Excellent!' replied Hibbert, knowing that he had the prompt book of his play even though he could not see it properly in the dark. 'Did you beat him well?'

'Very well. He'll not wake until morning.'

'Here's payment for you.'

Opening his purse, Hibbert thrust some coins into the man's hand, only to be grabbed by the shoulders and dragged swiftly into the inn yard. The hooded figure was Owen Elias, disguising his voice to sound like one of the ruffians who had attacked the book holder. Nicholas himself was waiting in the yard, hands on his hips.

'Send more men next time,' he suggested, 'for those two gave me nothing more than gentle exercise.'

'I have no notion of what you mean,' gabbled Hibbert.

'You've been discovered,' said Elias, giving him a shove. 'You set men onto Nicholas to steal his satchel and give him a sound hiding.'

'No, no, why should I do that?'

'We heard you loud and clear,' said Nicholas. 'When you took the play from Owen, you made a full confession. Let me have the book back.'

'It's mine,' insisted Hibbert, hugging it to him. 'I need it.'

'What you need is a spell in prison to contemplate your crimes. You are a liar, a villain and a fraud,' Nicholas told him. 'You signed a legal contract with a name that was not your own. You've lived like a lord here without any intention of paying your bills. Ever since you joined us, you've been a menace to the company. And worst of all, Master Hatfield,' said Nicholas, closing on him, 'you paid to have me cudgelled by two ruffians. One of them pulled a dagger on me and meant to use it.'

'Then I'll finish what he started,' said Hibbert, tossing the play into Nicholas's face and drawing his sword. 'You've been a thorn in my side since we met, Nicholas, and it's time I plucked it out.'

'Not while I'm here,' said Elias, drawing his own weapon.

Nicholas was adamant. 'This is my quarrel, Owen,' he said, putting the play on the ground. 'Lend me your sword and I'll give this rogue satisfaction.'

'I'll not be satisfied until I kill you,' said Hibbert, removing his hat and flicking it away. 'Come on, sir.'

'Leave some meat on him for me to carve,' asked Elias, handing his rapier to Nicholas. 'I've my own grudge against this knave.' Hibbert thrust wildly at him and the Welshman had to jump back quickly out of range. 'God's blood!' he protested. 'Can you not even fight like a man?'

'Let's find out,' said Nicholas, circling his opponent.

'I'm ready for you,' goaded Hibbert.

'How ready?'

'I'll show you.'

Hibbert thrust hard but Nicholas parried with ease. A second thrust and six fierce slashes of the blade were also harmlessly deflected. Hibbert came at him again. Light on his feet and well balanced, he was no mean swordsman. When he launched another ferocious attack, his rapier flashed murderously in the air but each stroke was deftly parried. Nicholas was happy to give ground, testing him out, lulling the man into false confidence, even giving a grunt of pain as if he had been wounded.

But the winner was never in doubt. Nicholas had studied the finer points of swordsmanship. He was stronger, faster and more nimble. He had had far more experience with a weapon in his hand than Hibbert. When he had taken everything that his opponent could throw at him, he retaliated with a dazzling series of cuts and thrusts that forced Hibbert backwards until he was up against a wall. Nicholas feinted, moved swiftly to the side, thrust again and twisted his wrist. Hibbert cried out as blood gushed from his hand. His sword went spinning in the air.

Nicholas rested the point of his blade against Hibbert's throat.

'Now, then,' he said, 'let's have some honest answers.'

'Run him through, Nick,' urged Elias. 'I'll swear you killed him in self-defence for that's the truth. He drew first when you had no weapon.'

'No, no,' begged Hibbert. 'Spare my life – please!'

'He'd not have spared yours, Nick.'

'Peace, Owen,' said Nicholas. 'Leave this to me.' He flicked his sword so that the point drew blood from Hibbert's throat. The playwright emitted a gasp of fear. 'A young woman lured Dick Honeydew away in that churchyard. Who was she?'

'In truth, I do not know,' replied Hibbert.

'Give me her name.'

'I would, if I knew what it was.'

'You know it only too well,' said Nicholas, remembering the letter he had seen, 'for you lived with her at one time. I think that she has learnt of your ruse. The woman is your wife.'

Hibbert gave a shudder and pulled himself back against the wall in a vain attempt to escape the pressure of the sword point. There was terror in his eyes and sweat dribbled freely down his face. All his hopes had been vanquished. He was caught.

'Admit it,' said Nicholas. 'Is she your wife?'

'Probably,' confessed Hibbert, 'but I cannot say which one.'

Richard Honeydew was mystified. From the various sounds he could hear from below and in the adjoining rooms, he was being held in a busy inn but he could not tell in which part of the city it might be. What puzzled him was that the woman who had fed him seemed to be alone. Since carrying him upstairs, the man had departed and stayed away all evening. The boy had heard a bolt being pushed home after his departure. When he picked up clear sounds that the woman was going to bed, he wondered why the man had not returned. The candle was blown out in the room and the tiny filter of light that came through the crack in the cupboard door was extinguished.

Stiff and aching, Honeydew was nevertheless relieved. The man posed the real threat. With him out of the way, the boy felt safer. He was also rescued from any embarrassment. Living in a crowded house in Shoreditch meant that privacy was almost impossible. Lawrence Firethorn was a lusty husband and Margery a vigorous wife. The noises that came from their bedchamber made the other apprentices snigger. They even put theirs ears to the floorboards to hear more clearly. Honeydew never joined them. Not really understanding what was going on in the marital bed, he did his best not to listen.

It was different now. He was less than six feet from a bed and could hear it report every movement that the woman made. Had the man shared it with her, Honeydew could not have blocked out the sounds of any love making that might have ensued. It would have distressed him. He did not wish to lose his innocence yet. In playing the part of Mistress Malevole, he had already been forced to grow up a little, finding sinister qualities in his voice and his manner that had never been there before. It had frightened him. He was still a boy with a boy's unclouded naiveté.

Honeydew remembered the evening when *The Malevolent Comedy* had had to be created anew and dictated to the scrivener. Nicholas Bracewell had felt certain that some of its characters were based on real people whom the author wished to ridicule. Mistress Malevole was one of them, a beautiful but devious woman who achieved her ends by all manner of trickery. Honeydew was hit by a sudden realisation. He might have met her. The woman who was keeping him prisoner had called him by the name of his character in the play, and there had been a sneer in her voice. When he looked at her, he was staring into a mirror. His captor was the real Mistress Malevole. He wanted to scream.

* * *

Lawrence Firethorn opened his mouth to let out a laugh of disbelief.

'Can this be so, Nick?' he asked.

'Owen was there at the time.'

'Saul Hibbert is a bigamist?'

'He admitted to three wives at least,' said Nicholas, 'and there may be more. It explains why he kept on the move. He would meet, woo and marry an unsuspecting bride, claim that he was sick and travel to another town on the pretence of seeing a physician there. After a lapse of time, he'd write a letter to say that he was dying and ask for money to repay his debts.'

'Who collected the money?'

'An accomplice who delivered the letter. He'd be paid a small amount for his work and the remainder would go to Master Hibbert – or Hatfield, as he was known in most cases. Our designing author preyed on women for a living. He boasted to me that he once earned eighty pounds in a year by such a deceitful means.'

'It was so with his play,' noted Firethorn, 'for what was that but a raid on gullible ladies who had once trusted him? He even gave us the full names of Rosamund, Chloe and Eleanor. Which one of them has learnt the truth about their husband and come after him?'

It was early and Firethorn had entered the city as soon as the gate had been opened. He and Nicholas met at the Queen's Head where the book holder had spent the night. In the light of day, the facial wounds that Nicholas had picked up during the scuffle looked even worse. The bruises were purple, the scar on his temple more livid and his lower lip almost twice its normal size. But there was no hint of self-pity. He was still exhilarated by the way that Saul Hibbert had been unmasked.

'Let me get my hands on the wretch!' said Firethorn, vengefully.

'You'll have to wait, Lawrence.'

'Why – where is he?'

'Lying in prison,' replied Nicholas. 'We had him arrested and taken before a magistrate. Owen and I bore witness to his crimes and he made a full confession. I also took the letter with me as evidence.'

'What letter?'

'The one he wrote to all his discarded wives or mistresses. I found the latest one when I searched his room yesterday. Depending on their circumstances, he asked the women for various amounts to clear his supposed debts. They paid up in the mistaken belief that their beloved was truly dying.'

'His letters served a double purpose, then.'

'Yes,' said Nicholas. 'It brought him money by cruel deception and ensured that none of the ladies came looking for him because they thought him dead. Until, that is, he wrote *The Malevolent Comedy*.'

'Did one of his "wives" catch wind of it?'

'Apparently so, though he can only hazard a guess at which one.'

'The rogue!' cried Firethorn. 'To use poor women so! When they discover that the lying knave is still alive, they'll come rushing to London with a pair of shears apiece.'

'They'll have to wait until the law has finished with him, Lawrence. He's charged with bigamy, deception, setting those ruffians onto me, and other crimes besides. When he married his last wife before a priest in Norwich, he did so falsely under the name of Saul Hibbert. That's fraudulence in the eyes of God. By rights,' said Nicholas, 'he should spend many years behind bars for all this.'

'That gives me some satisfaction but it does not bring Dick Honeydew back to us. He's still in the hands of those who kidnapped him.' He heaved a sigh. 'At least, I hope he is and that he's treated well.'

'They seized him to stop *The Malevolent Comedy* from being staged again. When they see we are performing something else today, they may release him. That's my prayer,' said Nicholas. 'My fear is that they'll hold him to ensure we do not present the play tomorrow or any other day.'

'Westfield's Men will never perform it again.'

'We know that, Lawrence – but they do not.'

'And they do not realise its author is now in prison.'

'Did they but know, that might content them. But I want more than to have Dick safely back with us again,' said Nicholas, resolutely. 'The two who took him from that churchyard must pay dearly for his kidnap, and for the murder of Hal Bridger.'

'Do not forget the theft of the prompt book, Nick.'

'Nor the release of that dog.'

'I'll forgive that piece of mischief,' said Firethorn with a chuckle. 'It added to the jollity to the scene and had Barnaby bitten on the bum. I took some pleasure from that.' He became serious. 'Murder and kidnap, however, deserve the hangman's rope.'

'That's what they'll get when I catch up with them.'

'Do you think they're still in London?'

'Yes,' said Nicholas. 'They'll stay to see that they accomplished what they sought. We must continue the search. Dick Honeydew is still in the city somewhere.'

They moved him not long after dawn. Still entombed in his cupboard, Richard Honeydew heard the woman get out of bed and begin to dress. He had slept fitfully and ached more than ever. There was a knock on the door and the woman unbolted it to admit the man. Honeydew heard a brief snatch of conversation.

'Has he been any trouble?' asked the man.

'No.'

'I'll take him out of here.'

'He's had no breakfast yet,' said the woman.

'Give it to him in the stable.'

'Is it safe to move him?'

'Yes, but I'll need your help.'

Honeydew tried to place the voices. Having toured the country often with Westfield's Men, he had encountered many local accents and even learnt to mimic some of them. The woman's voice had less trace of its region and he had been unable to identify it with confidence. The man's voice, however, had a more distinctive ring to it. Honeydew was certain that he had heard the accent during a visit to Lincoln and the surrounding countryside.

The door of the cupboard was flung open and a cloak tossed over the boy. Too afraid to struggle, he was lifted up and carried across the room. Then the woman opened the door and checked that nobody was about. Honeydew was taken quickly along the passageway and down the backstairs. He was soon lying in the evil-smelling stable with his feet tied once more. When he removed the cloak, the man had made sure that the boy did not see his face. Richard Honeydew quailed. He was at the mercy of a malevolent woman and a murderer from Lincoln. It was clear that they intended to keep their prisoner.

The search was resumed as soon as the actors had gathered. With more men at his disposal, Nicholas Bracewell was able to send some of them further afield, calling at likely hostelries and asking if a fair-headed man and a young woman were staying there while visiting London from the country. Nicholas himself went off with Leonard. Edmund Hoode was once again deputed to continue the hunt with Owen Elias. They returned to the point in Cheapside where they had abandoned their earlier search. The Welshman was bristling with curiosity.

'Well?' he said. 'Did you read your letter?'

'A hundred times, Owen.'

'Did she declare her love?'

'More than that,' said Hoode, suffused with joy. 'We are to meet.'

'A tryst?'

'Today at noon.'

Elias laughed. 'Well done, Edmund,' he said, slapping him on the back. 'You have wooed with more speed this time. In the past, you've waited months before you took a single step towards a lady.'

'Ursula is different.'

'Ursula? Are you sure it is she?'

'I sent her a sonnet in praise of her beauty.'

'Then you see things that I do not,' said Elias, 'for the woman is too homely for me. I'd not find one letter of the alphabet to dedicate to her beauty. If you found fourteen lines, then you have strange eyesight.'

'I looked into her soul, Owen.'

'Enjoy her body as well. Meet her, court her, board her.'

'There's no thought of that,' said Hoode, indignantly. 'This is no lustful conquest. I love Ursula and will treat her with the respect that she deserves.'

'Pursue this how you will, Edmund. Swear abstinence, if you wish. I'll not gainsay it,' said Elias. 'When I brought the sisters to you, I thought that the younger was more likely to arouse your affections. She'd be my choice, I know. Bernice Opie is a diamond of her sex that any man with red blood in his veins would yearn to possess.'

'I prefer opals. They sparkle less but have more depth to them.'

'Each man to his own desire. Whichever sister you pick, I hope that this new love will flourish.'

'It will, I feel it. Ursula and I were meant to be together. A tryst at noon!' cried Hoode, laughing. 'My heart sings at the very thought of it, Owen. And I know that Ursula will be looking forward to it with the same wild delight.'

* * *

'You must not even *think* of going,' said Ursula Opie with disapproval.

'But the meeting has been arranged.'

'Stay away from it. Convey your message by your absence.'

'No,' said Bernice, 'I gave Edmund my word.'

'You had no right to do so. A young lady of your upbringing should never see a man in private. It's against all propriety, all decorum. Imagine what Father would say, if he knew.'

'Father and Mother will be out of the city today, Ursula. That's why I thought it safe to see Edmund. I'll take Betsy with me,' she went on. 'I'm not so shameless as to go abroad on my own.'

'If you take Betsy, you turn a servant girl into an accomplice. She will suffer as a result,' warned Ursula. 'When Father hears of this deception, he'll dismiss Betsy on the spot.'

'There's no reason why he should hear.'

'I'll tell him.'

'Ursula!'

'I have a duty to look after you, Bernice, to save you from those random urges that always seem to afflict you.'

'This is no random urge. We love each other.'

'On so short an acquaintance?'

'The attraction between us was immediate,' said Bernice. 'Truly, I think that you are jealous of me. That's why you wish to spoil this tryst with Edmund. You are full of envy because no man would ever write a poem to you.'

'I hope that no man will. I'd find it mawkish.'

'Does that mean you must ruin my happiness?'

'No,' said Ursula, trying to be reasonable. 'I love you as a sister and want to protect you. You run too fast, Bernice. If it is true that Master Hoode would court you, then let him do so by more honest means. A secret meeting behind your parents' back is too immoral.'

'It was my suggestion and not Edmund's.'

'Either way, it must not take place.'

'You'll not stop me,' said Bernice, temper flaring.

'Then you'll have to suffer the consequences.'

'Gladly. An hour alone with Edmund, and I'll suffer any strictures from Father. I'm loved and admired, Ursula. I inspire poetry from the most wonderful poet in London.' Bernice folded her arms in defiance. 'I must go to him. It's my destiny.'

It was much easier in daylight. Being able to see an inn more clearly enabled them to decide whether or not it would be suitable for two visitors from the country with a taste for comfortable accommodation. Nicholas Bracewell and Leonard were able to move more quickly and go into more hostelries. The longer they searched, the further away they were taken from the Queen's Head. Nicholas became aware of the time.

'Let's turn back,' he said, reluctantly.

'Perhaps the others have had more fortune.'

'I hope so, Leonard. It may be that these people have friends in the city and stay at their house. If that's the case, we'll never find them.'

'Will they harm Dick Honeydew?' asked Leonard.

'I think not. There is no need.'

'There was no need to poison Hal Bridger.'

'That was done to bring a performance to an end,' said Nicholas. 'As long as they hold Dick, they know the play will not be staged. His role is too long and difficult for any of the other apprentices to learn in a day. Besides, we would not risk another performance or it might bring down their wrath on Dick Honeydew.'

'They'll have to endure my wrath when we catch up with them.'

'And mine, Leonard.'

They walked on and turned into Gracechurch Street, picking their way through the morning crowds. Nicholas was a big man but he seemed almost short beside the massive Leonard. He could see why he had not been ambushed in his friend's company the previous night. Leonard's sheer bulk would frighten most people away. But it also made him ponderous. While Nicholas strode, the other man sauntered. They were thirty yards from the Queen's Head when Leonard came to a halt and pointed a finger.

'That's him, Nick!' he said. 'I believe that's him!'

'Are you sure, Leonard?'

'I'm almost sure.'

Nicholas looked at the man ahead of them. He was tall, lean and wore the kind of decorous apparel that made him stand out from the market traders and their customers. Fair-haired and with a beard, he had the unmistakable air of a gentleman. When the man went into the Queen's Head, it was conclusive proof to Leonard. He wanted to charge in after him.

'No,' said Nicholas, holding him back, 'let's move with care. If it is the man, and he sees you rushing at him, he'll take to his heels at once. Let me go after him because he knows you by sight. If a mistake has been made, there's no harm done. If, however, he *is* the villain we seek,' said Nicholas, 'I'll drag him out. Guard the back door of the taproom in case he breaks away from me.'

'As you wish,' said Leonard, 'but I'd like to lay hands on him.'

'We all would.'

Obeying his instructions, Leonard went and stood by the back door. Nicholas, meanwhile, entered through the front. The taproom was busy, filled with spectators coming to the play that afternoon. The fair-haired man had found a table in the corner. He looked round to beckon a servingman. Nicholas closed in on him.

'Might I have a word with you, sir?' he asked, politely.

'Do I have any choice in the matter?'

'No.'

'Then speak on, my friend,' said the man with a bland smile, 'for I can see that nothing will stop you.'

'My name is Nicholas Bracewell.'

'I know that. You are the book holder for Westfield's Men and have been a mainstay of theirs for years. What would you have with me?'

'First,' said Nicholas, 'I'd like to know where you hail from. Those vowels of yours were not nurtured here in

London. They have a country sound to them.'

'I was born and brought up near Lincoln. Is that a crime?'

'It might be. Could I ask your business in coming here?'

'What else but to see a play?' returned the man, easily. 'And I hope to catch sight of Saul Hibbert, for I know he stays here.'

'You also know why his comedy has been cancelled today.'

'Do I?'

'You are playing games with me, sir,' said Nicholas, annoyed by the man's arch tone. 'Let's step outside and talk more freely there.'

'I mean to dine here first.'

'I think you'll come with me.'

'Take your hands off,' said the other, resisting as Nicholas lifted him from his seat. 'Is this the kind of hospitality you offer to your audience?'

Nicholas released him. 'We'll leave by the back door,' he said.

'I'd rather go on my own,' decided the man.

Without warning, he pushed Nicholas away and bolted for the back door, buffeting a few shoulders on the way. Nicholas went after him. When the man flung open the door, he ran straight into Leonard who enfolded him in a bear hug. Nicholas came out to join them.

'Let me go, you oaf,' cried the man, 'or I'll have the law on you.'

'Have no fear,' said Nicholas, 'officers will be called.'

'Get this man off me!'

'First, tell us your name.'

'It is Cyrus Hame and I'm a playwright with Banbury's Men. I'd certainly not work for your company if this is how I'd be treated.'

'Cyrus Hame?' said Nicholas. 'The co-author of *Lamberto*?'

'The very same.'

'Let go of him, Leonard.'

Leonard released him and looked at his face properly for the first time. Seen from a distance, there had been a strong resemblance to the man who had once questioned him in the yard. On closer inspection, doubts began to crowd in. Leonard's face fell.

'It's not him, Nick,' he said.

Edmund Hoode got there early so that there was no chance of missing her. The designated spot was close to St Paul's Cathedral. Before he reached it, however, he saw that she was already there, impelled by the same impatience that he felt. The servant girl beside her was sent away as he approached, retreating several yards to allow them privacy. Hoode's excitement robbed him of his voice. Ursula spoke first.

'You may be surprised to see me here, Master Hoode,' she said.

'The surprise is equalled only by the delight.'

'Delight?'

'It's a kind of ecstasy,' he said.

'I came to tell you that this is improper,' she said, briskly. 'It was foolish of Bernice to give you such an invitation but wrong of you to send her that poem in the first place. She is young and headstrong. When she wrote to you, Bernice did not know what she was doing.'

Hoode was despondent. 'Bernice?' he said.

'I came here ahead of her in the hope that I could speak to you first. Please, Master Hoode, I take you for a gentleman with high principles. I do not believe that you would lead a young lady astray.'

'No, no. I would not dream of it.'

'Then tell that to my sister.'

'Gladly.'

'And be kind to her as you do so,' said Ursula. 'I knew that I could count on your understanding.'

'You can count on anything I have,' he murmured.

'It is better to hurt her now than cause her deeper pain later on.'

'You show consideration to your sister,' said Hoode, realising that his sonnet had fallen into the wrong hands. 'I'll do the same I promise you. I can see now that I behaved impetuously and I regret it.'

'Thank you, sir. I appreciate that.'

He was tentative. 'Bernice told you of the poem, then?'

'She even showed it to me. It was well written, Master Hoode,' she said, 'but I would expect that of you. I admired its form while frowning at its sentiments. Had such a sonnet been sent to me, I would have blushed to receive it. It had a maudlin note.'

'I see.'

'Bernice was deeply affected. She has conceived a

fondness for you that she mistakes for something else. I felt it my duty to save her from any humiliation that might come.'

'That's very honourable of you.'

'I'm glad that we are in agreement, sir.' She offered her hand and he shook it. At her touch, Hoode felt a thrill throughout his whole body. 'Thank you.'

'It was good of you to come here.'

'It was the only thing I could think of doing.'

'You behaved like a dutiful sister.'

'I'll steal away before Bernice comes. Be gentle with her.'

'Rely on me,' he said.

'I will.'

When she turned away, he blew a kiss at her departing back. Hoode's dejection slowly lifted. His fulsome sonnet might have hit the wrong target but it had allowed him two precious minutes alone with the woman he loved. It had also given him an insight into her essential goodness and moral rectitude. Ursula Opie was not a woman to be swept into his arms by a mere sonnet. She was a goddess who had to be worshipped from afar, a wondrous icon, an ethereal being that was all the more inspiring for being so unattainable. Her rejection of him only served to intensify his devotion.

Meanwhile, there was another sister on her way. Bernice Opie came tripping along with a servant at her heels. When she caught sight of him, a broad smile lit her face. Ursula had asked him to be kind and gentle. It was an easy request to satisfy. Nothing would have persuaded him to send a poem of any sort to Bernice Opie. It had to be explained away as a foolish romantic gesture on his part. Hoode cleared his throat and began to rehearse his excuses.

Cupid's Folly drew a substantial audience that afternoon but it had nothing like the size or excitement of the crowds that had come to see the play it had replaced. It was one of the company's staple comedies, a sturdy and reliable war-horse on which they could trot happily for a couple of hours. With the inimitable Barnaby Gill in the main role, it filled the yard with laughter yet again. George Dart was promoted to hold the book, leaving Nicholas Bracewell free to watch the audience from the same upper room he had used before. He thought it unlikely that one or both of the kidnappers would be there, but he wanted to make sure.

Having met Cyrus Hame, he at least had a clearer idea of what the man he was after looked like. Nicholas had no qualms about the rough welcome that Hame had been given. He and John Vavasor were known to have done their best to lure Saul Hibbert away from Westfield's Men and deprive them of what had seemed to be a dazzling new talent. Hame and Hibbert had been birds of a feather, proud peacocks that liked to strut and show off their finery. The disgraced playwright would have little use for his wardrobe in prison.

Though he scanned the faces in the galleries, Nicholas could see none that looked as if it might belong to the man he sought. All that the kidnappers would want to know was that *The Malevolent Comedy* had given way to another play, and they could learn that from the playbills that had been posted up to advertise the event. When the play was over, he waited until the applause died down, and the yard began to empty, before making his way downstairs. The landlord intercepted him.

'I *knew* that he was a villain,' he said, wagging a finger. 'We owe you thanks for finding him out.'

'I'm glad that he had enough money in his purse to settle his bill.'

'And he's in prison now, you say?'

'Condemned for his many crimes,' said Nicholas.

'I hear that bigamy was one of them.'

'It was. Under two different names, he had at least three wives.'

'I do not know whether to be shocked or to feel sorry for him,' said Marwood, smacking his cheek to stop it twitching so alarmingly. 'One wife is more than enough for me. Two would break my back. Three would be something akin to purgatory.'

'The Queen's Head will be quieter without Saul Hibbert.'

'I'll say "Amen" to that.'

Nicholas broke away and went into the yard. Most of the spectators had left and the scenery was already being taken from the stage. Leonard waved and hurried across to his friend.

'Nicholas, Nicholas!' he called. 'I've seen her again.'

'Who?'

'The young lady who asked about the book holder.'

'Are you certain it was her?'

'Yes,' said Leonard. 'I'd swear to it.'

'You were certain about that gentleman this morning and he turned out to be Cyrus Hame. Let's not have another mistake,' said Nicholas, warily. 'You have to be absolutely sure, Leonard.'

'I am. She spoke to me again.'

'When?'

'Not two minutes ago. I came looking for you at once.'

'Had the lady been at the play?'

'No,' replied Leonard, 'she came to ask why *The Malevolent Comedy* had been replaced. I told her that it was out of favour with you.'

'Good. What else did you say?'

'That its author was in prison and likely to stay there a long time. She seemed pleased. She thanked me for my help then walked away.'

'You should have followed her!' said Nicholas.

'Not with these slow legs of mine. Besides, she knows me by sight and would have been warned of my pursuit.'

'In other words, she got away.'

'I'm not such a dullard as that, Nicholas.'

'What did you do?'

'I sent George Dart after her,' said Leonard, proudly. 'He's small enough to keep out of sight and young enough to run all the way back here to tell us where she went.'

Nicholas was thrilled. 'Excellent work,' he said, taking him by the shoulders. 'Saddle a horse for me at once. I want it ready for when George returns. And find Lawrence's horse as well. He'll want to come with me to set Dick free.'

Richard Honeydew had resigned himself to spending a whole day in the stink and discomfort of the disused stable.

The woman had given him breakfast and another meal at noon. To his profound embarrassment, she had released his bonds so that he could relieve himself in the corner, any hope of escape removed by the fact that the man stood outside the door with a drawn sword. During the afternoon, the boy had been left alone, suffering from cramp and twisting his body into all kinds of shapes in order to ease it.

He could hear the traffic in the nearby thoroughfare but remained cruelly isolated from it. Hours seemed to pass. It was late afternoon when he finally heard footsteps, accompanied by the sound of a horse's hooves. The stable door was open and his captors stepped inside. They were carrying leather bags.

'Why not leave him here?' said the woman. 'That's the best way.'

'No, he might be found too soon.'

'He knows nothing.'

'He knows your face,' said the man, 'and he's caught a glimpse of mine. It's safer to take him with us and leave him somewhere miles away from London. By the time he gets back here, we'll be long gone.'

'If we take him, he'll slow us down.'

'We'll do as I say,' he snapped, handing her his cloak. 'Wrap him in this and I'll throw him across my horse. Nobody will know that he's there. Tie it fast,' he ordered. Dropping his bag, he turned away. 'I'll fetch my horse from the blacksmith. He should be ready now.'

'Hurry back.'

When her companion went off, the woman crossed over

to Honeydew and looked down at him. Her voice gave nothing away but there was a tinge of regret in her gaze.

'You have to come for a ride,' she said, holding the cloak open. The boy shook his head and pleaded with his eyes. 'It's the best way. If we leave you here, you might not be found for days.'

He tried to shrink away from her but it was no use. She threw the cloak over him and wrapped him in a bundle, using more cord to tie the cloak in place. Honeydew heard the muffled sound of a horse's hooves as it was pulled to a halt nearby. He was to be taken out of the city and abandoned by the roadside. The thought scared him. But it was not the woman's accomplice whom he heard, coming to take him away. The next thing that reached his ears was the voice of Nicholas Bracewell as he came bursting into the stable.

'What do you want?' cried the woman.

'You dropped this in the churchyard,' said Nicholas, holding up the bloodstained handkerchief. 'I'm afraid that it got rather stained.' He saw the bundle, squirming violently on the ground. 'Is that you, Dick?'

Nicholas used his dagger to cut the cord and pulled the cloak away. Honeydew did his best to smile but it was impossible with the gag in his mouth. Nicholas tore it away.

'Did they harm you, Dick?' he asked.

'No, no.' He saw the woman, edging towards the door. 'Look out or she'll get away!'

Nicholas put out a leg to trip her up and she went down in an undignified heap on the floor. It was the work of a second to cut through Honeydew's bonds. While the boy rubbed his aching limbs, Nicholas helped the woman up from the floor. Another horse arrived at speed outside and its rider dismounted. Lawrence Firethorn stepped into the stable and, seeing Honeydew, rushed across to embrace him. He turned on the woman.

'You kidnapped Dick and killed Hal Bridger,' he said, angrily.

'We simply wanted to stop the play,' she replied.

'Why?'

'Because *she* is Mistress Malevole,' Honeydew piped up. 'My role was the counterfeit of her. Saul Hibbert put her on the stage.'

'He did more than that,' she said, baring her teeth. 'He married me under his real name and swore to love me. But as soon as I was quick with child, he left me and went to Norwich. Months later, a letter came from him.'

'I can guess at its contents,' said Nicholas. 'Your husband told you that he was dying and begged you to discharge your debts. How much did he want?'

'Thirty pounds.'

'Did you pay?'

'Like a fool, I did so,' she admitted. 'Then I learnt the truth.'

'How did you track him to London?'

'Quite by chance.'

'Where's your confederate?'

'I came alone.'

'She's lying,' cried Honeydew. 'There's a man with her. He went to fetch his horse from the blacksmith. They were going to take me with them. The man is dangerous. He'll be back at any moment.'

'Then he's all mine,' said Nicholas, sheathing his dagger. 'Will you take care of the lady, Lawrence?'

'Gladly,' replied Firethorn. 'Dick.'

'Yes?'

'How do you feel now?'

'All the better for seeing you and Nick.'

'Pass me a piece of that cord, will you? I think that this Mistress Malevole is one that Lord Loveless must reject. She's liable to scratch. I'll bind her wrists before we deliver her up.'

A horse trotted up outside. The woman screamed a warning.

'Fly, Robert!' she shrieked. 'They've caught me!'

Nicholas dashed out of the stable to confront the mounted rider, only to face a swishing rapier. As the man hacked madly at him, he moved back out of the way. He ducked as the sword was hurled at him. Wheeling his horse, his attacker then kicked the animal into life and sped off down the nearby street. Nicholas was in the saddle of his own horse at once, using his heels to take him at full gallop in pursuit of the other rider. People were scattered by the headlong race, diving for safety as the two horses clattered past them, protesting loudly and wondering why two men were riding hell for leather in such a busy street.

Heedless of danger, Nicholas pressed on, jabbing his heels hard to get more speed out of his mount. He began to close the gap between the two horses. The man's only thought was of escape but Nicholas was driven on by sharper demands. He wanted to avenge the death of Hal Bridger, the kidnap of Richard Honeydew, the theft of the prompt book and the accumulated damage that had been inflicted on Westfield's Men. He wanted blood.

The first horse powered on but the second was steadily gaining on it. When the man looked over his shoulder, he saw that Nicholas was only yards behind. It made him curse and kick his horse even harder but he could not outrun Nicholas. In a matter of moments, the other horse drew level and the man was knocked from the saddle by a flying body. Nicholas was determined to catch him, whatever the cost in cuts and bruises. The two of them fell heavily to the ground, momentarily winded.

Nicholas was the first to recover, getting to his feet and hauling the man upright before punching him in the face then throwing him against the nearest wall. Watched by a crowd of onlookers, the man responded by kicking out with a foot to keep Nicholas at bay while pulling out his dagger. Nicholas wanted him alive. Instead of taking out his own weapon, he spread his arms and waited for the attack. Both men were covered in dust and bleeding from gashes they had picked up during the fall. Nicholas could feel a pain in his shoulder but it did not hold him back.

'What was Saul Hibbert to you?' he asked.

'A cheat and a liar,' replied the man, breathing hard.

'Why make us suffer for his faults?'

'Because his play was like a child to him. In killing that, we could make him suffer in the way that my sister suffered.

He murdered her child so we wanted revenge.'

'Is that why you poisoned an innocent boy?'

'I'd have done anything to destroy that play of his.'

Pushing himself from the wall, the man lunged at him with the dagger. Nicholas danced out of the way and circled him slowly. Voices in the crowd started to urge them on as people took sides. Nicholas watched the other man's eyes, seeing the mixture of fear and bravado in them. Another lunge was dodged then he ducked beneath a sweep of the blade. As the man came at him again, Nicholas swayed inches out of reach as the point of the dagger went for his face. His hand shot out, grabbing the man by the wrist and swinging him against the wall with such force that the weapon was dashed from his hand.

It was Nicholas's turn to attack. After pummelling away with both fists at the body, he gripped him by the neck. The man spat in his face and tried to grapple with him but most of his strength had been drained away. Nicholas forced him back, banging his head repeatedly against the wall until blood ran freely down the stonework. A final uppercut sent his opponent slumping to the ground. Retrieving the fallen dagger, Nicholas dusted himself off. The fight was over.

Westfield's Men received the news of the release of Richard Honeydew, and of the arrest of his two captors, with complete rapture. They had something to celebrate at last. George Dart was, for once, the hero of the hour, having trailed the woman to the inn where she had stayed with her brother, then brought back the information to the

Queen's Head. They were quick to acknowledge Leonard's assistance as well. Instead of sweeping dung out of the stables, he was invited into the taproom and plied with ale. Even the landlord felt that it was a deserved reward.

Edmund Hoode stayed long enough to enjoy the festivities, pleased to hear that one of his own plays, *A Trick to Catch a Chaste Lady*, would return to the stage for the rest of the week. He was on the point of leaving when he noticed that Owen Elias was lifting a tankard to his lips. Crossing to the Welshman, he put a hand over his drink.

'You swore to stay sober for a month, if Dick was released.'

'Yes,' agreed Elias, 'but I did not say *which* month.'

'I might have known there'd be a trick involved,' said Hoode as the other quaffed his ale. 'Drink deep, Owen. I must away.'

'Another tryst already?'

'No, Owen. I'm eager to spend more time on my new play.'

'Would you rather scribble than hold a woman in your arms?'

'When I write my tragedy,' said Hoode, 'I can do both. Ursula was my inspiration. Though I work alone at my lodging, I feel that she stands close beside me as I do so.'

'I'd not want that long face of hers too close to me,' said Elias, 'but I'm happy that she has made you want to write again, Edmund. Only a woman can make you feel the spur that you need.'

'There was such a difference between the two sisters.'

'One was lively and gorgeous, the other was ill-favoured.'

'No,' explained Hoode. 'One was childish, the other was mature. One was full of silly laughter, the other was reserved and thoughtful. One sister lived for the moment, the other had a more purposeful existence. In short,' he went on, 'Bernice Opie was mere comedy while Ursula had elements of tragedy. *That* was what drew me to her, Owen.'

Elias was baffled. 'What man wants a tragic woman?'

'I do, if I can put her on a stage. Look to the last piece I wrote. *How to Choose a Good Wife* failed because it was a pointless comedy in which I had no real interest. With the same theme, Saul Hibbert's play put mine to shame. It was only when I saw those two sisters side by side that I spied my mistake. I should have spurned Bernice and turned to Ursula.'

'That's what you did do, Edmund.'

'I talk of my play. I should have abjured comedy and fashioned it into a tragedy. When I understood that, I started anew. Instead of lowborn country folk, looking for a wife, I have the King of Naples, falling in love with the daughter of his deadliest enemy. He, too, wants only to choose a good wife but she is kept from him by political intrigue.'

'What's the title?'

'*The Queen of Naples.*'

'Does the lady marry him, then?'

'Therein lies the tragedy,' said Hoode. 'She returns his love but will be exiled from her father if she disobeys him. The people of Naples respect their King but will not let him wed the queen of his choice. Does he abdicate and marry her? Does she defy her father? Will there be war as a result between Naples and its enemy?' He got to his feet. 'And it was all inspired by meeting Ursula. When you led her into my life, Owen, you created a wonderful tragedy.'

Notwithstanding his personal reservations about Ursula Opie, the Welshman was happy for his friend. Edmund Hoode's creative spark had been ignited once more. A true actor, Elias had only one concern.

'What part do *I* play in *The Queen of Naples*?'

The reunion with his friends was idyllic for Richard Honeydew but his ordeal had wearied him and he tired quickly. Lawrence Firethorn soon took him home to Shoreditch and Nicholas Bracewell went with them. Margery welcomed them all with cries of delight, reserving her warmest hug and biggest kiss for the apprentice. She fed him, washed him then joined the others in the parlour to listen to Honeydew's tale. Margery could not believe that any woman could treat a child so cruelly.

'She did show me some kindness,' said the boy.

'Well, I'd show none to her,' said Margery, roused. 'Leaving you bound and gagged in a cupboard all night? I'd not inflict that on an animal. What was the name of this ogress?'

'Celia Hatfield,' said Nicholas. 'At least, that was what she was called when she was married. Unknown to her, two other women had already wed the same man. Her maiden name was Malevant. When he met her, she was Celia Malevant.'

'Malevant to Malevole is but a short journey,' Firethorn

indicated. 'There was real malevolence in the lady. When we tried to tie her wrists, she cursed and spat like a fishwife.'

'Only a malign creature would seek such hideous revenge,' said his wife. 'She'll hang beside her brother for what she did.'

Honeydew grimaced. 'I feel pity for the lady.'

'After what she did to you?'

'And what she did to Hal Bridger?' said Firethorn.

'She told me that nobody was meant to die,' recalled Honeydew, 'and I believe her. She only wanted someone to be taken sick in the middle of the play.'

Nicholas gave a nod. 'It was her brother, Robert Malevant, who bought the poison and decided on its strength,' he said. 'He was always ready to go to extremes. When the letter came from her husband to tell her that he was dying, Celia Hatfield was so distressed that she miscarried and lost her baby. You can imagine how she felt when she later discovered that she had been duped.'

'She must have wanted to murder her husband,' said Margery.

'Her brother commended another course of action. It was he who learnt that Paul Hatfield was still alive and living here in London under another name. While visiting the capital on business, Robert Malevant chanced upon the intelligence. He sent to Lincoln for his sister,' said Nicholas, 'and they devised their plot.'

'To bring our company tumbling down,' said Firethorn.

'To ruin the author's dream. They knew how strong his ambition to be a playwright was. The brother described

The Malevolent Comedy to me as the child of its author.'

'So he and his sister decided to take its life.'

'An eye for an eye, a child for a child.'

'But that meant that we suffered instead of Saul Hibbert.'

'They did what they came to do, Lawrence,' said Nicholas. 'They killed his play and made him writhe in pain while they did it. His wife, of course, had another reason for revenge. In portraying her as Mistress Malevole, her husband was revealing the darker aspects of her character. When she saw herself in such an unkind light, she was moved to greater fury. Celia Malevant and her brother are two of a kind.'

'At least, we've seen the last of them now,' said Margery.

'And of Saul Hibbert,' added Firethorn. 'How would you like to share your husband with two or three other wives, my love?'

'I do that every time you step out onto a stage, Lawrence. Except that there are more than two or three. There's not a woman in the audience who does not imagine you as husband, paramour or both at once.' Firethorn laughed heartily. 'I bear them no ill will as long as you always come home to me.'

'And always will, sweet wife.'

There was a knock on the door and Margery went out to see who it was. Honeydew covered a yawn with his hand. Firethorn put a paternal arm around him. They were all surprised when Margery came back into the room with Barnaby Gill.

'We did not expect you to call, Barnaby,' said Firethorn.

'Nor I to come here,' said Gill, doffing his hat, 'but I bring you tidings that might cheer you.'

'To have Dick back with us is all the cheer I need.'

'This is a delicious rumour from Banbury's Men. I had it from a friend who works at the Curtain as a gatherer. From time to time, he feeds me such tasty morsels.'

'Go on.'

'Giles Randolph commissioned a new play.'

'Yes,' said Nicholas, knowledgeably. 'John Vavasor and Cyrus Hame were to be co-authors. When *Lamberto* was such a triumph, it was felt that they could repeat it with *Pompey the Great*.'

'My play, my character, my property!' asserted Firethorn.

'And likely to remain so,' said Gill. 'From what I hear, the play has been rejected as being unfit for performance. Giles Randolph thought the tragedy too slow and insipid, so the co-authors are out of favour.'

'This is heartening news, Barnaby. We owe you thanks.'

'We've lost one playwright but they've lost two.'

'Then we steal the advantage once again,' said Firethorn, happily.

'And we'll hold it,' said Nicholas with confidence, 'now that we have Edmund back again. He's found a new Muse. He's writing a tragedy that will overshadow anything that Saul Hibbert gave us, and push the memory of *Lamberto* into oblivion.'

'What more could we want?' asked Margery. 'The villains have been caught, Dick is safely back with us and Westfield's Men are set to rule the stage again.'

'I never ceased to rule it,' boasted Gill.

Firethorn cackled. 'You did when that dog bit your bum.'

'That made *me* laugh as well,' said Honeydew, giggling.

'Barnaby deserves praise,' said Nicholas, trying to appease him. 'Most actors would have quit the stage in fear. He turned the attack to good account and made it look as if it had been rehearsed.'

'Thank you, Nicholas,' said Gill, graciously. 'I struggled on in pain. A clown can turn anything into clowning if he has the skill. But I'm so relieved to see the back of Saul's play. It was the strangest comedy I ever saw. I never felt that it really suited us.'

'How right you were.'

'And you say that Edmund is writing a new play?'

'A tragedy,' replied Nicholas. 'I've never known him so excited about his work. He says that it will be his masterpiece.'

'And what is this new play called?' asked Gill.

'Who cares?' said Firethorn with a grin. 'It will be truly *ours*.'

If you liked *The Malevolent Comedy*, try Edward Marston's other series . . .